BOOK 7
THE PEAKS SAGA

WHERE all WORLDS END

M.F. ERLER

WHERE ALL WORLDS END, *Book 7, The Peaks Saga*
by M.F. Erler

Copyright © 2015, 2020 M.F. Erler
Revised Edition July 2020
All Rights Reserved

Published by

WESTWIND PRESS
an imprint of First Steps Publishing
PO Box 571
Gleneden Beach, Oregon 97388-0571
FirstStepsPublishing.com

ISBN:
978-1-944072-25-4 (hb)
978-1-944072-30-8 (pb)
978-1-937333-85-0 (pb/Amazon)
978-1-944072-26-1 (epub)

Bible quotes are from New International Version:
"Scripture taken from Holy Bible, New International Version (Registered Trademark) Copyright 1973,1978, 1984 by International Bible Society. Used by permission of Zondervan Publishing House. All rights reserved."

Lyrics to songs by Gregory A. DeMuth,
    Copyright 2005: Sacred Ground Music, used with permission
All other lyrics quoted are Public Domain, or composed by the author.

Cover illustration by Kabita Studios
Cover, interior design by Suzanne Fyhrie Parrott

Please provide feedback

10 9 8 7 6 5 4 3 2

Printed in U.S.A.

Praise for the Peaks Saga...

"I remember fondly reading The Lion, The Witch, and The Wardrobe *when I was in middle school.* The Peaks at the Edge of the World *has a similar mix of fantasy and adventure with a moral tale at its center. This is a book that's appropriate for a younger audience than most sci fi/fantasy novels. Enjoy the read!"*

—Kathy Dunnehoff
ZOLA AWARD-WINNING WOMEN'S FICTION WRITER

"...a page turner!" —Judith Seidel

"Ms. Erler puts religion in new settings as she uses the characters in both the past and the future to meld the consequences of a religion lost, then found, then challenged. The ride is exciting. The characters real and engaging."

—Charlene Hecht
BA MUSIC EDUCATION
LONGTIME WRITER, INCLUDING "GUNSMOKE" FAN FICTION

"M.F. Erler skillfully pioneers a new writing genre, mixing elements of science fiction, dimensional time-travel, and modern Christian spirituality. She uses likeable characters in well-crafted settings in which we can identify with their real-life struggles."

—Richard Bartlett, MA, PhD

"...[M.F.] Erler's book, with its futuristic sci-fi focus and true-to-life grittiness, is not your typical Christian novel. At times, it unabashedly describes the realities of the darkness of humanity in order to contrast it with the power of hope and love found in God's grace. This unique book is well worth your time to read and I highly recommend it."

—Pastor Kevin Bueltmann
TRINITY LUTHERAN CHURCH - ASSOCIATE PASTOR
TRINITY LUTHERAN CAMP - EXECUTIVE DIRECTOR

Books by M.F. Erler

THE PEAKS SAGA

PEAKS AT THE EDGE OF THE WORLD
Finding the Light

SEARCHING FOR MAIA

MOUNTAINTOPS AND VALLEYS

WHEN THE WORLD GROWS COLD

THE FOUNTAIN AND THE DESERT

BEYOND THE WORLD

WHERE ALL WORLDS END

THE JOURNEYS SAGA

JOURNEYS BEYOND THE PEAKS
Voices in the Past

Contents

"For I know the plans I have for you," declares the Lord, "plans to prosper you and not to harm you, plans to give you hope and a future."

— *Jeremiah 29:11*

ACKNOWLEDGMENTS

Thanks to the friends who have volunteered to read –and sometimes re-read—helping me with those words I tend to overuse and pointing out the typos and just plain wrong words:

Paul, Emilie, Mary S., Char, Delphia, Patty, and Richard.

Words cannot express how much I appreciate you!

FOREWORD

I can't 'make it happen' or summon it of my own will. Just like Danny's first call for help brought Jon and Jael through the GAP to help him and Ginna. It came on its own—when he needed it most—not when *he* wanted it. Perhaps this is why I formed my characters this way, reflecting an experience of my own:

Only once the vision came, while I was dressing for school in the attic bedroom that was mine alone. (We moved into this house when I was age 13, so it had to have been after this.) The only heat in this room came from a vent in the floor, beside the enclosed chimney that ran up to the roof from downstairs. On cold mornings I'd stand on top of the vent, dressing in the warm blowing air.

One particular day—I have no idea what was special about it—an image of a door opened above me. I saw light and heard songs I couldn't distinguish. Brightness flashed into my eyes, and I felt (rather than saw) the presence of a huge throng just beyond the light.

But the greater impression was a feeling of unspeakable joy—something I'd never felt before—or since. It coursed through my entire being in an instant. And then, as quickly as it came, it was gone—much faster than it takes to tell—like the door had suddenly closed.

At that moment, I knew this thrill of joy and peace had to be from God and his heaven. He had allowed me a glimpse of his reality—in the midst of my mundane, ordinary life. When fears and doubts seem to overwhelm me, I believe this vision was given to help console and strengthen me. When I begin to wonder if God is real, I remember those indescribable things I felt and saw. I think it is a reminder from God of *his* truth—something my mind can turn to when it's anguished and doubts his care.

So, I've analyzed this vision (for I do believe it was one) over the past 50 years (yes, I'm really that old—and I'm finding that with age some things, besides hair, tend to get thinner!—such as patience, endurance, and even faith), Yet, I think this is part of what the Lord was telling me back then, something he wanted me to carry through each stage of my life:

"Do not fear. I am here. I have prepared a place for you. There is more awaiting you than your limited human mind can fathom. I will bring you here to be with me when the time is right."

And so, I try to wait with hope, remembering the tiny taste of the Kingdom of Heaven that I was allowed. That glimpse was all my brain could handle at that time. But when I get to that place, I believe it's going to be wondrous—no sorrow, no pain—ever again.

M.F.E. 2014

The Sullien Family Tree

Dominic Sullien & Karina
(deceased)

(2 sets of twins)

Steph Sullien & Irina
(deceased)

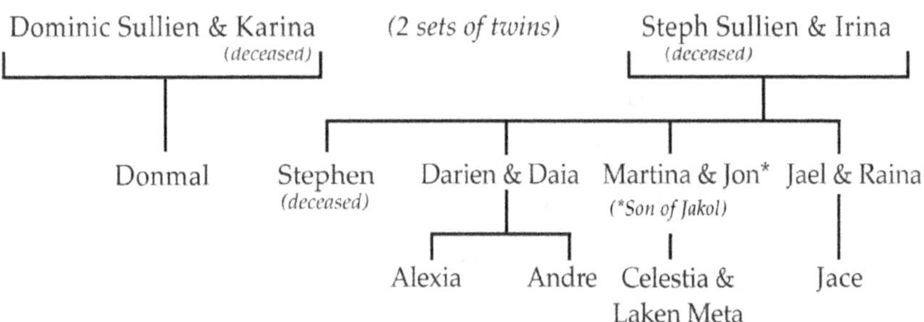

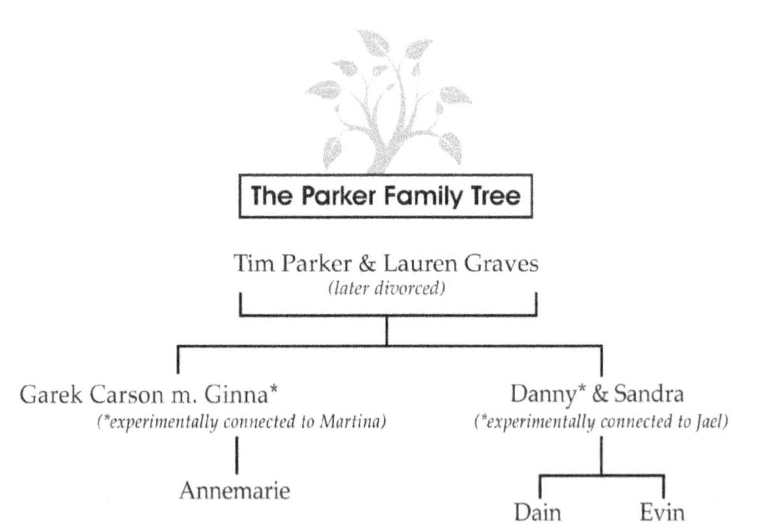

The Parker Family Tree

PROLOGUE

On good days:

Oh, that with yonder sacred throng we at
*   His feet may fall;*
We'll join the everlasting song,
And crown Him Lord of all!
>— Charles Wesley, 1707-1788

And bad days:

Dear Lord, if indeed I am thine,
*   if thou art my sun and my song,*
Say, why do I languish and pine,
*   and why are my winters so long?*
Oh, drive these dark clouds from my sky,
Thy soul-cheering presence restore:
Or take me unto thee on high,
Where winters and clouds are no more.
>— John Newton, 1725-1807

The Promise for all days:

**"Heaven and Earth will pass away,
But my words will not pass away."**

Jesus Christ

CHAPTER 1
The Secret in the Loft

Evin Parker bit his lower lip in an attempt to stop the tears gathering in his eyes. 'Not now,' he thought angrily. 'I need to concentrate.'

But despite his best efforts the tears soon filled his eyes and began to trickle down his cheeks. Glancing to his left, he saw his older brother Dain fighting back tears of his own. And it didn't help that he could hear his mother sobbing softly.

'What good are funerals anyway?' he said to himself. 'Why can't we just pick up and go on?' But even as he thought this, Evin knew it wouldn't be easy to get over his father's death. His mind began to run through the past five years—since they'd come back from the alternative universe with Shadow, their big black dog.

'I wonder if Dad was exposed to something there that caused his brain cancer,' he thought. 'But maybe not. Aunt Ginna, Dad's sister, once reminded us that their mother—the grandmother we never knew—also died of cancer.

Part of Evin's mind was desperate to find the answer to his dad's illness, but it wasn't easy to travel in the GAP. You couldn't just *go* somewhere in the space-time fabric— no matter how badly you wanted to. Shadow made this clear to him in one of their telepathic conversations. Evin was the only one Shadow communicated with in this way, so he could pass things along to his older brother or his parents if he chose to.

'There are things I don't tell them,' Evin mused. 'Have I kept too much back?'

'No, you haven't,' came the familiar low growl in his mind.

'Where have you been, Shadow? I've been searching for you for hours.'

'No need to be angry,' the thoughts came to him. 'I know what I'm doing, and I will tell you whatever you need to know.'

He turned and stared angrily at the black furry face behind him. 'Why do you always get to be in control? Maybe I need to decide for myself what's important now—after all I'm already thirteen years old.'

Suddenly he realized he'd said those last few words aloud. People were staring at him from where they were arranged around Danny's grave. Evin looked down at his shoes, embarrassed. Mom reached over and took his hand.

"Yes, Evin," she said. "You're a teenager, too—like your brother. I'm just sorry your dad will miss it—" Her voice dissolved into tears.

Other voices around them began to sing, and Evin recognized one of his father's favorite songs:

*Work, for the night is coming, work through the
    morning hours;
Work while the dew is sparkling; work 'mid
    springing flowers.
Work when the day grows brighter, work in the
    glowing sun.
Work for the night is coming when man's work
    is done.*

*Work, for the night is coming under the sunset skies:
While their bright tints are glowing, work, for
    daylight flies.
Work 'til the last beam fades, fades to shine no
    more;
Work while the night is dark'ning when man's
    work is o'er.*

He tried to join in the singing, but his voice refused to cooperate. Then as silence fell around him, he felt the arm of his older brother coming across his shoulders. "Come on, Ev," said Dain. "We can go home now."

They walked back across the hills and fields to the house. It wasn't far—only about a mile—since their mother decided Dad should be buried on their own land instead of in a church cemetery. Evin wasn't sure he could go into a church right now, anyway. Each time he thought about God, the huge question 'Why?' seemed to totally fill his mind with an endless ache.

Once they reached the house, Dain pulled him aside toward the barn. Inside, the smell of hay and horse manure filled his nostrils.

"Guess we'd better muck out Splash's stall today," said his brother.

"Yeah, and it's my turn," Evin sighed. He reached up and ran his hand along the black and white pinto's neck. The horse let out a nicker, and he reached into his pocket for a sugar cube—he always kept some there for his friend.

"We can do it together this time," whispered Dain, and Evin felt a slight warmth in his chest. "Let's climb up into the loft and take a break first, though."

So, the two boys climbed up the ladder to the hay loft above the stalls. They had just the one horse, who'd appeared seemingly out of nowhere, much like Shadow. Evin suspected Shadow had brought Splash to them—hadn't people in the other universe thought he might be Jael's horse? But Jael didn't live in this time—the early Twenty-first Century. Danny, his father, had known Jael very well, though. That was why the young woman and the older man had come to get Danny, just over five years ago. They said they needed his help to locate Jael. And they *had* found his father's friend—in a System prison, hidden in a Time Nexus.

"It all seems like a strange dream now."

"What does?" his brother asked.

"Oh, all the GAP-crossing and time travel Shadow took me on."

"Maybe it *was* just a dream, Ev."

"But I still hear Shadow's voice in my mind."

"Are you sure it's not your imagination?"

"Of course, I'm sure!" He couldn't keep the anger out of his voice. People asked him this way too often.

"Hey, it's okay."

He found himself calming down as Dain patted his back.

"I believe you," Dain said softly. "Dad did, too."

"Well, he'd traveled in time before—inside Jael—and knew things about GAPs no one else from our world could."

"I believe you—and Shadow."

Evin sighed and looked up into his brother's green eyes. With a start he realized he'd seen that color before—in Stephan's eyes. But now Stephan was dead, killed by the Red Dragon.

"What should we do now? I keep thinking of that song, 'Work for the Night is Coming'. If we need to work, how can we find out what to do?"

"I say we wait and see what Shadow tells us."

"But just sitting around and waiting is so hard."

"Here, Ev, I need to show you something."

"What?"

Dain brushed aside some of the hay, revealing the bare wood of the loft's floor. There were strange markings rubbed into the boards, and small stones arranged in a circle around them.

"What is it?" Evin said again. Below them, Shadow began to growl suddenly.

"Quiet, boy," he called to the dog. "He wishes he could climb up here, too," he shrugged to Dain.

"I'll find a way to show him this someday," Dain whispered. "He probably can shed some light on the parts I'm not sure about."

Evin crossed his legs into a more comfortable sitting position, but he didn't speak again, since he'd already asked the same question twice. Dain would tell him what he knew—in his own timing.

Dain was running his hands thoughtfully across the stones, his eyes closed. "Dad showed me this," he finally said. "A couple of years ago—I think he already knew then the cancer would take him."

He blinked hard to stop the tears again, and saw Dain was doing the same, as he said, "It's sort of like a miniature stone circle, isn't it?"

"Yeah," Evin said into his brother's silence.

"Didn't you say Jael's son told you instructions he got from some strange old man he met in a stone circle?" asked Dain at last.

Now Evin found his heart beginning to race, but he had no words to say.

"I don't know if this will help us reach that other place or not," continued Dain. "All I know is what Dad told me, when he arranged these stones and drew these letters."

"Can you read them?"

"Dad explained it this way—here, let me show you."

Again, he passed his hand gently over the stones. "They're like a stockade, see?"

"You mean like one of those old-time forts?"

His brother nodded. "A place to go for safety in time of attack— see, we're protected from all sides."

"By what?"

"Dad said it was a presence—like God—who encircles us."

"I wish I felt that presence."

"Dad said we couldn't always feel it, but it was still there. And he said not to give up hope, but to keep standing our ground."

"Standing our ground? Against what?"

"I bet Shadow can tell you the answer to that," Dain said, looking his younger brother squarely in the eye. "Ask him—"

'Shadow?'

'I'm here, Evin,' the dog rumbled. 'Yes, the True King will never leave you or forsake you—he's promised that.'

"But what are we standing against?" Evin heard his voice asking this question out loud.

'You've seen him—remember the Serpent?'

He closed his eyes and shuddered. "How could I forget the Red Dragon?"

"There's more," Dain said just then. He pointed his finger at a small figure drawn with charcoal in the middle of the circle. "See this?"

"It looks like a stick person." Evin tried not to chuckle.

"Well, it's not so easy to draw on these rough planks, I guess. But see his arms?"

Evin looked more closely and found himself nodding. "One arm is held up like he's making a fist."

Dain nodded and pointed to letters on the figure's left. "Can you read that?"

"*Semper Paratus*? What does that mean?"

"It's Latin," said his brother. "It means 'Always Prepared'. It's the motto of the U.S. Coast Guard."

"But we're in Colorado—nowhere near a coast."

"Still we need to be prepared for whatever the True King calls us to do."

Evin looked up quickly in surprise. He'd never heard Dain talk about these things before.

"You believe, don't you?"

"Of course, I do. Just because Shadow talked to you,

and took you with him doesn't mean I'm not important in all this."

"I'm sorry. I didn't mean to make you feel that way, Dain."

"After all, I am the firstborn—"

"So, you have the potential to be a GAP-crosser—don't you?"

Dain just nodded silently and pointed to the stick figure's other hand. "See this?"

He looked closely and saw a tiny sword in the figure's right hand.

"What's the sword mean?" he asked.

"Didn't Stephan have one—at the battle with the Red Dragon?"

"He did have a shining sword—and he said it was the Sword of the Spirit."

The words were barely out of his mouth before Shadow began howling below them.

"Sounds like Shadow remembers, too," Dain whispered tensely.

"Stephan's sword spoke words from The Book—he also called it 'The Sword Which is the Word of God'." Again, Evin heard himself saying aloud the thoughts Shadow sent him.

"So, we have three things here to remember," Dain sighed. "Dad told me to show this to you, after—"

"After he died?"

Dain nodded mutely. Both boys were fighting tears again.

"So, the first is to stand our ground, right?"

"Yeah. And the second is to always be prepared."

"And, what's the third one?"

Dain put his hand across Evin's as he spoke again. "Dad said we need to be ready to go the distance—whatever it takes."

"Like Stephan did." Again, Evin spoke aloud the words the black dog put into his mind.

"From what you've told me, Stephan was ready to give himself for the rest of you."

"And he did. He died to save us from the Red Dragon. But what do all these things have to do with us now—here in Twenty-first Century Colorado?"

"I don't know for sure—yet," Dain said softly. "But I have a feeling the battle isn't over.

"Yeah, that Serpent is still alive, Shadow's just reminded me."

"So, I won't be surprised if sometime, someday, one of those GAP-crossers is going to come back here—and we need to be ready."

"And since Dad is gone, it's all up to us now, isn't it?"

CHAPTER 2
SPLASH

Evin and his older brother were working all day in the back pasture, building a fence.

"You have to put that horse in a pasture," their mother had said. "He needs to be free to get some exercise—not just stand around in a stall all the time."

"But Mom," he'd replied, "We ride him regularly, and he gets plenty of exercise that way."

"Right now, it's enough," she sighed. "But when you two go back to school in the fall—especially to high school—you won't have as much time for Splash as you do now."

"She's right," his brother had said. "I know what the homework is like in high school."

"Okay," he'd said with a little frustration. "But Dain has to help. Splash seems to like him better than he does me."

Dain had smiled at him with his green eyes. "Of course I want to help, Ev, but I think Splash likes *you* more, since you ride him the most."

The fencing they'd bought was the least expensive they could find, just split wooden rails. Mom said it wouldn't be strong enough to keep Splash in, but they didn't agree. After all, only he and Dain knew what Splash really was—a time-traveler like their dog. In fact, he'd been brought to them by Shadow. And the two boys knew neither of their animals would leave them without saying good-bye.

As these thoughts flowed in his head, the time working on the fence passed quickly. He and his brother sang some of their favorite songs while they worked. But as the heat of the day began to build and their energy waned, the music fell silent.

Now at last, the end was in sight.

"Boy, I could've never done this without you," he groaned rubbing a blister on his palm.

Dain also took the opportunity to rest briefly. "No problem, Ev. Ever since Dad died, I need this brother-time."

Evin's throat tightened at the mention of their father. "Me too," he managed to say.

Just then Shadow came bounding up to them. Today he was just his usual size, which meant he wasn't planning on crossing a GAP in the near future. In a way, Evin was relieved at this, but a tiny shade of disappointment crept into his thoughts, too.

"What's up?" he asked quietly, knowing that since the dog could read his thoughts, there was no need to speak. Still he felt better expressing his thoughts aloud, especially when Dain was with him, because he knew his older brother couldn't hear Shadow.

'I'm just getting some exercise,' the dog's deep voice said in Evin's mind.

"Can I come with you?"

'I don't know—can you?'

"Oh, Shadow, don't be so picky with my grammar. I mean 'may I' come with you?"

Dain laughed lightly as he heard Evin's side of the conversation. "Your dog is worse than Mom."

"It's just one of the things he annoys me with."

"What are some of the others?"

"Oh, I can't think of an example right now. Sometimes doesn't tell me things I need to know." He reached over and patted the large dog, who looked like a cross between a Labrador and a wolf.

'I had to go alone this time.' Shadow's voice cut into his thoughts. 'But you and Dain need to practice riding bareback on Splash.'

"Why?"

'You'll find out when you need to.'

Then before Evin could say another word, the black dog bounded away.

"What did he say there at the end, Ev?"

"He said you and I need to practice riding Splash bareback."

Dain sighed. "You know I'm not very good with riding horses."

"Don't worry," Evin said to his older brother. "Splash is no ordinary horse."

"Like Shadow is no ordinary dog, huh?"

And so, every clear day through the rest of the summer, they rode Splash in the new pasture they'd fenced. At first, Dain was nervous, so they rode double, with Dain hanging onto Evin's waist.

At last, there were only three days left before school started for the fall.

"It has to be today."

"You mean I have to ride him alone?"

"Come on, you can do it."

Shadow barked loudly.

"Shadow even agrees with me—see?"

Evin boosted his brother onto the pinto pony's back.

"Just keep your legs pressed in tight, and let Splash do the rest. He won't hurt you."

As he stepped back, Evin could see his brother's hands trembling slightly. He gently patted Splash on the rump, and the horse set off at an ambling pace.

'Don't worry,' came Shadow's thoughts. 'He'll do fine.'

The horse began by circling the dog and boy, moving wider with each pass. His speed picked up a little with each circle, until he was galloping beside their fence, taking the full circumference of the pasture.

"Hey, this is actually fun!" Dain's voice called to them.

"Told you it would be all right," he shouted back. "All you have to do is stay on his back, and Splash does all the rest."

Dain was grinning from ear to ear as he continued riding around the grassy field. Suddenly Shadow nudged Evin's back.

'Come on. Time to join them.'

Before he could reply, Evin was boosted onto the black dog's back. Then Shadow morphed to twice his normal size, loping toward Splash and Dain.

"Shadow says the next step might be teaching you to cross the GAP," he called.

"When will I be able to hear him?"

"Shadow says you'll hear him when it becomes necessary."

"I already know that. But when?"

Evin didn't hear any reply from Shadow to his brother's question, so he just smiled. Soon he and the dog were galloping along parallel to Splash's path around the pasture.

At last both the dog and the horse slowed to a walk, and the two boys found enough breath to talk again.

"So, I guess this is part of what Dad meant when he left us the message that said 'Semper Paratus' – right, Ev?"

"Yeah, I think so. This is part of being always prepared." He nodded and tilted his head toward the dog's ears, "Is that right?"

'Yes—but there's one more thing we must do—practice crossing the GAP.'

"Right now?"

'No, tomorrow.'

Evin wasn't sure if he should repeat any of this to Dain, so again he smiled across at his brother.

"I got the hang of this a lot faster than I expected," Dain was saying.

"Our animals know what to do," he replied. "We just need to learn to trust them. Shadow says we'll do this again tomorrow."

"Okay."

Evin was glad to hear the enthusiasm in Dain's voice. 'He might not feel so confident if I told him what Shadow wants to do tomorrow,' he sighed to himself.

The following morning, they went out early because Shadow insisted it was supposed to rain in the afternoon.

This time, Dain was able to hoist himself onto Splash's back. In a short time, both boys were galloping along the fence line, riding comfortably on their animals.

'Soon,' said Shadow's voice.

"Already?"

'We don't have much time left,' the dog growled.

"Why not?"

'I'll tell you when you need to know, Evin.'

"Okay, okay." Now he realized how frustrating things must be for Dain—not knowing what their GAP-crossing dog was up to.

'See that large cottonwood tree ahead? When we get to the rail just in front of it, we're going to jump the fence.'

"What? We'll hit the tree."

'No, we won't. Just hold on tightly.'

"Dain," he shouted quickly to his brother. "Shadow says we're going to jump the fence—up by that big tree."

"What?"

"Just hang on to Splash's mane."

He didn't have time to get any more words out before he felt Shadow's muscles tense for the jump. Then the ground seemed to fall away beneath them, and he felt like he was flying.

"I remember this," he said quietly to Shadow. "This is how it felt when you took me to the Time Nexus."

'Correct.'

Looking toward his brother and the horse, he saw that they were still right beside him.

"What's going on?" Dain cried.

"Don't worry. Shadow is teaching us to cross the GAP."

"Cross the GAP?"

"Don't panic. Just hold on."

He tried to send positive thoughts out to his brother. Then he actually managed to reach over and pat him on the thigh, which was tensed and clinging for dear life to Splash's flanks.

Once he saw Dain nod, he felt better and looked around.

They were moving toward a small rocky planetoid. By the way the sky was turning above their heads he couldn't get any bearings, though.

'Don't worry,' came Shadow's voice. 'We're moving into a Nexus where no harm can befall—and no time will pass.'

Now the vertigo left him, and he realized their mounts stepped right onto the rocky surface as it loomed up to meet them.

"Where are we?" came Dain's nervous voice.

"I'm not sure, but Shadow says it's a Nexus—a place out of time."

"Wow, look at that."

Evin gazed at his brother's extended hand as he pointed to the sky above them. His jaw dropped as he saw the inky black nothingness, with ropes of stars spiraling toward it.

"What is it?" he whispered to Shadow.

'This is the Milky Way Black Hole,' the dog replied.

"I hear him!" Dain cried.

Evin heaved a sigh of relief. "Good, that will make things easier."

'All right, time for your galactic geography lesson,' rumbled Shadow.

"Will this Black Hole suck us in?" Dain asked nervously.

'No. There's no suction—only gravity.'

"But it's the strongest gravity in the universe, right Shadow?"

'Correct. If we weren't in this Nexus, the gravitational pull would be too strong to resist.'

The two boys stayed seated on the animals. Evin knew he was feeling fearful in spite of Shadow's assurances. 'Dain must be petrified,' he thought. 'He's never experienced any of this—like I did when Shadow took me to help rescue Jael.'

But to his surprise, Dain was now pointing and talking excitedly. "So, is this the Black Hole at the center of the Milky Way?"

'It is.'

"In science class last year, they taught us there's one of these at the center of every galaxy."

"Shadow says that's true," Evin added.

"I know—I can hear him."

"Oh, yeah—sorry. I'm so used to repeating what he says aloud."

His brother just grinned at him.

'The ultimate fate of your universe *is* Black Holes,' Shadow's voice was continuing in their heads. 'All stars large enough to produce this immense amount of gravity will eventually collapse into Black Holes like this one.'

"What about the smaller stars?" Evin asked.

'They will collapse into themselves, too. But their mass won't be great enough to become black holes. For example, your Sun will become a white dwarf, as much of its matter drifts off into empty space. The fate of a star depends on how large it is.'

"But what will happen after all the stars are burned out?" came Dain's puzzled voice.

'Astronomers aren't certain yet, but there are speculations about what lies on the other side of a Black Hole.'

"The other side? How can anyone know that? Once someone is pulled into a Black Hole, they can never get out."

'True,' barked Shadow's voice. 'We don't know anything for sure yet. This is all I can show you now, for we must return to your pasture.'

Everything around them began to whirl into a confusion of starlight and total blackness. Evin's heart began to race—'I don't want to go into a Black Hole,' he said to Shadow.

'Don't fear. That's not my intention.'

Still, everything was flying away from them as if blown in some cosmic hurricane. Evin's heart was pounding so hard he felt like it might push right out of his chest.

Then he was lying on dried grass, and slowly opened his eyes. Above him was a normal blue Colorado sky. They must be back in the pasture.

Sitting up gingerly, he saw Splash grazing nearby, with Dain seated on the ground close to him. Shadow was nowhere in sight.

"Are you okay?" he asked.

"Sure, I'm fine. What's wrong?"

To his surprise, Evin noticed Dain was quite calm about what had just happened.

"Did you see the Milky Way Black Hole? Didn't the GAP-crossing frighten you?"

"Not really," Dain smiled. "Maybe it's because I'm firstborn—and I was made for GAP-crossing."

"I guess that's so," Evin muttered, as he carefully stood and tried to walk toward Dain.

"Hey, careful there," Dain jumped up to keep him from falling over.

"I guess I'm dizzy," Evin sighed. "It looks like you're going to be better at this than I am."

"It's okay. That's why Shadow lets you ride him. He's the GAP-crosser of your pair—while I'm the one with Splash."

"Oh."

"Hey, don't be disappointed. You're the one who helped prepare me for this. And Shadow says you have a very important role to play."

"I do? He told you that?"

Dain was nodding and patting him on the shoulder now. "I don't know the whole story."

"Yeah, Shadow doesn't reveal much at a time," he said ruefully.

"It's probably better that way. Then we don't have as much to worry about."

"I'm glad you feel that way. Somehow, not knowing in advance gets me nervous."

"Well, try to trust Shadow—and Splash and me."

Evin nodded numbly and leaned against his brother's shoulder. Splash moved next to them and gave them both a shove with his muzzle.

"See, Ev? Even Splash says it's going to be all right."

"Is *he* talking to you, too?"

"No," grinned Dain. "I just know what he means when he does that. Wait, what's this bump on his head?"

"Where?"

"Here, feel it?" Dain placed his brother's hand on Splash's forehead.

"Yeah, there's a bony spot there. I don't know. Say, how come Splash is getting so many white hairs in his black patches?"

They both looked closely at the pinto's flanks.

"Gosh, I never noticed that. I wonder if it means he's getting old."

Evin shrugged, "I don't know. But it seems like it started recently."

Just then, Shadow appeared in a flash of sparks.

"Where have you been?"

'Be calm. I've just been consulting with Johan.'

"Is that the old hermit Jace and Jon talked about?"

'Oh, he's much more than that, boys. He's a Guardian of Guardians.'

"A Guardian?" they both said together.

'One who knows the Time Portals,' rumbled Shadow's voice ominously. 'Soon he will be summoning me and perhaps all of us.'

Evin felt a shiver run down his back, but Dain's eyes were still glowing in excitement.

"Will we be ready?" Evin asked.

"Of course we will," said Dain.

"Did Shadow just tell you that? I didn't hear anything."

"No, it's just something I know in my heart."

CHAPTER 3
Called from Afar

Ginna Parker Carson was trying to read a book, but her eyes kept lifting off the page and gazing at Garek, her husband. His hair had gone entirely gray now and hers was close behind. She wondered if he was experiencing some of the same aches and pains she was.

"Old age isn't for sissies."

Her mother, Lauren Parker, had said this often—especially near the end, when the cancer was ravaging her body.

Ginna shook her head and tried to stop the tears, but they'd already reached her cheeks. 'Too late,' she said to herself, as they blinded her eyes.

The next thing she knew, Garek was sitting beside her, his arm across her shoulders.

"You thinking about your brother Danny again?" he whispered close to her ear.

Shaking her head, she tried to respond, but her voice refused to cooperate.

"It's okay. It helps to cry."

"I know," she murmured, finding a faint raspy voice.

He gently kissed the top of her head and pulled her closer, both his arms around her now. She leaned against him, trying to absorb the comfort from him she so desperately needed. Soon his fingers were wiping at the tears on her cheeks, but more kept coming.

"Actually, I was thinking of my mother," she sighed at last. "I almost feel guilty because I think of her more than Danny."

"Well, that was another long good-bye, too. Didn't she die of cancer like your brother?"

All she could do was nod mutely against his chest—her voice drowning in more tears.

"Perhaps losing Danny has reawakened memories of her, too."

"I guess so. Mom's been gone over thirty years—I thought I'd gotten over grieving for her, but—"

"I don't think grief for a loved one ever goes away completely, Ginna."

She looked up into his face as he said this, and saw a hint of shine at the corners of his eyes. "Are you grieving, too, Garek? For your lost children?"

He half-smiled down at her. "How can I grieve for people who haven't even been born yet?"

"But you remember them—they're real in your mind, even if you did leave them behind to come to my time. I'm sorry I caused you this." Her voice broke abruptly, and she buried her face in his shirt.

"Don't feel bad," he murmured. "You've never caused me any grief."

She heard his voice rumble deeply in his chest, with her head against him like this. "But it *is* my fault." Again, her voice failed her.

"You're forgetting it was the Lord who sent me here with you, Ginna."

"I'm still sorry."

"Please don't be. You put way too much blame on yourself—blame that shouldn't be there."

She continued to lean her head against him, feeling the gentle circles his hand was drawing on her back. At last, her voice returned. "I'm glad you're here. These past few years have been the happiest part of my entire life— because of you."

"Well, the same goes for me." His voice was barely audible, but she could hear it in the vibrations of his chest. "Being with you, wherever you are, means more than any- thing—even the people I left behind—in the future."

"Do you realize how strange that sounds? You can't leave people behind who won't be born for nearly a thou- sand years."

Now his voice turned to a chuckle. "You're right. But they're still here in my memories, regardless."

"Time GAPs are almost beyond my comprehension,

Garek. I've spent a lot of time in that future—sometimes actually 'inside' Martina. So I have 'future memories', too."

"I know," he laughed softly. "That's how we met."

"You didn't even know I was there that first time, did you?"

"You mean when Martina and I had our 'little affair'? I wonder sometimes if it was you—there inside Martina's mind—that attracted me in the first place."

"Really?"

She felt him nod, but he didn't speak. Was his voice beginning to get lost again like hers?

"That's how I ended up having Annemarie."

"Our daughter," he added quickly. "And a beautiful young woman she's become."

"Not so young anymore. She's pushing forty."

"But we're pushing sixty ourselves."

"Don't remind me," she shrugged.

"Well, since I haven't been born yet, seeing that I'm from the future—maybe my age should be counted in negative numbers below zero."

"Oh, that's not fair," she began to laugh, in spite of her tears. "You always find a way to cheer me up."

"Speaking of the GAP, I saw Danny's sons paid you a visit the other day."

"It's hard to believe they're both teenagers already. Dain is nearly sixteen, and Evin just turned fourteen."

"And unfortunately, Danny won't get to see them grow up."

"It's sad for them, too."

"What did they want to know? Things about their dad?"

"No, actually they wanted to ask me about GAP-crossing."

"Really? Oh, I guess Evin did have that adventure with their dog, Shadow."

"He and Shadow 'crossed' into the future to help rescue Jael, Martina's brother. They told me the whole story."

"I heard it, too."

"I'm surprised at you—eavesdropping."

"It wasn't intentional. I just happened to be in the next room when they came to the door. I couldn't help but hear."

"Yeah, the walls in this old house aren't soundproof. That's for sure. So, did you hear the part about how they keep hearing Martina—and wondering if she's trying to call?"

"Have you heard her?"

"Maybe a little. She seems to pop into my mind more these days. Let's see, it's been at least five years since they found Jael."

"Is that five years in this century—or theirs?"

"All I know is how much time has passed here. But the time there usually passes in the same way."

"Except when they bring you back."

"That's true. It always seems no time passed here while I'm in the GAP."

"Do you think Martina may be calling you?"

"Either that or maybe J—"

She'd just begun to nod her head when the air across the room crackled with sparks. Then a hazy image of a slender, blond man began to emerge from the flashes of light.

Ginna stepped toward the figure in disbelief. "Jon? Is that really you? Did you cross a GAP? I don't think I called you, even unconsciously. What are you doing here?"

Before she could say any more, he pulled her into a firm embrace. "I need you, Ginna. I'm the one who called—for you."

"Wait a minute. What do you think you're doing with my wife?"

Jon stepped back and looked up into Garek's blue eyes. "I'm sorry," he muttered. "I have no intention of taking her against your will."

"So what is it?" Garek was standing at his full two-meter height with his hands planted firmly on his hips.

Ginna saw Jon take a deep breath and stand as tall as he could, though he was still looking up at her husband.

"It's Martina—she's acting so depressed." Jon said in the calmest voice he could muster. "I'm really afraid for her sanity, and I hoped Ginna could help reach her. I guess I should've asked you first, Garek. I'm sorry. Will you let me take Ginna with me—ahead to the Thirty-first Century?"

"That's my time, not Ginna's," Garek muttered. "But you don't want me to come?" Ginna could see his shoulders sag just a little, but then he pulled them up again and his voice came more firmly. "It's Ginna's choice. I won't interfere—if you don't need my help. I do care a lot for Martina—as a friend."

Now she saw Jon's eyes flash briefly. 'He's remembering when Garek and Martina had their affair, forty years ago. But that's in the future from here. Oh, this time travel gets so confusing.'

"Well?' both male voices asked, interrupting her thoughts.

She closed her eyes and took a deep breath before she spoke. "Okay—yes—I care a lot about Martina, too."

Before she stepped over to join Jon for the GAP-crossing, she stood on her tiptoes and gave her husband a tight hug and a lingering kiss. Her heart was beginning to race as she tried to pull herself away. "I won't be long," she whispered. "I'll miss you."

She felt, rather than saw, Jon take her hands because her eyes were blinded with tears. And then the ground beneath her feet seemed to fall away, like an elevator going down—except her body didn't go down with it.

CHAPTER 4
IN MARTINA'S THOUGHTS

I was lying on a cold stone floor, hugging my blanket, one of my few possessions. Sometimes I did this for hours on end, not having the energy to move even a muscle, hoping that if I sat like this long enough my body would just expire from disuse. But somehow, it always forced me to get up and feed it. Even though I wanted to die, my body refused to let me.

Outside I could hear the wind howling through the trees concealing the entrance to our cave. 'Another cold and blustery day,' I sighed. 'If only we could've gone back to Indonia. It was much warmer there, food was easier to find, and we didn't have to live in cold dark caves. But the System learned of the Indonia Out-clave from a traitor in our midst, so we can never go back there.' As these thoughts filled my mind, I could feel the darkness creeping into my body.

Many times, Jon found me like this and tried to comfort me. Right now, the thin muscles of my back seemed to be longing for his touch. But then my mind took me back to our most recent conversation:

"Martina," [he'd said angrily] "You need to snap out of this. I know our life has been really rough since we came back from Stephan's alternative-universe."

"I miss Stephan," I sighed, tears beginning to well up in my eyes. "He was like a father to me, the father I'd lost to the Galactic Wars almost fifty years ago."

"Please don't cry. I miss him, too."

"You should be glad I can cry today. Some days I feel so desolate that I can't, no matter how much I want to."

Jon didn't need to remind me why we were here again. After the battle with the Red Dragon, Johan had appeared and insisted we needed to return to Earth—to fulfill our mission. "The Serpent is still abroad," he'd said.

Now I sighed to myself with longing. Materna was such a beautiful place, all in shades of orange and gold with no green in sight. At first this had taken getting used to, but now the glaring colors of all the greens and blues of Earth seemed to jab my sight and grate on my nerves. I knew this was the first reason I'd retreated into the darkness of the cave.

"At least we have Jael back now," Jon had continued on that day.

I nodded and wished he'd give me a hug, but now he was pacing the floor of our small cave, his head coming dangerously close to the rocky ceiling.

"It seems like your moods lately are the ultimate in selfishness. You just dwell on yourself and how *you* feel—like you don't really care about anyone else."

"That's not true."

"Well, you never go to visit Jael and Raina, and they live just a quarter mile away."

"I don't want to interfere," I sighed, realizing my tears were already dry. The numbness filling all of my soul returned. "He and Raina need to get reacquainted, after all the years he was in the System prison, believed to be dead. And I feel like I'm just a burden in their way."

"You've even cut yourself off from Celestia and Laken."

"They have each other and need to get adjusted to being married now. I'm glad Johan sealed their vows of marriage before he brought us back here." I heard the envy in my voice and wondered if Jon did.

"Celestia needs her mother, too. You know that as well as I do."

"When *I* needed my mother, she was taken from me."

"There you go again—with your 'oh poor me' attitude. Sure, you lost your mother when the System took her away, but that was long ago on Terres. And you were restored to her when your Uncle Dominic found her and brought her to Earth."

"But I had to watch helplessly as they both died in the battle on Luna—when the System and the Serpent attacked us."

"Still, that made it possible for us to escape to Materna. You do realize that, don't you?"

Again, I felt my eyes trying to cry, but no tears would come.

He moved closer to the cave's entrance. I wanted to reach out to him, feel his reassuring touch, but none of my muscles would cooperate.

"I can see you want to wallow in your own 'pity party' here, so I'll just leave you to it." Then he was gone.

***

That was several weeks ago now, but even reliving the moments of this encounter with my husband couldn't bring the tears I so desperately wanted to shed. My mind was almost totally numb now. I couldn't pray, either. There was nothing in my mind and heart that even seemed alive anymore.

'God, if you're real, why don't you speak to me?' I moaned to myself. It was getting more and more difficult to think at all.

I knew this was how my mother had been right after Father died. She'd just sat in a corner on one of our floor cushions, staring into space with an empty gaze for hours on end. I knew I was experiencing depression, just as she had. But that didn't help me at all. I was trapped in a deep, dark place—and there was no way out.

'That's a lie,' came a voice from somewhere in my memory. Who was it? Perhaps my oldest brother, Stephen? He'd died not long after they'd taken Mom away.

'Our family was torn apart by the System back then,' I sighed. 'Where were you when I needed you, God?'

Only silence met me.

'Well, if you don't care enough to answer me, maybe I'll just stop asking.' Feeling anger was better than the total numbness. And a voice in my mind seemed to say, 'It will be much easier to stop believing in the True King. Just think, you could return to the real world. No more hiding or trying to please anyone. No more having to be good or caring about any of those people who could care less about you.'

This was almost refreshing. Maybe the voice was right. Where had it come from? Was it my own thoughts or someone else's? I had no idea, but it reminded me that I was still alive.

But I wasn't sure I even wanted to be alive anymore. There seemed to be no hope left in me. The best part of my life was over. Maybe it would be better for everyone if I just ended it…

I must have fallen asleep with this thought in my mind because when I woke it was still there. But there weren't any means convenient. Jon had taken our only knife, folded it and put it in his pocket. Was it that same day as our argument? Most likely. Other than finding a cliff to jump off, I had no other means of ending my life.

'That's probably why I'm not eating,' I thought. 'All I have left is trying to starve myself.'

But this kept backfiring. Every time I woke, I was ravenously hungry and usually ate whatever was in sight. This time I managed to rummage up some venison jerky and fruit leather.

As I munched, I realized Jon was the one doing all the work around here. 'He's the one who hunts the game, cures it, and makes what food we have. I'm not doing anything but be a burden.' And so, my mind brought itself full-circle, back to the idea of suicide.

After my meager meal, I must have curled back into the blanket, trying to pull any comfort out of it I could. My eyes were closed when the crackling flashes started. I heard them before I saw them.

As I stared at the other end of our small cave, I saw two figures beginning to emerge from a shower of sparks and flashing amber light. One was the lean, tall frame of my husband, and the other looked vaguely familiar. I blinked my eyes several times before I recognized the woman who, like me, had streaks of gray appearing in her brown hair.

Then, it was like a small light appeared in my darkened mind. "Ginna? Is it really you? Or am I dreaming?"

"Martina? You look awful!"

For the first time in ages, I was aware of how tangled my hair must be—and began to wonder if I smelled unwashed. "I'm sorry, Ginna."

"No, don't worry." She moved to my side and hugged me tightly. "I want to help you."

"I'll just let you two get reacquainted," came Jon's voice, fading away as he left the cave.

CHAPTER 5
DESPERATE MEASURES

I knew Jon meant well when he brought Ginna to the cave. And she did, too, as she tried to draw me out of my deep, dark well of depression. But the more either of them talked to me, the deeper I sank.

'Can't they see talk is hollow?' my mind kept saying. 'Why don't they just leave me alone?'

I'd been down in this pit so long it was a strange comfort to me, and if they just left me alone, I didn't have to think, groping for words to answer their incessant questions. Anything besides lying wrapped in my blanket was just too much effort.

'Now I understand how it was for my mother—why she couldn't come back to us from her despair. This was nearly fifty years ago, and light years away from me now. If Mom were here, maybe she'd know how to help me. But probably not. I don't know if she learned anything from the time she was deep in her depression.'

I hoped tears would come to my eyes as I thought of my mother, lost to me now in death. 'You'd think I could cry for my own mother.' But once again, the tears refused to fall.

There's one day I remember more than the rest. Ginna was seated on one side of me and Jon on the other, while I was wrapped tightly in my blanket-cocoon, refusing to let either of them touch me. 'Touching is too risky,' thoughts were saying inside my head. 'You might lose it—if you let anyone touch you.'

"I wish you'd let me help you," came Ginna's whisper, close to my ear. I could hear tears in her voice, and this filled me with envy.

'Why can she cry for me, when I can't even cry for myself?'

Jon's voice came next, "Martina, please. Don't lock yourself away like this." Anger was beginning to edge into his voice. "We love you."

'What do either of you know of love?' I asked myself. 'You think you love me, but I'm the lowest, most unlovable creature that exists.'

Jon was trying to rub my back, as he often did when I was tired or stressed. But today the thought of his touch filled me with dread. 'Perhaps he'll see all the darkness in my soul if he touches me. I'm too ashamed to let that happen.'

After my continued refusal to let either of them comfort me, Jon finally rose and began to pace the floor. The heaviness of his footsteps reverberated with his frustration.

Ginna, however, remained at my side sitting patiently. Finally, Jon left with a huge sigh, and I rolled away from Ginna. This gave her the opportunity to rub my back unimpeded.

My first reaction was to cringe and try to draw away, but she persisted. And at last I began to feel a trickle of comfort move across my shoulders.

"We really love and care for you. Why can't you let us in?"

'Doesn't she see? I can't let anyone in. It would show them the face of my total despair, my shame that I can't get escape it.' I didn't say any of these words out loud, but somehow Ginna sensed them:

"I know how this deep pit of depression feels, Martina. I've been there myself. Can you imagine a seventeen-year-old girl—pregnant and with no one to turn to? She doesn't even understand how it happened because she was 'within' another human's psyche—"

"You were inside me, weren't you, Ginna?"

"It was part of Jon's Parallel Universe experiment." Now anger was creeping into her voice as she continued. "I didn't know what to think—except wonder if somehow I'd been raped while I was 'in' you."

"But now you know the truth, don't you?" My voice

was a barely audible whisper.

Ginna's hand kept its slow circles across my back. "Yes, I know you didn't intend for anything to affect me when you had your affair with Garek. But sometimes consequences can be much more than we expect."

Another wave of fear and despair swept over, and I pulled myself out of her reach. 'How can she care about me? I'm the cause of all her problems. I don't deserve to go on.'

Again, she seemed to sense my thoughts. "Please don't blame yourself, Martina. Sure, I experienced some pain, but now that we've learned the truth, I have joy, too. Garek and I are happily married and sharing life in my time and place—Twenty-first Century Colorado."

"And your daughter Annemarie?"

"Thanks to the Lord's amazing provision, she and David are also married and building a life of their own. Perhaps someday I'll—or rather, we'll—have a grandchild or two to love."

"Okay, so the True King has fixed what I messed up, but this doesn't make it better. I still feel guilty."

"The Lord has forgiven you, and so have I. Why can't you forgive yourself?"

Suddenly my empty shell filled with unexpected emotion, the first I'd felt in a long time. But it wasn't the release Ginna was expecting. Instead, I leapt to my feet, almost bumping my head on the low ceiling of the cave.

My entire body was trembling in anger.

"How dare you think you can come back into my mind. That was many years ago, when we were both much younger. I don't want you to invade me like this anymore. Jon should never have brought you. It's like he has no care for my true self. He has to bring you back into the picture to find any love for me in himself."

"That's not true. He loves you for you. He just hoped I could reach past this wall you've built between yourself and the rest of the world."

"Maybe this wall is the only safety I have left."

"If you'd just let me in for a moment, I could help you see what's missing."

Now I was the one pacing the rock floor with my blanket pulled tightly around my shoulders. I was clutching it like a drowning person grabs at a would-be rescuer, dragging him down with her. "Just go away," my voice screamed. "I don't want to talk to anyone."

I heard the scrape of shoes on stone as she rose to her feet and began to move toward me. "Please don't shut me out."

"No! Take your so-called sympathy and go away. All I want is to be left alone."

"You may think that right now." Ginna's voice was growing louder, and frustration was beginning to give it a desperate edge. "But even if you don't know it, you need someone to help you through this."

"No, I don't!" Now my voice was almost a scream. "If you won't leave, then I will." I edged myself toward the entrance of the cave.

"Okay, okay." I could hear her trying to put a smooth calm back into her voice. "I'll leave for now. But I'm not giving up on you."

"Just get out of here," I muttered through clenched teeth.

I turned my face toward the rocky wall, hearing her as she walked away and went out of the cave. 'Do I hear tears in her voice?' I wondered. This thought made my anger turn to envy. 'Why can she cry—and I can't? It's just not fair.'

After Ginna left, I continued to stand unmoving. In a strange way the anger was a relief. At least I was feeling something for a change. I think this realization planted the germ of an idea in my mind.

She and Jon came and went over the next few days. In the darkness of the cave, I really didn't know whether it was day or night. I pretended to listen to them sometimes, but all their words were just like water flowing over and around me, having no effect. Whenever one of them brought me food that wasn't perishable, I ate a tiny bit and managed to hide the rest beneath my blanket.

Finally, the day arrived when I had enough stored. Once Ginna left, after trying unsuccessfully to give me a hug, I wrapped the fruit leather and jerky inside the blanket and found a way to tie it across my back, with the slight bulge of the food secured in front of me.

'The only reason I'm taking this is so I have enough energy to get far away from here,' I muttered to myself. 'Once I get there, it won't matter whether I go on living or starve to death.'

As I silently slipped out of the cave, I saw the sun setting in a flood of pink, orange, and purple clouds. Their contrast with the pale blue of the evening sky was dramatic, and I felt a slight thrill at the beauty of it. But now my mind was made up. I was leaving this place and these people forever—so I wouldn't have to deal with any emotions, ever again. Or so I hoped.

***

By the time I reached the open fertile fields east of the montane forests, a shell of a plan developed in my mind. Knowing I had no clothing appropriate for anyplace except a Rebel Out-clave, my story had to be good if I was going to escape capture and imprisonment.

'Prison would be no better than the life I'm running from,' I muttered to myself. 'But if I say I was captured by Rebels, that could account for my appearance.'

I walked along doggedly all through the night. In some strange way, I didn't fear the darkness. In fact, it was comforting. As the sun began to rise ahead of me, I resented its presence, much like I'd resented Jon and Ginna's presence back in my cave.

But my path was set. I had no other plan. As I walked through the fields of tall ripe grain, I began to see the skyline of a city in the distance. Since I'd paid no attention to where our cave was, I didn't know which city it was. But it didn't really matter.

As the day wore on, and the city drew gradually closer, I saw the outline of the tower—a structure that made a pang of regret stab into my mind. It looked exactly like Neptune Spire, the tallest building in Terres-City. But that was on a distant planet long in my past. From what Jon and Jael had told me, it was destroyed in the disaster that overtook our old home planet, when a passing star captured our sun, Regelian.

'Why should I feel something for this long-gone place? How come I feel for things that no longer exist, but nothing for people who are close to me now?'

My only answer to these thoughts was total silence in my soul.

As I continued to progress toward the city on the horizon, I focused my eyes on the tower. 'I feel like it's calling me. That makes no sense, but at least I'm feeling something.'

Other parts of the city's skyline began to take shape as I trudged on. I would stop occasionally to eat a few bites of the food I'd brought, telling myself it was only to give me energy to reach the city. Because of the tower, I felt confident the city before me was Tornatoh, one of the chief cities of Old North America.

Ginna and I had been there once—hoping to rescue our daughters, Annemarie and Celestia, when they'd tried on their own to locate Garek.

'If I'm honest with myself, it was exciting to see Garek back then, after all those years. There were still seeds of attraction to him. But he seemed to think Ginna was who attracted him all along. He said her presence within me was what he'd felt, even far in the past when we were working together here on Earth.'

In spite of myself, I let out an audible sigh. 'Even the one person who I still have feelings for has none for me. Ginna is the lucky one. And as usual, I'm left with the meager crumbs.'

Perhaps this made sense in a twisted sort of way. 'Am I still in love with Garek? Maybe I'll find someone in Tornatoh who cares about me.'

As expected, I came to a high fence when I was still several miles from the outskirts of the city. A guardhouse stood near a heavily armored gate. 'What are they afraid of? The remnant of Rebels and Believers out in the wilds is no match for them.' My mind couldn't grasp any answers to its own questions, so I just shrugged and walked up to the structure.

When I was still about fifty meters out, a figure emerged from the shadows.

"Who goes there?" His voice seemed too young to sound so sharp. And I almost smiled at the same classic greeting used by soldiers and guards for eons.

"Oh please!" I didn't need to make my voice sound desperate—it did that on its own. "Help me! I've escaped from one of their prisons."

"Prison? What prison?"

Stepping a bit closer so he could see the ragged clothes I wore and the disheveled state of my hair, I looked at the ground— a classic pose of submission. "The Rebels captured me." My mouth was having trouble working, but it didn't matter. It only added to the effect of helplessness.

"Wait there."

I continued to stand gazing at the ground as he approached me and poked at my makeshift pack sack. "That's just a few bits of food I stole," I whispered.

"How long have you been walking?" His voice still sounded suspicious.

"Oh—several nights—and most of today, sir. I had to travel in darkness at first, in case they sent anyone after me."

He stared into my face, but after glancing up into his eyes for an instant, I dropped my gaze to the bare sandy ground at my feet.

"That fits,' he muttered. "Just about the right distance to that Rebel Out-clave in the mountains."

At this question, my stomach began to heave. 'Does he know where the caves are? The System could wipe us out whenever they want. But wait! He thinks our caves are days away and doesn't know I've come a much shorter distance.'

As I let this fear pass over and through me, I found it gave me an odd sort of courage. "I escaped," I began again. At least I wouldn't be the one who gave our out-clave away. "Please take me to a place where they can never snatch me again."

"What did they do to you?"

"I was kept in a totally dark cave, with only this blanket." I shifted the blanket so the small packet of food now rested on my hip.

"Did you hear anything that might be good intel?"

"No sir. I'm sorry. I only saw two people the entire time. There was a tall man, blond hair speckled with gray—and a woman he sometimes brought along to question me."

This, I knew, was the best way to fabricate my story—with as many true facts as possible. Then I wouldn't have to remember what I said.

"How did you escape?" His voice still sounded suspicious.

Somehow, I needed to convince him I had something that made me worth keeping.

"I watched their patterns for weeks, sir. And hid bits of the food they brought in my blanket. Finally, one day at sunset no one came, so I slipped out of the cave. I could hear angry voices in the distance, and no one was paying attention to me."

"They had no guards at this cave?" Again, the voice was incredulous.

"There always were before," I added quickly. "I think the guard was drawn away towards the sounds of argument. I just ran into the forest, and never paused to see."

With this statement, I raised my eyes and looked directly into his. My heart jumped when I saw green eyes looking much like my younger brother's. The one we'd thought dead until he was rescued and restored to his family.

'But he had no space in his heart for me,' I muttered to myself, even though I knew this wasn't true. Jael's mind was badly damaged by his ordeal in a System Time Nexus.

I pushed these thoughts angrily away, even as I heard Jon's voice echo accusingly in my mind: 'It's not Jael who's turned his back on you, Martina. You've turned your back on him.'

"You don't understand," I'd cried. "You never have understood what Jael and I shared from our difficult childhoods."

That happened before I began to sink into this well of despair, back when I could still sort some of my thoughts into a semblance of coherence.

Now I shook my head ever so slightly—I didn't want these memories clouding my mind.

Just as I thought this, another voice boomed from above our heads:

"Well done, Corporal Shei. Bring her into the holding area."

'Shei? Is that his given name or surname?' I'd barely thought this when he grabbed me roughly by the arms, pulling me into a small fenced area beside the guardhouse.

"There's no need to be so rough, Corporal Shei," I murmured close to his ear. "I'm seeking your help, and I mean you no harm."

I almost found myself wanting to laugh. How could someone in my present condition harm anyone?

Perhaps Shei sensed my weakened condition as he pulled my arms, for the next thing he did was seat me on a bench standing just inside the guardhouse.

"You do seem very weak." His voice became suddenly more solicitous. "Can I get you anything?"

"Just water." I could barely speak now, and my throat was suddenly aching and dry.

He stepped back toward what appeared to be a kind of cooler, pulled out a small bottle and handed it to me. I noticed he was careful not to take his eyes off me.

"This isn't some kind of truth-serum, is it?" I tried to laugh casually.

"No," he smiled. "Just good old H-two-O."

I took a tiny sip at first, but my mind didn't seem to be affected—so I took a few swallows more. As the cool water entered my system, I began to feel more clear-headed.

"So, Corporal Shei," I began.

"Just call me Shei. What should I call you?"

"Tina. What do you propose to do with me?"

"Maybe I should take you to the Infirmary, Tina. You look very pale."

As he said this, the room took a large spin in my vision. Had he drugged me after all?

But as he helped me to my feet, my vision cleared enough to sense him leading me to a door on my right. We stepped into a brightly-lit hallway. My eyes were so unaccustomed to bright lights that they closed instantly. All I could see was a throbbing orange around me.

Then he pushed me into another doorway. I tripped on something, opened my eyes, and discovered I was in darkness again. The echo of a heavy door locking filled my ears.

CHAPTER 6
ONCE AND AGAIN

Laken Meta woke to the sound of heavy breathing close to him. Their cooking fire had burned down to fading embers, so he could see only a vague shape above him.

The feeling of surging adrenalin caused him to sit up too quickly, and he knocked the shadow above him to the ground.

"Ouch!" came his wife Celestia's voice.

"I'm sorry," he said to the darkness. "What's wrong?"

"I need your help, Laken." This was a deeper voice that he hadn't expected.

"Who's there?" He shoved long strands of black hair out of his face.

"My dad," Celestia replied. "My mother has disappeared."

"What?" Laken shook his head, still in the grogginess of sleep.

"She's gone," Jon said again, and now Laken could

hear the panic rising in his father-in-law's voice. "You know how moody she's been. I think she's run away, but God only knows where."

'Yeah, only God knows—that's for sure,' he thought. 'And I'm not God. How am I supposed to help?' By this time, he'd found a piece of twine to tie his black ponytail in place.

He didn't say anything aloud, though. Instead, he shifted to feed the fire with a couple of the split pieces of wood he'd saved here in the cave—ones he'd intended using to take the chill off tomorrow morning. Something in Jon and Celestia's voices told him this night wasn't going to be spent in sleeping.

Gradually the flames began to lick at the wood, and the three of them moved closer to the fire-ring, holding their hands out to catch the warmth.

"It's really scary," Jon began. "She did this back in her teens, when she ran away from Terres City to join the Redlarks in the Wilds."

Laken was thinking words he knew he shouldn't say: 'But now Martina is an adult woman, not a frightened and confused teenager.'

"Wasn't that the time she left her little brother all alone?"

"Right, daughter. Jael was barely ten Standard Years old."

"Why did she run away then?" Laken asked softly.

"I'm not really sure," sighed Jon. "At that time, I hadn't met either of them."

"But later you met Jael and helped him find her."

"It wasn't easy though. Without the King's help, we never would have gotten her back."

"Mom gives you a lot of the credit, you know."

"Well, Celestia, I don't think I could have done any of it alone."

"Okay, you two, we need to think." He couldn't contain his impatience any longer.

"There are some similarities to last time," Jon said softly. "She's been acting disoriented and depressed. She seems to have inherited that tendency from her mother."

"Yeah, when her husband died, back when they all lived on Terres, Grandma went into a deep depression, didn't she?"

Jon nodded to Celestia. She reached for his hand and squeezed it. "You've done the best you can."

Laken could hear the pain in their voices and wished he knew how to help. "What she needs is a real trained counselor," he sighed.

"But there's no way to get such a thing—now that we're all hiding in the wilds of Earth."

"I know, Hon," Laken said to his wife, trying to keep the frustration out of his own voice. 'I know how Jon feels—that's for sure,' he added silently.

"Maybe she'll find some help where she's gone."

"But where has she gone?" sighed Jon.

"My best guess is the nearest city," said Laken. "I don't think she could survive alone in these mountains."

"What is the nearest city?" asked Celestia.

"Tornatoh," Laken said flatly, fear coming into his voice, too.

By now Jon's brown eyes were closed as he nodded and squeezed his daughter's hand.

Celestia fought back tears. "What about Ginna—was she any help?"

"Not yet."

"But maybe she has a role to play that you've missed."

Jon nodded silently, unable to speak again.

"Perhaps Laken and I can help. Laken's had experience working undercover."

"Sure have. Maybe we could go into the city to search."

Jon turned toward Laken as he finally found his voice again. "I don't want you two in danger. It would kill me to lose both my wife and my daughter."

Laken was momentarily at a loss for words, but then he replied, "Please trust me with your daughter, Jon. She's my wife now—and as dear to me as Martina is to you."

"I know, I know. But I still have a father's fears—you have no experience of that. I can't let you take the risk."

Celestia decided it was time to change the subject before the two male egos collided further. "Does Ginna know Mom's run away?"

"I don't think so," said Jon. "She's staying with Jael."

"He probably reminds her of Danny," Laken added.

"Especially now that he's died."

"Danny died? You never told me that."

"Sorry. I guess I've been too wrapped up in my own problems."

"Oh, Dad." She tried to give him a hug, but it was awkward in the cramped cave, with them all clustered around the small fire.

"When I went back for her, Ginna told me Danny died of brain cancer a few months ago."

"I wish I'd known. I would have talked to her sooner than this."

"Like I said, I'm really sorry."

"I think we need to see if she can help us find Martina," Laken interrupted.

"You're right. I've been in such a panic since Martina disappeared—thanks for helping me gather some of my scattered thoughts."

"Let's go talk to Ginna."

***

Laken had met Ginna back in the Twenty-second Century, when Celestia brought her—with her daughter, Annemarie—to find the Fountain in the Desert. But they fell into a Time Well, and ended up in his time by mistake.

Now, as they made their way quietly through the

forest toward Jael's cave, he could see the last quarter of the Moon dropping into the western sky.

"Sure is hard to believe we were up there not too many months ago, isn't it?" he said.

"I was just thinking the same thing, you mind-reader," Celestia replied.

"Sh! Not so loud," hissed Jon.

"Oh, right. But there haven't been any Patrols here since we came back, have there?"

"No." Laken patted her back gently. "But it's always good to be careful."

She stopped now and was gazing up at the silvery half-circle. "I sure wish we could go back there—or even to Materna."

"Materna wasn't our home," he sighed. "It was an alternative-universe, so we couldn't stay there forever. And the Portal on Luna was compromised." He nudged her to begin walking again.

"By the Traitor," said Jon.

Laken was surprised at the anger in his voice. Apparently Celestia noticed also, for she turned toward her father and added:

"I feel sorry for all the things that happened because of the Traitor."

"Yes, some died that might not have."

"Like my grandmother and her husband." Now she was sounding angry, too.

"Branden was used by the Serpent because of his intense grief for his first wife, but you were the one who brought him back from the edge of destruction," Laken murmured to her.

"I'm glad the King was able to use me for that," she sighed. "And now it appears we have another crisis."

"I hope this one won't have more bad effects on Jael and Raina," Jon said quietly. "They're barely getting back to normal."

"As normal as it ever gets out here in exile," muttered his wife.

By this time, they'd reached the entrance to Jael's cave, and the dawn was barely beginning to brighten the eastern sky.

Jon called softly, and Jael appeared quickly in the opening.

"It's my sister, isn't it?" his question came with no prologue.

"How did you know?" Laken asked.

"I just had a strange dream about her—a sort of flashback to when she abandoned me in Terres-City. Has she run away again?"

"You're right as usual," said Jon.

"I think the connection between you and me is being reforged, Jon."

At this, Jon pulled Jael to him in a tight embrace. "Thank you, Lord," he breathed.

Jael also seemed to be feeling this way, because he held onto Jon tightly. In a short time, Ginna and Raina were wakened by the commotion. Raina's voice came first:

"Come in out of the cold. I have the fire restarted."

Soon all seven of them were gathered around the fire pit in the center of the cave's main room—joining Jeal's wife Raina, and Jace, their nearly-grown son.

"Sure is a good thing your cave has more space than ours," Jon sighed. "I don't think we'd all fit in there."

"Ours either," Laken added.

"Maybe the True King knew we'd need this," Celestia whispered.

Laken heard her, then reached over and squeezed her hand.

"It's a bit tight, but we just fit," came Jael's voice. "So, what can we help with?"

"Well, as you've guessed, Jael—Martina's disappeared. We think she may have run away to Tornatoh."

"That's just the opposite of what she did on Terres. There she fled the City to go into the Wilds," said Jael.

"Right," Jon nodded to his friend.

"I can see a pattern in it," Ginna began. "The first time she was running away from grief and depression. Now that those same feelings have returned, she probably hopes to reverse them by running back to the kind of life she left the first time."

"There's some logic in that," said Laken. "Do you

think perhaps you're sensing some of her feelings?"

"Because of the connection we had when I was 'within' her mind?" Ginna finished for him.

"That time on Terres, it took Jael's love to bring her back to her senses," added Jon, looking into his younger friend's eyes, "Right, Little Brother?"

Laken saw a slight smile play at Jael's lips as he nodded to Jon. "It's good to be back in my right mind," he said. "I hope what I experienced those eight years in the System's Time Nexus can help us reconnect with my sister."

Jon looked down then to hide tears, but Laken saw Jael grasp his hand firmly.

An uncomfortable silence settled around them, broken only by the crackling of the wood on the fire. At last, Ginna spoke:

"I think my brother had a premonition of this."

"How's that?" Laken finally spoke. He'd been waiting on the others to speak their thoughts first—since he hadn't known Danny very well.

"He told me shortly before he died to talk to his sons, Dain and Evin," Ginna continued.

"Dain is the elder one, isn't he?"

"Right," nodded Ginna.

"I met the two boys briefly, when my other-universe grandfather, Stephan, took me to Danny's home," Celestia added.

"And that's how you found Jael, at last." Raina's voice

was heard for the first time since they'd settled around the fire.

"But Dain wasn't with us then," said Jon, "Just his younger brother, Evin."

"And his big black dog," added Laken.

Jon nodded quickly. "That's right. Shadow was a great help. He had some special powers, didn't he?"

"Sure did," Laken cut in. "He could cross GAPs like no one I've ever met—except maybe Johan."

"I think I need to go back to my time and fetch both Dain and Evin," Ginna interrupted. "Let's not get off the subject here. I was *trying* to tell you my brother said Dain inherited his role of communication—because their names were based on the same meaning."

"What meaning?" asked Raina.

"I remember talking with Danny about the meaning of their names just before he and Evin left with Shadow," said Celestia, excitedly. "Both Daniel and Dain mean 'God is my Judge'. And Evin is an ancient form of 'Jon'."

"Really? My name?"

"Yes, Dad."

"So perhaps these two brothers have the kind of connection Jon and I have?" asked Jael.

"It could be," Laken nodded.

"Then it sounds like they *may* be able to help us." Jon's voice sounded a bit more hopeful.

"I think we need Shadow, too," said Laken.

"Jon, if you help me, we can go back for them," Ginna said.

"I don't want to force these risks on you," he replied. "I think I should just take you home to your own time. I shouldn't have brought you to this dangerous place, but I was desperate for someone to reach Martina."

"Obviously that didn't work," Ginna interrupted.

"Still, this isn't your problem. You belong back in your own time with Garek—in Colorado."

Ginna was staring directly into Jon's eyes now. "I know what the King has called me to do, Jon, so don't try to interfere."

At this, Jon nodded mutely.

"What should we do now?" asked Jael.

"Jon and I go back for Dain and Evin," Ginna said firmly, reaching out and taking both of Jon's hands.

A sudden electric shock seemed to flow between them, and both of their eyes went wide in surprise. Laken heard a sizzling sound that didn't come from the fire. Then both of them closed their eyes and disappeared in a flash of golden light.

"Wow," cried Jael, "That was fast."

Laken nodded. "That crossing seems like the ones Johan can make."

"Johan! I remember when Martina, Jon, and I met him—when we were fleeing Terres in the space ship we found," said Jael.

"I've met him, too, Dad." Jace had been listening so intently that they'd forgotten he was there.

"That's right," said Celestia. "He helped us when we were searching for the Traitor."

"I know," Jace replied. "We met him the circle of standing stones, remember?"

"Perhaps there's a way Johan can help us now," said Laken. "Celestia and I could try to find him. But he's often elusive."

"Wherever you go, I think I need to come with you," Jael cut in. "After all, Martina is my only sister and the only other survivor in my family."

"But Jael, we've just gotten you back." There was an edge of anger and panic in Raina's voice.

Jael gently pulled his wife closer to him. "I have a feeling this is the reason I was brought back, Honey."

Raina was fighting back tears and just nodded slowly.

"Can I go, too, Dad?"

Jael turned to look at his son, noticing for the first time that he was becoming a man. "Jace, your mother needs you with her."

"But Dad!"

"It's something I just know somehow, Son. Your part to play in all this is here, with Raina."

Jael's wife nodded mutely, her face still pressed against his chest. "Please don't leave right now," she said suddenly. "Let me at least fix you some breakfast."

Jael smiled at her. "That's my ever-practical wife. You're right, we'd better have something to eat and make some plans. We can't just jump into any old GAP, like Jon and Ginna just did. Especially since I'm not first-born."

"Well, they knew where they were going," said Celestia. "And knowing Sandra, they'll get something to eat there."

"Still, I wish they hadn't disappeared so quickly," sighed Raina.

Laken patted her arm. "I think that was a 'Johan-thing'—judging by all the sparks and flashes of light."

"You should know. You've worked with Johan before," said Celestia.

"Yeah, I was part of his Time Guardian Circle—and perhaps I still am."

"At least he hasn't whisked *you* off to parts unknown," she murmured.

"Not yet, anyway," he half-smiled.

***

Laken found himself getting increasingly agitated as Raina cooked their breakfast. She put flatbread on hot stones, and a piece of some kind of meat was on a make-shift rotisserie above the fire.

'I never realized how much I'd miss fast food and mi-crowave meals,' he sighed to himself.

As he watched his wife, he realized she didn't have

the same memories he did. Most of her life was lived like this, on the run in the wilderness. Sometimes he actually envied her. 'She doesn't know what she's missing, and that probably makes it easier.'

Celestia soon seated herself next to him on the rocky cave floor. "You're getting restless, aren't you?" she smiled.

"Is it that obvious?"

"Probably only to me—I know you, Laken Meta."

"You think so, Mrs. Meta?"

She almost laughed aloud. "I still have to remind myself of my new name."

"You're right, though. I feel like we need to get going if we have any hope of finding your mother."

"I'm feeling the same way. But I also know we have to let Raina become used to the idea of Jael's going."

"Do you really think he's up for travel?"

"If he says so, then I think we have to believe him. And I agree with my dad that having Jael along will make it easier to get through to Mom."

"Yeah, I hope so. Sounds like none of the others close to her could break through—not Jon, Ginna, or even you."

"I know," she sighed, leaning against his chest. "Why can't we just have normal lives?"

"What's normal?" he chuckled. He could feel her sigh again and pulled her into a closer embrace. "I'll do my best to take care of you. I always have."

"Yeah, you've promised my dad that many times," she

smiled. "I love you, Laken. I'm so glad the True King sent us to this time together."

"You weren't saying that a few years ago."

"Well, a girl can admit when she's wrong, you know. And besides, the more I've gotten to know you the more I like—"

"You'd better stop, or I'll be getting a swelled head."

"You? Not a chance."

Just then Raina announced breakfast was ready.

As the five of them worked on the roasted meat and hot bread, there was little conversation. By the way Jace was eyeing Jael, it seemed to Laken that he was wondering if his father would suddenly disappear.

'Knowing how things have worked with GAP-crossings before, I'm not surprised he's worried. He's too young to deal with all that's come his way in the past few years.'

At last, the food was all eaten and no more delay was possible. Laken took a deep breath, knowing he was about to upset another applecart.

"I know we've talked about going to seek Johan's help, but I feel we need to take more direct action first."

"Like what?" His wife turned her dark brown eyes on him.

"Don't give me that look. You know I'm trying to do what Johan would tell me."

"And what is that?" Raina asked, almost too sharply.

"After thinking things over, while we ate your delicious

breakfast, Raina—I feel Jael, Celestia, and I should slip into the city undercover."

"How can we do that?" asked Jael.

"I've been in deep cover several times before," replied Laken. "I can help you two prepare."

"Weren't you in deep cover when I met you in Tacoma?"

He just nodded to his wife.

"And you said you didn't know anything of your past, or who you really were?"

Laken nodded again but still didn't speak.

"Jael and I don't want to lose our memories. If we do, we can't help reach Martina."

"Oh, I see your meaning," Laken smiled. "We won't have to go that far. But I will need to instill some new memories to overlay your old ones."

"How does it work?" she asked.

"I'm sure you remember the Mind-sharing we did in Toronto—"

"How could I forget? I don't want that much pain ever again."

"Don't panic. I won't hurt you this time."

"You'd better not," she grumbled.

"What exactly do you propose?" Jael cut in.

"All I need is your willingness to open your mind to mine, just for a few minutes. Then you'll each have a new 'identity' so to speak, and we won't be obvious as Rebels once we enter the city."

Celestia saw Jael looking into her eyes searchingly. "What do you think?"

"I've been through a lot with Laken," she sighed, "Not all of it good—but I've come to trust him and his special abilities."

"Why do you have to go to the city?" Raina asked then.

"I just have a feeling it's the best way to get closer to Martina," Laken shrugged.

"I still wish we could consult with Johan first," said Jael.

"He's not always available," Laken replied.

"So, we have to go with your expertise, I guess," said Celestia.

"I do have more experience than you know of," he said to his wife. "Sometime I need to fill you in on more of it."

"If we ever have a time when we aren't dealing with an emergency."

"Well, I can't argue with you on that."

"Okay." Jael suddenly sounded impatient. "Let's get on with this. I want to find my sister."

Laken turned to his wife first. "I need you to put both of your hands on my head and close your eyes."

As she obeyed, he reached over and took Jael's hands in his. "I need you to see what she does, so your stories will match."

As the three of them seemed to go into a trance, Jace pulled his mother with him into another section of the cave. "We'd better not get in their way," he whispered to Raina.

CHAPTER 7
RAINA AND JACE

Jace had a plan he hoped would help cheer his mother up. As they moved deeper into the cave, he began to talk casually:

"You know, Mom, some of these caves have a lot more passages than we ever use."

"I know," she replied, "For one thing, we have to keep our cooking fires close to the entrances, so the smoke can work its way out."

"I guess so. But being close to the cave-mouth makes it easier for us to be seen by the wrong eyes, you know."

She sighed but apparently had no words to add.

As they spoke, they went through several junctions, where small passageways and tunnels went off in various directions. Finally, Jace stopped and handed his mother one of the head-lamps he'd brought.

"What's this for?"

"I want to show you something I found one day when

I was exploring."

"Jace, I wish you'd tell me when you're going off alone like that. You could be hurt, or lost, and no one would know where you went."

"Don't worry, Mom. I always let someone know where I'm going—usually one of my friends, like Andre."

"But I need to know."

"Okay, I'm sorry." His voice just barely showed the hint of aggravation he was feeling about this. 'I wish she could treat me like an adult. I'm not a little child anymore.' He wasn't ready to say this aloud to her, though.

To change the subject, he took hold of her hands and guided her to the opening he'd been looking for. "Close your eyes," he whispered. Gently, he turned her to face into the oval opening. "Okay—now open them."

Jace watched his mother's face to see her reaction.

And just as he'd hoped, her eyes were wide with wonder, as she exclaimed, "This is the most beautiful thing I've ever seen."

He smiled and turned his eyes to the scene, gently squeezing her hand. Before them, a room full of sparkling crystals shone in the light of their head-lamps.

There were all kinds of shapes. Tall slender stalagmites gave off a rainbow of colors in their lights. From the ceiling there were newly forming stalactites looking like hundreds of tiny hollow tubes, each with a hanging drop of water. Occasionally one of these drops would fall, either on their heads, or onto the top of a little pile of mineral forming beneath.

"It is really amazing, isn't it?"

"Totally."

"The first time I saw this room, I had only a small hand-lamp, so I couldn't get the full effect like we are now," he added. "And look at the pillars over there." He pointed to their right. "Those stalactites and stalagmites have been forming long enough to meet each other and form columns."

"But they're so fluted and wavy, Jace. It's like each one has its own unique form and decoration."

"Each one is like a snowflake," he whispered. "No two alike."

"And like people, too—each person unique."

"Right, Mom."

After they'd stood and gazed around them in wonder for several minutes, Jace moved his mother toward a low shelf of rock where they could sit.

"Why did you bring me here, Jace?"

"I thought perhaps all the beauty would cheer you up."

She hugged him around the shoulders quickly. "Thanks."

Again, silence settled between them.

"This reminds me of a verse your father used to quote often: 'The heavens are telling the glory of God, and the

Earth shows his handiwork.' Do you remember?"

"Yes, I do, though I was really young then. It was a long time ago, before—"

"Before he was captured by the System," she finished for him.

"But everyone thought he was dead, didn't they?"

"Yes, even I did."

"Mom," he began in a quiet whisper, "I think it's sort of like this room."

"How do you mean, Jace?"

"Well, it was forming down here all along in total darkness. No one had seen it, until I came along with a light. Maybe I was the first to see it."

"I know what you mean. The only one who knew about it was the Creator."

"And even though it hadn't been seen by human eyes, he made it amazingly beautiful, just because that's the way he is."

"I think I understand." She turned and looked into his eyes, surprised again at how they were on a level with hers. He was growing up so quickly. Then she took a deep breath before she spoke aloud. "Sometimes things that seem dark and ugly can turn out to be the most beautiful places—in the right light."

"There's another verse I heard Dad quote often. It says, 'God has made all things beautiful in his time.' We never know how something will look in the future—even things that seem really horrible now."

He rubbed his hand across the back of her neck, the way he'd often seen his father do.

"Sometimes it's really hard to believe that," she sighed. "Why did we have to go through all those years of believing Jael was dead?"

"I don't know. But I still believe there will be a small flash of beauty within the pain—somehow."

"Well, there is my daughter Morgan, born to Branden and me before he died."

"Where is she now?"

"She wanted to visit Andre and Lexi, and since Daiah's cave is so far from here, they won't bring her back until the next full moon."

Looking over at her again, he saw tears were trickling down her cheeks now. Wordlessly, he pulled her into a hug.

"I wish I were a strong brave person, like many others here in the Out-clave who've also lost loved ones. I feel unworthy of them."

"But you've been as strong as you could. You were always there for me when I needed you."

"Sometimes I think it was you being strong for me."

"We had each other, and we always will. Besides, we even have Dad back now."

"But I'm so worried about Laken taking him away," she cried. "He's still not completely healed and very weak."

"Laken knows. He was there when we found Dad in

the System prison. He won't allow anything that's beyond him."

"Isn't there a verse in The Book that says something like that?"

"I've heard Dad say it. I think it goes, 'The Lord won't allow you to be tempted beyond what you can bear, but will always provide a way out—' "

"I'm so fortunate that you and your father have put so many verses into your memories."

"You never know when you may need one, and there may not always be a Book with you."

"Especially now that the System has come back to Earth, and begun to ban books—like they did on Terres."

"What was Terres like?"

"Oh, it was much like the cities of Earth are now. Still, I like Earth better than Terres, even though we're forced to live in caves. But sometimes I feel like the Lord is sending me more hardship than I can handle. Then I doubt that verse you quoted, especially the part where it says 'He will never send more than you can bear.' I guess my faith is just too weak."

"I think we sometimes put too much emphasis on the wrong part of this verse, Mom. It's not how much we can bear on our own, it's how much we can handle with the King's help."

"I think I see."

"There's another verse which really says it: 'I can do

all things, through Him who strengthens me.' It's not our faith that matters, Mom. It's what we put faith in. I could believe with all my heart I could walk through a solid stone wall, but that wouldn't make it so. But if someone told me there was a secret passage in a certain corner, then I *could* 'walk through the wall' so to speak."

"I'm so blessed to have you, Jace. You have so many of your father's strengths and abilities. I'd be totally lost without you."

"Thanks, but I think it's more God working through his Spirit."

"I guess."

"Try not to worry so much. The next turn may look dark and foreboding—"

"But it may reveal a room full of beautiful crystals, right?"

"Yeah, you've got the message now."

"I just wish there was something I could do to help Jon and Martina. She seems to have fallen back into the depths of darkness she experienced with the Redlarks, back on Terres."

"Was her time that much worse than yours, Mom?"

"I don't really know, but she seems to be very prone to despair. Jael says she's like their mother."

"And she lost her mother on Luna, in the battle," he added in a murmur. "I think when we got Dad back, she felt envious."

"But it's not as though we flaunted it in her face. She should've been glad she'd gotten one of her brothers back."

"I'm sure she was. I think she's just fragile, because of all of the troubles she's been through."

"I feel guilty I haven't been able to help her."

"Please don't. You did what you could. It's her own fault that she's shut everyone out. You're making a sacrifice to help her, by letting Dad go with Laken."

"How can one so young have so much wisdom? You are truly gifted."

"Each of us has our own gift. We're unique —remember?"

"Like snowflakes," she smiled.

"And stalactites and stalagmites," he added.

CHAPTER 8
INTO DARKNESS

I must have been asleep, for my whole body ached from lying on a cold stone floor. 'Where am I?' My mind reeled for a few moments, as I wondered if I was back in our cave. Then I heard the sound of heavy breathing beside me.

"Who's there?" my frightened voice blurted out before I could stop it.

There came more snorting sounds and then a growling.

A faint light was coming into the room from a small square opening in the door. With all the strength I could muster, I jumped up and began pounding on the heavy door with my fists.

"Please, help!" I screamed. "There's some animal in here. Let me out—I'll do anything you want!"

'You must be in pure survival mode,' my thoughts said. 'A short while ago, you wanted to die.'

But despite my mind's trying to stop me, I kept

pounding on the door. Blood began running down my wrists and arms from the force of my fists beating on the rough stone and wood.

Then the door opened. Outlined in the light streaming into the room, I recognized the uniform of Corporal Shei.

"All right, Tina," he said in a sickening-smooth voice, "It appears you've passed the first test."

A low rumble came behind me, but I clung to Shei. "Please, I'll do whatever you want," I gasped.

"Truly anything?" his voice gave me a sick feeling in my stomach, but I didn't let go of him.

Shei didn't say any more, but merely nodded and took hold of my elbow. I noticed his touch seemed a bit gentler and more familiar than before, but a wave of fear passed through me. He was definitely expecting something.

Once we'd passed through the heavy door, it closed with a scraping sound behind us, but there was no clicking of a lock this time.

"You can be my dessert," he grinned, turning me to face him.

"Aren't you a little young for an old woman like me?" I tried to tease.

"Oh, I prefer my food well-seasoned, and aged like fine cheese or wine," he chuckled. Then in a quick movement, he ripped my tunic from top to bottom, leaving me fully exposed before him.

By now he was running the back of his hand across my cheek. "You can't be that old—not very many wrinkles."

"Just good clean living," I shrugged, before I realized this might be taken as my living in the wilds. "My captors let me out to exercise fairly regularly," I added.

The shadow I saw in his eyes cleared quickly. Without a word he pulled me to him tightly and began kissing hard on my lips. "So now I know you're not one of those prudish Believers," he breathed in my ear. "I can help you get back into real civilization—if you give me what I want."

At this, I understood even more clearly the reasoning behind his shutting me in the cell with his unknown beast. I had no choice but to surrender in order to live, and now I knew Shei expected the same cooperation. As much as I wanted to resist, I was too weak.

Again, my mind went into pure survival mode. Nothing else mattered except staying alive. He was too strong for me to fight off, and I didn't want to die anymore.

"It's so refreshing to meet a willing female," Shei said, caressing my neck with his lips. "Most of what we get here are captured Rebels, those who would rather die than compromise their so-called morality."

"I gave that up long ago," I murmured against his cheek, hoping he believed me. I inclined my head so he could kiss my neck. To myself I was thinking, 'That's at least partly true. I gave myself up to Jason on Terres, and to others in the Redlarks' Camp.'

I forced my mind to stop there, not wanting to be reminded of the vows I'd made to Jon, or the sins I thought I'd left behind at the Fountain in the Desert. 'None of that made my life any better,' I told myself. 'Nothing has been easy since then. Things just keep going from bad to worse.'

Realizing I was turning my back on all I thought I believed, I began to kiss Shei desperately, pulling him with me onto a bench along the wall. Perhaps it was the one he'd sat me on before. I didn't care. I just wanted to get this over with—so perhaps I could get on with a more normal life. If there was such a thing.

***

My mind was drifting slowly back from some distant place where it had been wandering in sleep. Vaguely, I remembered snippets of a dream. I was riding a large brown horse—a very docile and plodding animal barely needing reins. I was seated on a heavy blanket, but no saddle was on his back.

Somehow, even without stirrups, I was able to guide him—which was fortunate because we were picking our way through a series of cluttered rooms filled with broken furniture. One I remembered most distinctly was full of musical instruments that seemed to be playing by themselves. This was the first room in my dream with any kind of light—in the others the horse and I were stumbling in darkness.

At last, we came out of the maze of rooms, and before us stretched a grassy meadow dotted with tall evergreen trees. I tried to dig my heels into the horse's side to get him moving faster, but as soon as I did, he collapsed onto the ground. I pulled on the reins in my hand, but there was no bit or bridle, and the horse seemed unable to move. Anger and fear moved into exasperation, and I tried to pull him up again, to no avail. Then I awoke.

I was lying on my back, on a low sleeping platform between smooth cool sheets. It was such a long time since I'd slept in a real bed, and the feeling of comfort sent a shiver of shock through my body. That's when I noticed I was totally naked. Turning my head, I expected to see Shei lying next to me, but there was no one else in sight.

Now panic was beginning to build and I sat bolt upright. Then I saw Shei standing silhouetted against the light of a window. By the looks of the colors in the clouds, the sun was either rising or setting.

"Welcome back, my sleepy beauty," he grinned, turning to face me.

Instinctively, I pulled the bedclothes up to cover myself.

"No need for that. I've investigated all the parts thoroughly, Tina."

I felt warmth rush up into my cheeks. "Did I prove satisfactory?" I made my voice as sarcastic as I could, but I could feel my insides quivering.

"Of course," he murmured, stepping back toward the bed.

I sat frozen, not sure what to do.

"I prefer to ration myself, though, so I'm going to make you wait until tonight," he grinned. "If you can stand it."

"I think I can manage," I said lightly, hoping my voice was casual enough. "Do I get to wear any clothing between now and then?"

"You might as well, since the day is just beginning. Otherwise *I* might not be able to manage." The smirk on his face sent chills down my spine, but I couldn't tell if they were all fear—or partly excitement.

'It sure hasn't taken you long to fall back into your old bad habits,' a voice in my head began to say.

"Stop it," I replied to my alter-ego. "I've tried to live your way, and all it's brought is darkness in my soul. Leave me be."

By this time, Shei tossed some underclothes and a loose-fitting tunic onto the bed beside me. "Get dressed, so we can get something to eat," he grinned. "My body needs at least two kinds of sustenance."

As soon as I slipped into the clothes, he pulled me up into his arms and kissed me.

"You're not controlling your appetite very well, Corporal."

"Call me Shei, please. Besides, there's no rule against eating a few snacks now and then."

As we stepped into a brightly-lit hallway, I tried to push any lingering fears out of my mind. 'This won't be so bad,' I told myself. 'Adequate food, warm place to sleep, and the price isn't all that high.'

'Only your whole belief system.'

I gritted my teeth.

"I'm going to get better at overcoming you, old self. Just leave me alone."

Shei didn't react to my words, but he must have felt the chill that crept into the hand he was holding.

"You're cold again. Do you need a cloak?"

"Yeah, I guess so. I never got used to the damp chill in the caves my captors kept me in."

He stopped briefly at a door on our right in the long hallway. Opening it, he pulled out a fleecy blue jacket, draping it over my shoulders. Then he pulled me toward him and kissed me much longer this time.

"I'd call that a bit more than a snack," I murmured, as I tried to pull away from him. "I need some real food before I can even think of dessert."

"Okay," he chuckled. "Hopefully a well-fed woman is what I really need."

In a few more steps we came to a 'T' junction in the hallway, and he led us to the left, stepping into a brightly-lit room. Around the walls were rows of various food replicators.

"Choose anything your heart desires," he grinned. "Just be sure to save room for dessert."

"Uh, sure." I tried to return his jovial attitude, hoping no fear in my eyes was giving me away.

'You've made your own bed, now you have to sleep in it,' came the ominous voice in my head.

CHAPTER 9
BACK TO MAIAR

Jon and Ginna found themselves standing on a rocky ridge overlooking a narrow valley. Gazing along the ridge crests on either side of them, Ginna saw how the jagged lines of rock were actually mirror images of each other. To anyone seeing this ridge from a distance, the valley between them would be virtually invisible.

"I've seen this before," Jon said in surprise.

"When?"

"Remember when we came here with that spaceship from Terres?"

Ginna searched in the deeper recesses of her mind—back to the time she'd been living Martina's life 'within' her consciousness. And suddenly the picture flashed before her eyes.

"I do remember, Jon. The ship nearly crashed, but you were able to land it here."

"The propulsion crystals had gone bad."

"And Johan helped us. Is this really his little planet, the one he called 'Maiar', his 'motherly place' ? Did he snatch us from the cave? I thought we were going back to my time to get Dain and Evin."

"It looks like Johan has other ideas, Ginna. Come on, I think I see his secret pathway down."

Just as they began their descent, a large bird swooped over them with a hawk-like cry.

Both ducked instinctively.

"What was that?" she cried.

"Strange," said Jon. "I feel like I've seen that bird before, but I can't remember when."

As he said this, the winged creature dropped between the cliffs and disappeared.

"Its tail and wings were so red, they almost seemed on fire," Ginna added.

"I think it was just a trick of the light here," he said. "This little planet's sun is very distant. Come on, we need to get down into the valley."

"Before something else comes along."

With Jon helping her down the steep carved path, Ginna felt a bit safer than if she'd been attempting this alone. His arms were strong and steady, seeming not to have aged with the rest of his body.

'My mind was here,' she thought, 'But not my body. I don't remember this.' Her legs were beginning to feel rubbery, and her insides began to quake and quiver like a bowl of gelatin that wasn't quite set. 'That's a metaphor from my time for sure.' She couldn't help but half-smile to herself. 'No one in this century—especially the exiled Believers—has likely ever seen gelatin.'

These thoughts calmed her, and before she knew it, they were at the valley floor, though it was only a slightly wider path between the cliffs. Ahead of them, she heard a trickle of water dropping into a pool.

"It's good to see you again, Jonahkan," came a deep rumbling voice.

At first, Ginna was startled. The voice sounded ominous echoing off the rock walls above them. 'Is this really Johan—or an impostor?' her panicked mind said.

Apparently sensing her fear, Jon took her hand and squeezed it gently.

"We're happy to see you, Johan—'The One Who Shows the Way'."

"Your wife may not agree with that name for me."

"Martina hasn't been well."

"I know—and I've already taken some action in an attempt to reach her."

"How did you know?" Ginna blurted out.

Johan turned his sparkling eyes toward her. "Ah Ginna, it's good to see you in your own body."

"Are you truly Johan?" She still felt suspicious.

"Yes, my dear. I thought perhaps you'd remember me from before."

"Uh—I don't think I ever met you, except when I was 'within' Martina."

"Perhaps."

She could hear the smile in his voice, even though his mouth was hidden by his thick white beard and mustache.

"So you know Martina ran away," Jon cut in. "We think she returned to the city and the System. Can you help us?"

"Perhaps she thinks she's gone full circle."

Jon only nodded, his voice apparently overcome by his emotions.

"Of course I can help," the old man chuckled, "If you really want the kind of help, I can give."

"You helped us find Maia—Mother Earth."

"But that didn't turn out to be the paradise you'd hoped for, did it?"

"Well, no," Jon stammered.

Ginna felt doubts beginning to rise again. Was the old hermit merely a madman, after all? Hadn't Martina thought he was a wizard, at their first encounter some forty years ago?

"Do you doubt me, Ginna?" came the old man's voice.

She stepped back in surprise. Was he reading her mind?

"I've only just met you," she managed to say at last. "How can I know what you truly are?"

"So you say, but perhaps this will help."

His form began to shimmer and fade away like a mist on a sunny day. Then suddenly a bright beam of golden light shone down from above them. As it hit the ground, a tall shining figure appeared within it.

She blinked at the brightness, and Jon reached up to shade his eyes.

"Do you prefer to see my powerful side—or my kindly side?" a low voice rumbled.

Now she was nearly hiding behind Jon. "The book says Satan can disguise himself as an angel of light," she whispered. "This doesn't prove who this man or creature is." She hoped Jon could hear her.

"We'll take whichever you prefer, sir," Jon murmured.

No sooner had he spoken than the light beam shot back upward, and the white-bearded hermit reappeared.

"How do we know you're not the Serpent in disguise?" Jon asked.

Ginna looked at him quickly, thankful that he'd heard her.

"As the Book says, 'By their fruits you shall know them.' What fruits have I given you?" The man seemed to be looking directly into each of their minds, which wasn't giving Ginna any more confidence in him.

"Well," Jon began hesitantly, "You did give us a copy of The Book."

"Do you think the Serpent would have done that?"

"No, of course not." Ginna finally found her voice. "He hates and fears God's word."

Johan nodded and smiled slightly.

"And you repaired our ship," Jon added.

"I'm glad you remember that. And how is Jael?"

"He's much better since we rescued him from the System. Gradually he's coming back to his old self. But he's very upset that Martina abandoned him again—like she did when they were children on Terres."

Suddenly Ginna spoke. "My nephew says you helped them find Jael, using their dog, Shadow."

Johan smiled enough that they could actually see his open mouth above his beard. "I'm glad to hear he shared with you. So how are the sons of Daniel?"

"They miss their father very much, sir."

"I'm very sorry that Daniel had to leave your time."

"You mean he's still alive somewhere?"

"Not in the sense you think of life, my dear. His soul is with the True King, and he will have a new and perfect body when The Day arrives."

"The Day?" Jon's voice sounded puzzled.

"You need to read the last part of The Book, Jon."

"You mean *Revelation*?" Ginna added. "I've read it several times, but it's so confusing."

"Just read with an open heart and mind—and watch for the signs of the times."

"But Johan, can you help us find Martina?" Jon's impatience was increasing, and his voice showed it.

"Calm yourself. Help is almost here."

"What?"

The man didn't reply, but turned and pointed to the far side of the pool behind him. A sudden shower of sparks and a crackling sound filled the air. Then two large shapes began to emerge—a huge black dog and a black and white horse.

"Splash?" Ginna cried. "That's my nephews' horse."

"Shadow!" Jon was exclaiming at the same moment. "You sent him to help us find Jael."

Johan was grinning from ear to ear now, but before he spoke two young voices spoke simultaneously:

"Aunt Ginna?"

"Jon!"

As she heard these words, Ginna's eyes saw the two small figures on the animals' backs.

"Evin and Dain—" her voice cracked.

By the time she spoke, Dain had swung down from the pinto's back. As he did so, the size proportions of the boy and his mount shifted into the balance of a normal teenager and a horse.

He ran to her without hesitation, grabbing her into a tight embrace. "Where are we, Aunt Ginna?"

"You're safe with us," she whispered into his ear. She was beginning to feel Johan wasn't a threat after all.

In the meantime, Jon strode over to the huge dog and reached up to the boy perched high on his back. "It's good to see you again, Evin—and you too, Shadow."

As Evin took Jon's hand and jumped down to the ground, his size grew, and the dog's shrank to a normal size for a Labrador, or perhaps a Newfoundland, for his fur was too shaggy for a Lab.

"Don't worry, Dain," Evin's young voice said calmly. "These are friends. This is Johan," he turned his eyes toward the old man. "Why did you bring us here?"

'How can he be so calm?' wondered Ginna.

"It's good to see you face-to-face at last, boys." Johan stepped up and shook each of their hands. "Jon and Ginna—who I think you've met—need our assistance. Jon's wife has disappeared."

Evin quickly took Jon's hand and looked up into his eyes. "She's been in a depression, hasn't she?"

"How did you know?"

"I'm not sure. I just know. Maybe Shadow put it in my mind."

"Our mom has been really down, too," added Dain. "She's in a lot of pain with grief."

"She will heal, my sons," rumbled Johan. "But I fear Martina's flight may cause peril for many others as well as herself."

"What should we do, sir?"

"Ah, yes—my brave Evin," Johan half-chuckled.

"Actually, I'm just passing on what Shadow tells me."

"So he still communicates with you?"

"Yes, sir—and with Splash, too. Though I can't hear what the horse says, only what Shadow tells me."

"I can't hear either of them," Dain sighed, "One time I heard Shadow though, the first time we crossed a GAP with him.

"Don't fret, my child. You'll hear him when it's necessary."

'Does he mean if something happens to Evin?' This thought of any harm coming to her nephew sent a chill into Ginna.

***

Ginna woke suddenly, wondering where she was. For a few moments, panic rushed through her body. Then she heard soft breathing—one other person? No more than that. Glancing beside her, she saw Jon. So that was the lower-pitched snore she'd heard.

As her vision widened and her mind cleared, she made out the smaller shapes of Dain and Evin. Their breathing had the deep evenness of sound sleepers. For an instant she felt envy. Oh, what a joy it would be to sleep with the peacefulness of a child again. But that time in her own life was much too distant now to be revisited. And besides, all the GAP-crossing she'd done since then must have muddled her mind—for all too often she found Martina's memories rising into her brain instead of her own.

Just as she was about to touch Jon to see if he would wake, there came a crackly electric sound beyond where the four of them lay. When the sound stopped, there stood

Johan, dressed in shining white that matched his bushy beard and hair.

"Where have you been?" she heard her voice ask. The sound of it felt strangely unfamiliar. She must have spoken louder than she realized, for Jon sat up suddenly, rubbing his eyes.

"What's going on?"

Before she could respond, Johan spoke, "I've been through the 'back door' for a bit."

"What door?" Ginna asked.

"The one into Tornatoh."

"Have you seen Martina?" Jon asked quickly.

"I have."

"Why didn't you bring her back?"

"As I've said before, Jon. The time isn't right yet."

"But I thought you were going to help us get her back." Now the desperation was rising in Jon's voice.

"Don't fear, I will—when she's ready. But we cannot push the river, Jon."

"I've heard that before," he sighed. "Long ago, in a vision I had in the Redlarks' Camp. I thought everything I experienced there was an illusion."

"Not all of it," Johan whispered. "In order for Martina to return to you safely—and without causing greater danger to the rest of you Believers—we must do something else first."

"Johan," Ginna began, "Can you tell us anything about Martina?"

The old man nodded, "I've talked to her, but I can't reveal any more right now."

"But is she okay?"

"She is, all being considered. I've had confirmation from my friend, Kai."

"I remember meeting him—with Martina."

Jon was staring from Johan to Ginna, confusion in his eyes. "What's all this about?"

"Remember when Annemarie and Celestia took off to Tornatoh, trying to find Garek?"

Jon merely nodded.

"When Martina and I went to find them, it was Malakai who helped us—the same old man who told us how to find the Fountain all those years ago."

"The old man on High Street, near the Temple of the Way? How do *you* know him, Johan?" Frustration filled Jon's voice.

"Like I said, I go to where and when the True King sends me—and sometimes I have to disguise myself."

"So what did my wife say to you?"

"I can't reveal anything yet, Jon. You must be patient. She has a long way to go before she'll be free from the present darkness within her heart."

"Why can't you help her now?" Ginna cried, desperation in her voice.

"It would do more harm than good to force these things. I've talked to her, and we'll talk again, I'm sure. I've promised to be there for her." Johan's voice was deep and calm, and gradually Ginna felt some of the calmness creep into her body. She glanced at Jon, hoping he was feeling this also.

"Hey, where are Splash and Shadow?" she asked then.

"No need to fear. They're in my cave behind the waterfall. It's a larger accommodation for a dog and a horse."

Almost as if on cue, the two boys awoke and went behind the small waterfall.

"What's up?" Dain asked sleepily, as they came back.

"Nothing yet," smiled Johan.

Dain patted his brother's back but didn't speak again.

"Are your animals resting?" Johan asked. "I see you just checked on them."

"Yes sir, just as you told us. But, Johan," Dain added, "Splash looks strange."

"How so?"

"His black patches are turning white."

"And there's a strange bump on his head," Evin cut in.

"Bring him out," was all Johan said.

The boys disappeared behind the waterfall again. Soon, Dain led out a glowing white creature that still looked somewhat like a horse.

"What's that?" Jon asked. "Where's Splash?"

"This *is* Splash," Dain replied.

"No way!" cried Ginna. "That's a unicorn. See the spiral horn on its head?"

As Dain turned to look back at his horse, his eyes rounded in astonishment.

"Remember how we saw the white hair in his black spots one day?" Evin said.

Dain nodded mutely.

"Now, don't get excited," Johan smiled. "He's still Splash, but for this task we need a unicorn's power."

"You can change him like this?"

"Of course, I can, Dain," the old man shrugged.

"Johan says he's seen Martina," Jon cut in.

"And talked to her," Ginna added, "But he says it's not the right time to bring her back."

"Besides, I have another task for the four—or rather six—of you," said Johan.

"So, Splash and Shadow are part of the plan, too?" Evin spoke at last.

"They're absolutely necessary, especially Splash in his new form."

"What do we need to do?" Dain asked.

"I'm thankful for your strong sense of purpose, boys. Your father must have taught you well."

"Yeah, he left a message for Dain to show me after he died." Evin was trying his best to keep all fear out of his voice. "It's in the hayloft of our barn."

"I know," Johan nodded. "I helped him with it."

"Oh—" both boys spoke at the same time.

"Then what do you need us for?" asked Jon. "Dain and

Evin seem to have a strong connection—like I did with Jael. But what help can Ginna and I possibly give, especially considering the powers Shadow has. I saw him in action back in the System Time Nexus, when we rescued Jael."

"Well," Johan almost smiled. "Dain follows in his father's footsteps, except that he's firstborn and has the potential to be a GAP-crosser like you. And Evin—whose name means 'Jon' in Welsh, by the way—has the ability to focus on others and guide crossings, the way Jael does."

"Hmm," murmured Ginna, "That's kind of the opposite, isn't it? I mean, Jon is the firstborn and yet, it's Dain who has the ability. And though Evin's name means 'Jon', he isn't the firstborn in this pair."

"Very perceptive. That's one of the skills we need."

"Uh—okay."

"And Jon, you have the strength and experience given you through the many trials you've faced. That kind of ability isn't inborn, so we must rely on someone like you."

"Okay—thanks, I think."

No one spoke for several seconds then. Each of them knew somehow that Johan would reveal his plans in his own time. There was no point in asking too many questions.

"Thank you for your patience," the old man said at last. "That shows me you're ready to hear my plan."

The four glanced around at each other, wondering what this meant. Then they realized Shadow and Splash were each standing by the boy who was his rider.

"I need you all to jump to the center of our Galaxy, the Milky Way. The Serpent is hatching a dreadfully dangerous force there, and he must be stopped. Otherwise, everything any of us has done will be in vain."

"Can *we* stop him? He's terribly powerful," said Jon.

"Yes, he is," Johan said firmly. "You must have the power of the True King with you—and you will. Just be willing to step out in faith, my children." He motioned to all of them with a sweep of his hand, even the black dog and the shimmering white unicorn. "He will provide what's necessary, exactly when you need it most."

"You mean we just have to go there on blind faith?" Jon's voice had an edge of anger.

"Remember what the King has done with you in the past. Has he ever let you down in the end?"

"No sir." Jon hung his head, but Ginna reached over and patted his shoulder.

"Then, you know whom you have believed—that he is able to help when it's needed most. And he will."

"Is that what you meant by needing Jon's experience?" Dain asked.

"Exactly right, young man. There's an ancient hymn born out of times such as these—when Believers were facing similar opposition from the Serpent."

"When was that?" Ginna asked.

"As you number time, it was the Sixteenth Century."

"That's nearly sixteen hundred years ago—from my time," cried Jon.

"Even from the Twenty-first Century, it's a long time," Evin added.

"What does this hymn say?"

"I will sing it for you," smiled Johan. "I have a feeling most of you have heard it, for it's one of those songs which endures because it's true. Believers of all centuries have faced trials by the Evil One. These tribulations may not appear to have the same form, but they still come from the same force—the original Father of Lies and Evil—"

"The Red Dragon?"

"Correct as usual, Evin."

Then Johan closed his eyes and seemed to draw within himself. Ginna found she was actually holding her breath. But the tightness in her chest eased when she heard the words Johan began to sing:

*"A mighty fortress is our God, a trusty shield and
   weapon;
He helps us free from ev'ry need that hath us now
   o'ertaken.
The old evil Foe now means deadly woe;
Deep guile and great might are his dread arms in
   fight;
On earth is not his equal.*

*Though devils all the world should fill, all eager to
   devour us;*

*We tremble not, we fear no ill, they shall not
    overpower us.
This world's prince may still scowl fierce as he will,
He can harm us none, he's judged, the deed is done;
One little word can fell him."*

"I've heard that," mused Ginna. "The words were a bit different, but the meaning is the same."

"Those words were penned by a Believer named Martin Luther, in the early Sixteenth Century," said Johan softly. "Originally the lyrics were in German."

"I learned a little German in school," added Dain.

"So, can you translate *'Ein feste burg'?*" Johan looked directly into the young blond's eyes.

"They mean 'a mighty fortress, or stronghold'—just like the words you sang."

"My favorite part is the last words," Ginna said. "Where it says that we need not fear the Evil One—'one little word can fell him'."

"And what's this powerful word?" Jon finally spoke.

"The word is Kristos, isn't it?" said Ginna.

This time Johan merely nodded.

"I remember when Stephan used the name of the Lord to stop the Red Dragon's attack on us—back when we rescued Jael," said Evin. "But he was killed. Why didn't the Lord's name protect him?"

"Well, there's one more verse I think you need to hear," Johan said.

Again, all were silent as the old man held his breath briefly, and then began to sing:

> *"The Word they still shall let remain nor any thanks*
> *have for it.*
> *He's by our side upon the plain with his good gifts*
> *and Spirit.*
> *And take they our life, goods, fame, child and wife,*
> *Though these all be gone, our vict'ry has been won:*
> *The Kingdom ours remaineth."*

"So even if we do die in battle, like Stephan did, that's not the end of hope?" said Dain.

"For Believers there is always hope—if they don't cease to believe."

Ginna felt her heart jump as she thought of Martina. She almost spoke, but before she could Jon did:

"What if someone loses their faith? Do they lose hope, too?"

"Sometimes, Jon. You're thinking of your wife, aren't you?"

He nodded, staring fiercely at the ground.

"There's still hope for her. She's still asking questions."

"Why can't we go get her now?"

"Because she's not ready. And because we must face the Serpent first."

Now Ginna was staring at the ground also, then she felt Jon touch her with his chilled hand and tried to send a little warmth to him. "I'll do anything I can to get her back, Jon," she whispered.

"All right, everyone." Suddenly Johan's voice took on a commanding tone. "It's time for you six to get into a GAP Circle."

They quickly obeyed him. Jon kept his hand in Ginna's, while Dain mounted the unicorn, and Evin climbed up onto Shadow's back. Ginna reached her other hand up to take Evin's, and Jon took Dain's.

"Now Jon, let Shadow take charge. And Evin, you are the one to guide."

"But who am I guiding to?"

"Not a person, and not the Dragon. Instead concentrate on the center of our galaxy, the Milky Way. That's why Shadow took you there before."

"Oh, now I understand."

At this, Johan patted Evin on the head and then Shadow. As he stepped back, they all closed their eyes. Soon stars seemed to be whirling around them in spirals. Long tails of stardust swept over and around each of them.

Above them was a shining nebular cloud. From its center ropy-shaped trails swept toward them. Each was like the spokes of a wheel, except they weren't straight or smooth. Instead they made a corduroy vision across the black sky, and each seemed to pull toward the central Nexus from which they extended.

Ginna began to hear the sound of howling wind. 'How can there be wind with no air? We're supposed to be in the vacuum of space.' Then she remembered hearing about Solar Wind once in science class. 'Perhaps that's what it is. Somehow my ears can hear it here, while they couldn't on Earth.'

The clouds seemed to be swelling as they moved closer, and when they actually touched them, she felt a sudden chill. It was as though fingers of ice were pulling at her body. To try to stop the pain, she gripped the hands on either side of her even tighter.

As she did this, there came a flash so brilliant it blinded her. Then everything was black all around. Some force was trying to tear her away from the hands she was gripping—Jon's and Evin's. Then at last all feeling ceased.

Opening her eyes, all she could see was blackness. 'Are my eyes really open?'

"What is this?" she heard Dain's voice ask.

"We're at the center of the Galaxy," said Evin. "Remember how Shadow told us every galaxy has a Black Hole at its center?"

"But won't we be swallowed up by a Black Hole?" Ginna's voice was full of fear.

"Shadow says not to be afraid," came Evin's calm voice again. "We're protected."

But just as he said this, a serpentine shape began to move across the blackness before them. It was flaming red, and there was no need to say anything. They all knew it was the Serpent, the Red Dragon.

CHAPTER 10
MARTINA'S DEEP CAVE

Deep in my subconscious the knowledge was still there. I was living a lie. But I kept pushing the thought away, and gradually a numbness took its place.

'You're fortunate Shei has taken you under his wing,' my mind kept telling me. 'Except for him, you might have been sold as a slave to someone who sees people from the wilds as mere animals.'

And I knew these thoughts were true. My captor—for I knew I still belonged to Shei—was beginning to show signs of actually caring about me at least a little.

Once we left the border outpost, he kept me with him, and I knew this was by his choice. Now he'd even found a flat for me, which he visited quite regularly. There was only one price to pay—giving him the pleasure he demanded. I tried to convince myself he actually had feelings for me, and this made the cost easier to bear.

'You're such a mess, Martina,' the voice inside my

head would try to argue. 'You might as well admit you're just his sex-slave.' No matter how hard I tried to drown these thoughts, this voice inside my head just wouldn't stop reminding me. But I was beginning to get better at ignoring it.

"You expect too much, self," I often argued. "I have food and shelter—and even a bit of pleasure. There's nothing else I need."

I desperately needed to convince myself of this, to keep any calm in my heart. Of course, I was totally dependent on Shei—he'd engineered it that way. There was no one else I could go to for food or other basic necessities. I had no choice but to do his will.

After a few weeks, Shei gave me permission to walk the lakeshore, at least as far as the Temple of the Way. That's the name I remembered, though others now called it 'The Temple of Unity.'

One particular day, I set out walking along this huge lake bordering the city of Tornatoh. It was the smallest of five original inland lakes. I remembered words I'd found in one of my parents' antique books:

"The Great Lakes," it read, "are the remnant of an enormous inland sea left when the glaciers of the last Ice Age melted. Even today they are larger than some saltwater 'seas' in other parts of the world. Since European settlers came to North America, they've been referred to as 'lakes'—though in fact they are inland freshwater seas."

But I found out later that the shallowest of the lakes described in this ancient book had dried up, consumed by a waterfall which crept its way back, as the cap rocks supporting it eroded away. So, this meant the lake I saw now was called Omato, the former Lake Ontario of the millennium before my time.

As these thoughts floated through my mind, I sniffed the moist air and realized it definitely didn't have the same smell as the ocean near our Indonia Out-clave. That had been a sharper scent—an infusion of fish, rotting seaweed, and salt. But this air was different. There was the same sense of water, but none of the fishy-salty smell of the ocean.

This only made me feel a sharp pang of regret. "Why did I run away?" I muttered to myself. Fortunately, no one was close enough to hear me over the sound of the rolling waves. 'You've been stupid, but it's too late now,' my alter-ego voice cut in.

"Maybe if we'd been able to go back to the more hospitable climate of Indonia, it would've been easier," I told the voice. "But the long, cold winters of North America always seem to drag the life out of me. I go dead like all the dry plants and flowers. And each year when they come back to life, I seem to feel less of the hope of spring. I think I've lost all my hope."

'You spent too much time reading in your youth,' the voice in my head interrupted. 'Can't you think of anything better to do? You're back in a real city. Get on with a more normal life.'

"What is normal?" I said aloud, trying to drown out the voice in my head. "Was my life in the wilderness with the Believers the real normal? Why did I feel I needed to come here and leave behind all the people and things I knew?"

There, I'd finally said it aloud. But neither the voice nor my own thoughts seemed to have any answer to give. With a shrug, I walked down the sandy beach to the water's edge. The day was sunny and warm, so I took off my shoes and waded into the gently lapping waves of the inland sea.

At least the sun was out again—after several days of rain and wind, beginning as soon as Shei brought me into the city.

Shei. Now here was a thought that brought many mixed emotions to me. He was a likable enough young man, and not a bad lover. But it had been a long time since I'd been able to have this kind of casual intimacy without feeling soaked in guilt.

'You're feeling guilty now,' said the voice. 'You just don't want to admit it.'

"Shut up!" As I said this aloud to myself, another wader nearby looked at me in surprise. But I just shrugged and walked a bit farther out from the shoreline.

'So why are you here?' My inner voice seemed to be in the mood to analyze me.

"All right," I muttered to this other self, "I don't know exactly why I'm here. I just couldn't go on living in dark caves, always wondering where my next meal would come from, and whether we were in eminent danger from Patrols. Isn't that enough?"

'But you've left all your family behind. Doesn't that matter?'

"I don't know." This conversation with myself was beginning to feel like I was talking to another real person. Perhaps I *was* going crazy.

"I think my only choice was either to run away or kill myself," I muttered at last.

'But you *have* let part of your true self die, just by denying all you said you believed in and cared for.'

"I just couldn't do it anymore." Luckily as I shouted these words, the wind whipped up and blew them toward the open lake, an expanse of water so vast I couldn't even see the other side. "You know," I murmured more calmly, "My life was like this lake, and I got tired of not being able to see the other side. The uncertainty was wearing me down to dust."

'You are such a weakling.'

Why wouldn't this voice in my head leave me alone?

"Okay, so I am what I am. No one seemed to understand or try to help me back there. So, I did what I'd done as a teenager back on Terres—I ran away. Except this time I ran *to* the city, instead of away from it."

'And left your little brother alone again.'

"No. This time he has Raina and Jon."

'What about Jon? Doesn't he love you?'

"If he really loved me, he would have helped me—instead of lecturing me all the time."

'Maybe he was just doing the best he could.'

Suddenly I heard a gull crying overhead, and on impulse I imitated his raucous call: "Heaa-aah-aah." Two gulls plunged down to the water close by, and again I imitated them by throwing myself into an oncoming wave.

The water wasn't warm—in this large body of water, it probably never was. But the sudden catch in my breath from the chilling plunge seemed to clear my mind.

When I stood up, dripping and wondering why I decided to get my only clothes wet, I still felt a sort of exhilaration—like I was somehow cleaned within.

Wiping my wet hair out of my eyes, I noticed I'd moved far enough down the shore to be in sight of the Temple. It was many years since I'd first seen it—when our daughter was just a baby. Then Jon and I felt a desperate need to find this True Fountain we'd heard could cleanse us body and soul. And so, we'd left Celestia in another woman's care and made the journey here.

But the Temple of the Way, as they called it back then, was only a show. The fountains were beautiful, but they had no power. Then we found the old man on High Street who told us where the True Fountain was—in the desert, far to the east.

Gazing up, I could see the Temple grounds were still well kept. The buildings shone with a golden luster and the gardens were full of many multicolored flowers. There was a covering of mist where I knew the fountains to be. My feet took me toward the steps climbing up to the gate of the grounds.

'Why are you coming here?' I asked myself. 'I thought you didn't believe any of this anymore.'

I could think of no reply and so continued up the steps to the main level. Soon I could see the platform where Jon and I had stood in the mist so many years ago. As soon as I saw it, I knew there was no point in climbing all the way up there. I'd been to that platform before, and all I'd gotten was wet. Thinking about this brought a heavy feeling into my chest, and my eyes began to burn. But no tears came.

Turning away from the fountains, I made my way toward the upper entrance of the grounds. This was the way we'd come in that first time, I realized. "So here I am doing another thing I've done before, but once again doing it in reverse."

'Maybe you're hoping doing things backwards will reverse your whole life?'

Inwardly I groaned. "Are you back again, voice?"

'I'm part of you. I go where you go.'

This time I refused to let anything come out of my mouth, and tried to block all thoughts from my mind.

So, for several minutes I wasn't even noticing where I was going.

When I finally started to pay attention again, I found my feet walking up a steep, but familiar street. 'High Street, I'm sure,' I said to myself.

"Well, I should recognize it. I've been here twice before—once over thirty years ago with Jon, and the second time only a few years ago with Ginna."

'When you came looking for Celestia and Annemarie.'

"And we found Garek."

At the thought of him I felt a great longing. It was an actual pain in my chest. 'Is this a heart-ache?'

"Guess so…"

'How can he still mean anything to you after all this time? And you say you knew all along he was meant to be with Ginna. Were you just trying to fool yourself into believing you and Jon still belonged together—even after what you'd done?'

"When are you going to stop lecturing me?" I muttered angrily, barely keeping myself from shouting the words aloud. "Okay, I admit there are times when I wish I could hear Garek's deep caring voice again, and feel one of his warm reassuring hugs. There I've said it. Are you satisfied now?"

'Well at least you're finally being honest with yourself. I'll shut up for awhile.'

Stopping on the steep pavement, I looked around, but no one else was in sight. Then I saw the familiar doorway, just a few meters beyond me. Even though I knew there was no way the ancient old man could still be alive, I found myself walking up to the dust-covered door. Very little paint was left around the glass, which was so smudged I couldn't even see through it.

Yet I pushed at the latch and to my great surprise, the door creaked open—with the same familiar squeak. As I stepped into the gloom of the shop, I saw the empty shelves, now covered with a thick layer of dust. It looked like no one had been into this place for several years.

But still I walked toward the back, where I remembered the old man having a little room of his own. Then I heard my voice calling the name I remembered from my visit here with Ginna:

"Kai? Malakai? Is anyone here?"

Silence was the only reply. Just as I'd expected.

Then there came a rustling sound. Was it a mouse, or perhaps a rat? I knew I should just turn back and leave this piece of my past behind.

What was I doing here, anyway? I didn't want things from my past confusing me anymore.

Then a loud crash startled me right out of my skin. I was shaking in fear, and then I saw the bent old form and heard a familiar raspy voice:

"Who is it? Can't an old man rest in peace?"

Stepping closer to the sound, I saw the same face I'd seen with Ginna. How could he still be living here? He didn't seem as though he'd changed at all.

"Malakai? Is that you?"

"That's a name I use," came the gravelly voice. "What name do you use?"

"I was Martina," I muttered. "But now I just want to be Tina."

There was a shuffling sound as he moved closer. "Ah, now I can see you. Have we met before?"

"Well, if you're really Malakai, then I've met you twice—once a few years ago with my friend Ginna."

"Oh yes."

"And many more years before that, I was here with my husband and brother and a feier-cat, and—"

"Looking for the Fountain—yes I remember you now."

"How can you still be alive?" I couldn't help but ask. "How old are you?"

"Older than the hills, as an ancient saying goes," he chuckled. "So, what brings you here this time—uh—Tina?"

"Nothing really. I was just wandering this morning by the lakeshore, saw the Temple and came up to see if it had changed. Then somehow, I ended up on High Street at your shop. That's all."

"Oh, I don't think that's quite all, now is it?" he whispered.

"Not you, too," I moaned.

"What?"

"You sound like the voice in my head that keeps questioning and accusing me."

"Accusing you of what?"

"Doing the wrong thing."

"And what is it that you've done?"

"I've run away from home—again."

"And not just from the home, but from the loved ones, the beliefs, the faith—your whole life. Correct?"

"How do you know this, old man?" Now I couldn't keep the anger out of my voice.

It seemed like everything was against me today. I was wishing I'd just stayed in the little flat Shei rented. But sometimes it felt so lonely, and the walls seemed to be closing in on me. Shei came and went on an unpredictable schedule. He kept promising to find a better place—and even a job for me. But the words never came to anything.

'You just don't want to admit you've made a terrible mistake,' my inner voice said.

"All right!" I shouted suddenly. Kai's eyes flashed, but he didn't seem surprised at my outburst. "I admit it. I've really gotten myself into a mess this time. I thought if I came back to the city, I could just forget everything about Believers and being persecuted. I wanted to live like other people do here in the Thirty-first Century. Is that too much to ask?"

"I guess it depends on who you're asking," he murmured.

"I don't think I'm really asking anyone anymore," I sighed. "I don't even believe in answers."

"Yet, your feet still brought you here."

"And I don't even know why. How can I be sure you're the real Kai? Perhaps you're a spy or secret police sent to root out Believers here in Tornatoh."

He actually smiled then, and something in his eyes was vaguely familiar. "That isn't my intention, Tina."

"What are your intentions then?"

"My, for someone who doesn't want answers, you really ask a lot of questions."

All I could do then was sigh.

"Come in and have some tea," his voice said. There was something kind and warm in his tone, and I felt drawn to him.

'Be careful, it could be a trick,' I said to myself, but still I went through the shabby door into an even shabbier room.

In a short time, I was seated across from him at a battered wooden table, sipping hot tea, and marveling at its taste. It had been a long time since I'd had real tea.

"So last time you were here, you and your friend were looking for your daughters, correct?"

"You do remember, don't you?"

He smiled and nodded. "Did you find them?"

"Yes, but not in the way we expected."

"But you did all get safely back to your place, didn't you?"

Now I was the one nodding and wondering. "How do you know?"

"When you've lived as long as I have, you hear all kinds of things—often from unusual sources."

"So what else do you know about me?" I wasn't sure I wanted to hear the answer to this question, but it was too late to take it back.

"I know you still think you love Garek Carson," he whispered.

My breath was taken away so quickly that I felt faint. "No, I don't!"

"Are you sure? Isn't that perhaps part of the reason you decided to come to this city—to see if by some chance you might reconnect with him."

"But my daughter said he went back with Ginna, to the Twenty-first Century." As soon as these words were out of my mouth, I regretted it. 'This GAP-crossing and time travel isn't something he'll understand,' I thought.

"So I've been told," he smiled. ('Does he understand after all?') "But still you wondered if perhaps he might be here."

I took a long, deep breath while I tried to find an answer for this old man who knew much more than he should. "Okay, I guess there is a part of me that longs to see Garek again. When Ginna and I found him, he was preoccupied with getting to know the daughter he'd never known. Then he and Ginna seemed to be forming a deeper connection. I couldn't interfere with that."

"And so, you had to stand by as their lives merged without you."

Tears were beginning to form in my eyes now as I slowly nodded. As more teardrops fell onto the rough surface of the table, I felt a sense of relief—I was actually able to cry again.

"I know it was wrong of me to love him. I was promised to Jon. And yet there's something in Garek that's always attracted me."

"What is that?"

"Well, he listened to me better and understood how I really felt. Talking to him was so much easier than—well than almost anyone else."

"Including your husband?"

"I'm ashamed to admit it."

"You're not the first wife to feel this. But I can assure you Jon does love you—the real you—faults or not. Yet it isn't easy for him to communicate it."

"How do you know Jon so well? You only met him briefly that first time, when we were seeking the Fountain."

"Actually, I've met you other times before that—in other places."

As I tried to grasp what he meant, his form suddenly began to glow and fade in and out—hiding in a golden mist. When the mist cleared, he'd changed. He was still an old man, but no longer bent and worn. He had a much fuller white beard and long hair. The two nearly covered his face. All I could see were his flashing eyes and a smiling mouth.

"Now do you recognize me?"

At the sound of this strong voice, my eyes were suddenly opened. "Are you Johan?"

"Yes, I am."

"But how did you get here? Has it always been you—here in this old shop?"

He nodded and smiled. "Your daughter can tell you sometime of the other places she's seen me. I can go to many places, if I choose to."

"If I ever see my daughter again. Why did you come here, Johan?"

"To help you."

"Why me?"

"Your destiny is interwoven with mine and many others, Martina. Right now, you're walking in the dark, but it won't always be this way. The light will come again, when it's time. And until then, I'm here if you need me."

As I heard these words, I felt like I was melting. Tears flooded my eyes again, and I heard my voice sobbing, though it didn't sound like myself at all. I couldn't even understand the words I was saying. It seemed like some strange unknown language. My eyes ceased to focus, and I slumped into a soft cushion of darkness.

***

Gradually I came back to consciousness, out of whatever daze I'd been in. Johan was holding me in his arms, and they seemed much stronger than I expected. He didn't seem like such an old man anymore. I actually felt safe—for the first time in a long time.

"So, what should I do now, Johan? I can't just run back to Jon and the others. It will lead the System to them, and they'll be captured—or worse."

"That's true," he sighed. "And I think perhaps there are other things you need to learn before you go back."

"If I ever do go back."

"Well, that's another possibility. You're correct."

"Should I go back to Shei?"

"As a moral person my answer would be no," he said. "But there's also your safety—and the others'—to think of. And in that scenario, you must go back to Shei, whether you want to or not."

His answer told me, even without my saying a word, that he already knew all about my relationship with Shei. My stomach ached, thinking how ashamed I was Johan knew the truth, that I was nothing more than a slave to a dark master.

"I'm sorry, Kai—uh—Johan—"

"It doesn't matter which you call me. I'm both of those people. And if you don't mind, I'm still going to call you by your true name."

"I guess it's okay," I shrugged. "But it hurts, because it makes me think of who I used to be. Sometimes I feel I've already lost that life, and I'm dead already."

"That's another possible outcome, but not the one I hope for, Martina. I hope you'll rediscover your old self—and be restored. But it will take much time and effort."

Looking toward the front of the old shop just then, I realized the shadows outside were lengthening. "The sun is already setting. How did this day go by so quickly?"

"Time is like that sometimes," he smiled.

"I think I'd better get back to my flat—in case Shei—uh, is looking for me."

"Yes, I think that's the best option at this moment. But please remember, you can find me here at any time."

"You're just going to be sitting here waiting?"

"Not exactly. I can travel in ways your husband the GAP-crosser has never even dreamed of. But that doesn't concern you. Whenever you need me, come to this shop and I'll be here."

With these words he stood up suddenly, much more quickly than the old man Kai could have. Taking my hands in his, he smiled and closed his eyes. I felt myself sinking into the floor beneath my feet. And when I opened my eyes, I was standing alone in the middle of my flat.

CHAPTER 11
BURDEN OF PROOF

I can't tell you how much time has passed. Every day is nearly the same. Sometimes Shei comes to be with me, and sometimes not. Otherwise, I sleep. I eat when I have to—though I don't seem to enjoy it—and just exist. 'How different is any of this from your life before?' that persistent voice in my head keeps asking.

I thought once I was away from the deprivation of the wilderness, I'd be able to enjoy life as it was meant to be. No more scouring the forest and meadows for edible plants, no more starving when the game became scarce, and most of all no more living in fear.

Anyway, after a long time passed here in Tornatoh, I came to a wall one day—an impenetrable thing that knocked all the wind (and nearly the life) out of me:

I was listening to the System Terminal all day—there was nothing else to do in my tiny flat. Of course there were no books, no way to make music—not that I couldn't have hummed or sung to myself. But any urge to make joyful sounds seemed to have drained out of me, along with my strength.

"What I don't want to admit is I'm bored," I sighed half-aloud.

'How can you be bored?' that voice asked me. 'No one here tells you what to avoid—or what to fear—not like the fear you've lived in most of your life. You're free to choose now.'

"Am I really free?" Here I was again, arguing with myself. And lying to myself.

'You must be going insane, Tina—always talking to yourself like this.'

"Well, there's no one else to talk to."

'Go out and find someone then.'

"Oh, be quiet." I was remembering how Jon used to tease me about talking to myself as I worked—cooking or gardening, any of the daily chores.

I'd find myself blushing, and then he'd add, with a grin, "At least you're not crazy yet. When you start answering yourself back, then it's time to worry."

'And that's exactly what you're doing now—carrying on a two-way conversation with yourself.'

A deep chill swept over my body as I thought this. Perhaps I really was becoming insane. Shuddering at this thought, I jumped up from the floor cushion I'd been sitting on and began to pace the tiny main room of my flat. Shei hadn't been by to see me for several days.

'You're a fool, you know.'

"Oh, shut up, self!" As I screamed these words, I grabbed one of the smaller maroon-colored cushions and threw it against the wall. It ricocheted into a lamp stand, and the lamp crashed to the floor, shattering into dozens of pieces.

I just stood and stared at them for a long time. Then suddenly, I realized what luxuries I was throwing around. None of the Believers in hiding had cushions or lamps.

'There's no way you'll be able to repair that,' I thought. 'Shei will be so angry.'

"So what if he is." The thought of Shei showing any kind of emotion was suddenly novel to me. "He never shows his feelings," I muttered to myself and to the broken pieces on the floor. "He's a true offspring of the System."

As these thoughts gelled in my mind, it hit me how I truly had come full circle from my life as a child long ago on the planet Terres.

'There we were taught to avoid expressing emotions—especially negative ones. Strict control of one's mind was the mantra of the Galactic System back then. Apparently, it still is, now that the System's 'rediscovered' Earth.

'On Terres and other System planets, Earth was degraded to nothing but a myth. It didn't exist, we were taught. But then Jon and Jael and I were led to find it, by the old hermit, Johan.'

"Oh, him again?"

'Remember the hopes of finding answers to all our questions here? But it didn't turn out that way. After our first decade or so, the System again reared its ugly head, and those who refused to prostrate ourselves before it fled the cities to live in the wilderness. Your mind is sure wandering today.'

"Well self, it's partly your fault."

Sitting back down on the floor, careful to avoid the broken pieces of lamp, I let my mind go back further than I had in a long time—all the way back to my childhood:

My parents taught us to doubt the System's indoctrination. Instead they told us emotions were a normal human experience—not something relegated to the hidden nights of the Underground. They even taught us to read the many books they'd stored in our home. No one else had books by then. Everything was on the System Terminal, and every home had at least one.

Our parents also talked of a True King who was the embodiment of all things good—especially love, something sorely missing on Terres, outside of our home, that is. There was even a song they'd taught us:

> *The King of Love my Shepherd is,*
> *His goodness faileth never.*
> *I nothing lack if I am his,*
> *And he is mine forever.*

Father often sang for us when we were small children. And he read words to us from an ancient-looking book.

All books were forbidden by this time, and so his books were precious to him. But I remembered how Father treated this particular book with the greatest reverence. When I asked once what made this book so special, he replied:

"This is The Book, Martina. It isn't like any other books we have. All the others are merely the opinions of humans, and of course that's important, too. But The Book—this book—he touched the cover with great respect—is inspired by the True King himself. He inspired its authors down through the ages with his own Spirit."

Evidently, I was too young then to absorb what he truly meant, but the sound of his voice and the look in his eyes made a great impression on me. Jael, my youngest brother, was only a tiny baby when this conversation took place. Over the years, as Father read to us from The Book every evening, my respect continued to grow, and I began teaching these things to my little brother as we played together.

When I was a teenager, and Jael was still a small child, our father suddenly disappeared from our lives. Mother told us he'd been conscripted to fight in the Galactic War—battling against a rising force called the Rebels.

Unsure of what this really meant, I turned to my eldest brother—named Stephen, after our father—for the guidance, love, and leadership that I'd gotten from Father.

Stephen did his best, reading to us from The Book every night and singing the old songs. Mother sat beside him, nodding and smiling—though sometimes I saw tears in her eyes. Jael was so young that he sat on her lap. I would sit across from Stephen, where I could look into his shining green eyes. Our other brother, Darien, sat between Stephen and me—just as he was between us in age.

Now, as these old memories bubbled to the surface of my mind, I found tears streaming from my eyes. How I longed to go back to those days of my childhood. Back to the time when I felt cared for, loved, and secure.

'You know that's impossible,' my inner voice snapped. 'Not even a GAP-crosser can bend time like that.'

"I know."

'Are you sure what you remember from that distant time is real?'

"Why wouldn't my memories of things I experienced be true?"

'You were a child. How could you understand reality?'

"A child-like faith and trust is the purest. The King says so in The Book."

'How convenient. The Book says to us—and to it-self—that it's true. And how do we know this to be true? Because The Book says so."

By now my eyes were blinded with tears. My hand found another cushion to throw. A loud crashing sound told me something else had broken.

Still unable to see clearly, I stumbled out the door and into the small courtyard between the flats in this section. Wiping angrily at my tears, I finally made out the gate to the street—and dashed through it.

The sun was bright but the air was chilly—a typical Tornatoh day. Without even thinking about it, my feet took me in the direction of the grimy little shop on High Street.

***

Somehow, I knew the old man would be there. This time he was again in the guise of Malakai, the bent ancient man with a balding head and a sparse, ragged beard on his face. But the eyes and voice were the same as I remembered from my previous visit, when he revealed himself as the white-bearded Johan—the hermit we'd met all those years ago—Jon, Jael and me.

Just thinking about my husband and younger brother at this moment brought a tight knot into my chest. 'Why did you leave them—again?' my accusing voice asked. I tried to ignore it.

"Well, well," the old man said as I entered the creaking door. "It's very good to see you again. How are you faring?"

"Not too well," I shrugged. "When I left the wilds and came here to the city, I wanted to start over. I was so sick of all the trials and tribulations, the fear and the hunger."

"And so, you tried to come back to what you'd fled all those years ago on Terres."

"The System," I sighed, barely audibly. Tears were flooding my eyes again. "I don't think I believe in anything anymore. Why can't I put it all out of my mind, and just live for today?"

"Many have succeeded in doing just that," he half-smiled. "But it doesn't appear to be working for you, does it?"

"I doubt the truth of everything my parents taught me. How can some ancient book really contain the truth about our complex Universe? No one can fathom the four dimensions we live with every day. So how can some book of stuff handed down from person to person for eons, really be what they say it is—the Word of the King. Perhaps the writers each added their own ideas."

"Ah, I see you've been on the System Terminal again, haven't you? What you don't realize is these same questions have been asked all through the lifespan of The Book. Can it be trusted? How can we be sure? Must we only accept it on blind faith?"

"I know. Faith is all most people can fall back on. But I feel like my faith has dried up and blown away."

By this time, I was seated beside him on a low floor cushion and leaning my head against the rough cloth of his tunic.

"There now. You are correct in part. Faith is important, but it doesn't have to be totally blind. There are tests of historicity—historical proof—which can be applied to all knowledge, including The Book."

"What do you mean?" I asked at last.

"You know what scientific proof entails, don't you?"

"Well, yes. A scientist develops a hypothesis and sets up a controlled experiment to test it. The results of the experiment either prove or disprove his hypothesis. If true, it becomes a theory that other scientists can also test by controlled experiments."

"Very good. How do historians test their ideas and theories?"

"I guess in the same way."

"No, not really. A historical event can't be replicated in a controlled experiment. All we have to go on is accounts of people who saw the events."

"Eyewitnesses, right?"

"Correct. But sometimes we can't talk to an eyewitness ourselves."

"So, we rely on accounts written down by the witnesses who were there—that's what my father always said."

"But what if none of the accounts we have are by eyewitnesses?"

"I don't know, sir."

"Well, people who are serious about knowing the truth will look for the most recent account of the historical event—I mean the one that is written closest in time to when the event occurred."

"Okay."

"And then they'll try to find as many accounts of this event as they can. That way they can compare and see if the accounts are similar, or totally different. Do you see why that's important?"

"Yeah. If the accounts are too far out—too different—then they probably aren't accurate. But what does this have to do with The Book?"

"It is more than just a devotional book, you know."

"It is?"

"Yes, it presents the history of God's interactions with humans through the course of several thousand years. And it passes some of the most stringent of historical tests."

"Really?"

"Here, let me show you an example." At this he stood and reached up onto a barely visible shelf high above our heads. When he sat back down beside me, he was holding a very ragged, ancient book.

"What's that? Another copy of The Book?"

"No, this is another very ancient book, by one of the great Greek philosophers—Plato."

"I think I remember my father mentioning that name when he was studying with me once."

"Plato's works were highly respected, back when people still used books," he smiled.

"Did he help write The Book?"

"No, he didn't even know of its existence during his lifetime."

"So what does he have to do with The Book then?"

"Patience. Let me show you."

With that, he carefully opened the fragile leaves of the book. In large letters, it read: "Plato's Tetralogies—written 427 to 347 B.C."

"Wow! That's over three thousand years ago!"

"Yes, but look at the fine print."

Under the large letters, was smaller type that read: "Translated from the most reliable manuscripts available – seven copies transcribed in 900 A.D."

"Hey, those were the 'most reliable'? They were over 1000 years after the originals were supposedly written. Okay. What's the point?"

"Well, for centuries, scholars have never questioned the authenticity of these writings by Plato. But these same people have continually questioned the accuracy and authenticity of The Book. How do you think it stands up to the same tests these books have had—the number of copies available to compare with, and the length of time the copies are from the actual events?"

"I have no idea," I shrugged.

"Okay, the part of The Book originally written in Greek (which is also the language of Plato, by the way) has its oldest known manuscript dating from 125 A.D., which is less than 100 years from when many of the events it records took place."

"That's pretty impressive. How many copies have they found, maybe fifty?"

"More like twenty-five thousand-"

"What? You're kidding!"

Kai merely smiled his partially toothless smile. In his sparkling eyes I could see Johan's.

"There's no comparison." I felt my mind whirling. "How come people believe the words of Plato, when the manuscripts have such a lack of evidence—but then question The Book, when it stands the test of historicity much better?"

"Well, why do you think?"

"I'm guessing it has something to do with the System."

"In part, that's correct."

"And people don't like to be told what The Book says about God and humanity."

"And neither does the Serpent," he added.

"Oh, yeah-"

I realized with a start I'd forgotten about our encounters with the Red Dragon, especially back in Stephan's alternative universe.

"So is the Dragon—or the Serpent—behind the System?"

"Oh, yes. He's behind everything that teaches people to question their Creator—everything that tries to convince humans they can be their own gods and masters."

Now I could feel a great lump rising in my throat, as I recalled times when Jon, Jael, and I discussed these things—especially after we met Johan, and as we read The Book he'd given us. "I've been a selfish fool, haven't I?"

As I said this, a bright beam seemed to penetrate the cobwebby ceiling above us. And in an instant, Kai was transformed into the image of Johan I remembered so well.

"How could I have been so blind?" Now tears were covering my face, and I wanted to hide from this powerful being.

But he put his hand on my head, and I felt a bit of calm flow into me. "You're not alone, my child. Many others before you have made the same mistakes. And more after you will do the same. All humans are flawed. It's The Book which helps us see that—and face up to it."

"But what can I do now? It's too late for me to go back."

"That's true. But The Book also tells us what God did to solve our problem."

"What?"

"You've forgotten already?"

I hung my head in shame, and nodded.

"He sent his only Son."

"Okay—I remember people saying the Son came to show us how to live the way the Lord expects."

"He did much more than that."

I looked up slowly and saw his eyes shining into mine as I asked, "What did he do?"

"The Son of God took our place. He took the punishment we deserved and paid the price to set us free." The old man's voice suddenly sounded younger and stronger.

Now my mind was pulling out an image from over thirty years ago—the shining cross we'd seen in the sky as we approached the Fountain in the Desert. "How could I forget something so important?" I moaned.

"Because you're only human," he whispered. "That's why the Son came down to help us, because we were powerless to help ourselves."

By then I'd lost my voice and all control of my emotions. Soon I realized I was sobbing onto Johan's shoulder, overcome by shame.

"What shall I do?" I was finally able to ask. "Is it too late for me? Have I run away once too many?"

"No, child. As long as this world exists, it's not too late. Just trust in what you've been taught. Now you can see what *is* true—that's stood the test of time."

"Okay, but what do I say?"

"You don't have to say anything. He knows your heart. He knows your grief for turning away, and he knows you repent."

"Still I feel so awful, like I've gone past the point of no return."

"These very feelings show you haven't gone too far— yet. Now just talk to the King, and tell him what you're feeling."

I tried to do what he said, but I felt like my insides were turning to mush. My lips couldn't form any words, and my mind became a blank page of black.

"Oh, L-Lord—" I began. But no other words would come. I sobbed on Johan's shoulder. "I can't say anything."

His deep voice rumbled through my entire body. "You don't need words, Martina. He's told us his Spirit intercedes for us—with groans too deep for words. Just let go and let him help."

I thought I was doing the best I could, but still the deep aching chill remained. In a sudden burst of anger, I pulled away from Johan and jumped to my feet.

"It's not working. I don't feel any different."

"Sometimes that takes time," he said calmly. "You can't base your faith only on feelings."

"But something should be helping me feel better."

Before he could reply, I stormed through the creaking shop door and began running down High Street.

CHAPTER 12
UNDERCOVER

The wind was moaning in the conifers above them, and Laken was thankful the trees were providing some shelter from this raging storm. As they entered a clearing in the forest, the gusts increased, threatening to push him to the ground.

"I've never felt wind this strong." His wife's voice came only faintly, shredded by the wind.

"Me either," her uncle Jael added, cupping his hands to try and focus his sound.

Retreating back into the shelter of the pines, Laken stood still long enough to catch his breath. "It's a wild and blustery day, for sure," he said, once his voice returned.

"I don't suppose you know how much my mother hates this sort of weather," he heard Celestia mutter.

Stepping over, he took her hand before he spoke. "Does she?"

"Absolutely. She doesn't like to be cold at all—and wind gives her headaches—or so she says."

"Hmm—I wonder if the long winter we had this year was one of the triggers of her depression."

"I suppose. I guess it's good the past few days have been milder than today."

"Or not," he added.

"What do you mean?"

"I'm thinking that if she encountered weather like this, she might have turned around."

"And come back home," she sighed.

"*We* may need to turn back if this gets any worse."

Just then Jael moved toward them, so quickly in fact he nearly knocked Laken over. "Sorry," he said breathlessly. "I think there's a cave near here—one Raina and I once used."

"When was that, Uncle?"

"Back before I was captured, when we were trying to keep the children safe."

She nodded, but her reply was ripped away by another hurricane gust. By now the wind was blowing so hard it almost blew Laken off his feet. He grabbed onto both of his companions and pulled them down on their knees beside him. The sound of the roar in the tops of the pines nearly drowned out the end of Jael's reply.

Laken looked at him with a questioning gaze, and Jael responded by jerking his head to his left. They followed him as he crept on hands and knees through the prickly juniper bushes.

Just as Laken was about to tell him this looked like a dead-end, he saw the dark mouth of the cave. The next thing he knew, they were crawling inside, grateful to have some respite from the storm.

'It's a good thing Jael knew of this place,' he thought. 'Otherwise we'd be too exhausted to think, let alone walk anymore.'

In fact, both his companions were soon sleeping soundly in exhaustion, so he stretched out next to his wife and joined her in the peaceful oblivion of slumber.

***

The sounds of birds singing woke him. Sitting up suddenly he tried to remember where he was. The low rock ceiling of the cave reminded him.

"Ouch!"

Celestia stirred, "What's wrong? What happened?"

He reached over and took her hands in his. "Don't sit up too fast. The ceiling in here is low."

"The what?"

"We're in a cave," came Jael's voice. "If we keep closer to the entrance there's more headroom."

"Wish you'd told me that before," he said ruefully.

"Sorry, Laken. There wasn't much we could do in the storm."

"That's for sure. Is it over?"

"I'd say so," said Jael.

Laken helped his wife sit up carefully, while Jael moved into the yawning opening of the cave.

"Is that birds I hear?" she asked.

"I believe so," he smiled at his wife and gave her a quick peck on the lips.

He could feel rather than see the affection this triggered, and couldn't help thinking how much he wished the two of them could be alone together. 'In time—be patient,' he murmured to himself.

Jael pulled some fruit leather from his pocket and passed a piece to each of them. "This won't last long, Laken. I guess we should've brought more supplies."

Laken shrugged and tried not to take this as a personal criticism of his leadership. "Yeah, I assumed we could make it in a day. Not so smart, I guess."

"It's all right," said his wife. "We don't have weather forecasters anymore to let us know about storms like yesterday's."

"Still, if I were more wilderness-smart, I might've read the signs in the sky or the forest. Just before the wind came, the forest animals suddenly went silent, remember?"

"I guess I didn't notice," she sighed. "So don't feel bad. I should've paid more attention, too."

"That's all past now," Jael cut in. "No point in going over ground we've already covered."

"Except to learn from our mistakes."

"Well, you've got me there." Jael patted her shoulder and smiled into her eyes.

"Now we just need to get moving toward the city," Laken said quickly, before they could get off on another subject. 'There's something about this family,' he thought to himself. 'They have a circular way of thinking—and seem to go off on tangents.'

Both his companions nodded and finished their fruit leather. "It's a good thing this stuff gives extra energy," she said, once her last bite was swallowed.

"We should be able to reach the city today," Laken said. "Come on, you two. We need to get moving if we're going to have another meal anytime today."

Laken watched his companions carefully as they all walked through the conifer forest. He knew they needed to be as quiet as possible to avoid capture by System Patrols. 'I hope they're getting used to their new identities,' he thought.

He did his best to keep their roles as close to their real lives as he could. Celestia (now 'Starla') was still his wife, and he kept his own name. 'Since I'm from 900 years ago, no one here will know me anyway.'

His wife's Uncle Jael chose to go by the name he used long ago in the Redlarks' Camp—Stel.

"Daiah gave it to me," he'd smiled as he told them about it. "She said it meant I was the child of the stars. Especially the new Double-star in the Terres sky, from when a passing star captured our sun, Regelian."

Laken had never been to Terres, and neither had his wife, but it seemed more than coincidence that Celestia's new name and Jael's both meant 'star'.

"My dad told me how much significance the Doublestar had for you," Celestia said.

"It did for Jon, too," 'Stel' replied. "Its coming was when I finally got him to help me find my runaway sister."

"Martina," Laken chuckled. "I sure hope it brings us as much luck on this search for her."

Jael smiled, "Me, too. Besides, I'm thankful to have most of my memories back. I lost so many during those years the System held me captive."

"It's good to have you back, Uncle—I mean Stel."

"It's good to be back—uh, Starla."

Laken smiled. "You two need to always call each other by your new names, so it becomes a habit. Slip-ups can be deadly."

"At least you're still Laken, and still my husband." She reached over and gave him a big hug. Then he kissed her, holding her close for several seconds.

But when he saw Jael standing alone, he broke away sooner than he really wanted to. "I'm sorry, Stel."

"It's all right. You two need to be convincing. I'm supposed to be the 'older and wiser' one in this scheme. But of course, it's just the opposite. You're the one with the most experience in undercover operations."

"He's been alive longer than both of us put together," Starla smiled.

"Those were other lives in other places, distant in space and time," Laken shrugged. "I don't have full memories of most of them. That's just the way it is with Time Portal Guardians."

"Is that what you truly are?" Stel asked.

"That's been my chief role down through the centuries. But I don't think we'll be using any Time Portals on this mission."

"You never know," added Starla. "We need to be prepared to do whatever the situations call for. And we all need each other, with our different strengths and past experiences." She turned to look at Stel. "Doesn't it say somewhere in The Book that 'a three-strand cord is not easily broken.'?"

"Yes, in a book called Ecclesiastes," he replied. "Johan quoted another part of that book to us the first time we met him, remember? 'To everything there is a season, and a time to every purpose under heaven'."

"Uh, I've heard it, but you were the only one who saw Johan on the first flight from Terres," she said.

"Oh, I guess I forgot. You remind me so much of your mother that sometimes I think of you as my sister, instead of my niece." He was looking down at the ground in embarrassment, stopping the progress they'd made walking through the forest.

She reached over and took his hand in hers, feeling there was still some weakness in his body. 'I hope you can handle this mission, Uncle.'

"Don't worry. Just remember to use my new name, Starla."

"Anyway, that part about the 'three-strand cord' is a true saying," Laken cut in. "So hopefully the three of us will be stronger together than we would be apart." Then he looked squarely into their eyes and said, "Okay, you're Starla, my wife, but what else are you?"

"I'm a medical worker. So I'll be working in an infirmary, helping to heal people—hopefully."

"And you, Stel?"

"I'm a technician who repairs electronics and terminals."

"Are you sure you can do that? It's been a long time since you worked with a computer," she said.

"Don't worry, you two, he's my assistant," said Laken.

"Okay," sighed Stel. "And I know you're always working with some kind of technology."

Laken looked from one to the other—his wife looking beautiful, even in a white lab coat. Her brown eyes were shining, and he found he really liked the way her long, dark hair looked when it was let down, falling across her shoulders.

Jael—or rather, Stel—was still thin from his prison ordeal, but his eyes had regained their old sparkle, and his blond hair had grown back from a shaved head. But he was getting gray at the temples now.

"Is Raina okay with all this now?" he asked, pulling his mind back to the present.

"She's come around. She understands it must be done, but she hopes you can alter time, so when we get back it will seem little time has passed for her."

"I can't guarantee anything, but I'll do my best," he replied.

By now, they'd left the environs of the mountains and reached the edge of the forest, where the hills settled into gently rolling swales. Soon they came to open grassy prairies, and before long, Tornatoh appeared in the distance.

Laken decided to cross the GAP when the city was in sight. "There's less chance of errors this way. And hopefully we'll be able to reappear in a more deserted part of the city."

"Why can't we just walk all the way?" Starla asked.

"There are fences and guard posts, I'm sure. We can't afford to be questioned closely." He'd tried to keep his voice calm and nonchalant speaking these words. But in his own mind he was envisioning all the dangers they might run into.

When they were close enough to Tornatoh, the towering spire became the most distinctive part of the skyline. It had been here over 900 years ago—the last time he'd been in this city, back in the Twenty-second Century. 'And Celestia was with me then, though we'd barely just met, introduced by Darroch.'

He stopped his thoughts right there. The reminder of his friend Darroch's betrayal sent a flash of anger through him. 'I can't afford this kind of distraction,' he told himself. 'Besides, there are things I did then that I prefer to forget. I'm just fortunate Celestia has forgiven me for the pain I caused her.'

"Okay, folks," he said aloud to clear his mind. "I think I can see a more residential area to focus on, just to the north of the densest part of the city. It appears to have some smaller office-type buildings—not like the skyscrapers downtown. Hopefully there won't be as many people walking those streets. Let's get into our circle."

He reached over and took his wife's hand, kissing it quickly. Then he grabbed Jael's hand—reminding himself to call him 'Stel'.

Holding hands, he could feel they all were ready. There was an electric excitement running back and forth between them.

All three closed their eyes. Laken and Starla were the first-borns, and Stel had the ability to focus on a certain person. This first time, however, Laken had cautioned him not to concentrate on Martina.

"We need to check out the whole situation before we try to focus on her. Otherwise, we might cause her—and ourselves—a lot of trouble."

Giving his wife's hand an extra squeeze, he focused on what he hoped wasn't a busy street. Then the ground fell away in the familiar GAP-crossing sensation.

In the next instant, they found themselves standing

on pavement. Laken knew immediately they were in the middle of a street because horns were blaring at them.

Quickly he pulled his companions into an open grassy area nearby.

"Whoa, that was close!"

"Sorry, Stel."

"So much for not being noticed," sighed Starla. "Here comes some kind of law officer."

Sure enough, a young man in a uniform was approaching them. "Are you okay?"

"Yes sir," the three companions said almost together.

"What did you think you were doing—standing in the middle of the street? You're not some of those protestors we've been having lately, are you?"

"Oh, no sir," Laken said quickly, trying meanwhile to think of a plausible excuse.

"It's my fault, officer," Starla spoke up. "I was trying to practice what I would do in a traffic emergency, but the street was busier than I realized."

The officer frowned, but Laken saw his wife showing her most winning smile.

"Are you a healthcare worker?"

"Yes, sir. That's exactly what I am."

"And these two are friends of yours?"

"You could say that. Laken is my husband—and Stel is my uncle."

"Ah!" His eyes opened wide and his eyebrows raised

up to where they almost disappeared into the brown hair covering his forehead. Laken thought he saw a hint of disappointment that Starla was married. "Well, you need to practice in a safer place," he was saying. "And your name is?"

"Oh sorry, officer. My name is Starla."

"All right—I'm letting you off with a warning. But I must take your husband in for questioning."

"Why?" she blurted out.

"Just the rules," the officer shrugged. "We've been plagued with protests recently."

Laken turned to her quickly. "It's okay, dear," he whispered. Then he extended his hands toward the officer in a submissive pose. "I'll come peaceably, sir. Meanwhile, try to find a flat for us, Stel," he added over his shoulder.

He could see the confused and stricken looks on his companions' faces as the officer put binders on his wrists and led him away.

"There's really no need for these," he murmured to the officer.

"Must follow the rules, though," came the reply.

Laken just nodded mutely.

***

He expected to be thrown into a prison cell with no questions asked. Instead, the officer seated him next to a short, dark man with piercing black eyes.

'A Questioner,' his subconscious told him. Apparently, he'd encountered one of these before—in another of his lives.

The man didn't speak but stared intently into Laken's eyes, never blinking. Suddenly, a sharp pain coursed through him, almost like he'd been pierced with an ice-cold blade. His vision blurred and his head began to throb.

From some distance he felt a pair of chilling hands resting on his head. Then he was engulfed in total darkness.

When a small pinpoint of light began to pulsate before his eyes, he found himself lying on a cold metal bench. His head felt like flames were smoldering just below his scalp. As his eyes finally adjusted to the dimness around him, he made out vertical bars along one side of the tiny room he was in.

'Ended up in a cell after all,' he sighed to himself. 'Have I been unconscious? Maybe I'm in a Time Nexus, like Jael was in his System prison.'

Finally, he heard a sound besides his own breathing and pounding heart—footsteps coming toward his cell.

In the dimness he could make out a face above a uniform. It wasn't until the voice spoke that he recognized the young officer who'd arrested him.

"Well, Mr. Laken," the voice said, "I'm sorry to have inconvenienced you."

'Much more than inconvenience,' he muttered to himself. But he didn't speak, moving cautiously toward the bars. His head was still throbbing, and as he moved the room spun sickeningly around him. "You're sorry?" he managed to say.

"Yes. Our Questioner has found no subversive thoughts in your mind."

Laken stood stock still, not wanting to reveal his dizziness—or his emotions.

"You're free to go, Mr. Laken."

With a screech of metal against metal, the barred door swung open. He stepped gingerly past the threshold and restrained himself from cringing when he felt the officer's hand on his shoulder.

"Well, I won't report you to your superior for this insulting behavior," Laken muttered, "—just this once. But don't let it happen again." He hoped his voice sounded more indignant than surprised.

The hand on his shoulder was quickly withdrawn. "Oh, thank you, sir." The young officer's voice was almost a squeak of fear.

Taking a deep breath, Laken hoped the room around him wouldn't start spinning again, as he walked away from the cell. The sound of quick shallow breathing faded behind him as he made his way down the hall, retracing the officer's approach.

Once into the outdoors, he was thankful to see the sun had just set. 'How am I going to find the others?' he mumbled to himself.

Just then a sharp hiss to his right startled him, and he turned to flee.

"Stop!" came a deep male voice.

'Is this a trap, after all?' But then he heard another higher-pitched voice:

"Don't run. Please."

He froze in his tracks, not recognizing either voice. "Who are you?"

"Friends."

Laken hoped this speaker was honest. Before another thought could materialize in his mind, however, strong hands grabbed him from behind.

CHAPTER 13
THE CITY WITH THE SPIRE

Laken woke feeling quite sore. His neck, back and head throbbed, and his first thought was 'Who hit me? And why?'

The room he saw, once his eyes began to adjust, was dim and smelled musty. He heard another sound of breathing, and froze his movements. Waiting a few minutes longer helped his eyes adjust to the lack of light. Now he could see a form lying on the floor next to him, and he was surprised to find that he wasn't tied or shackled in any way.

"Where am I?" he finally said aloud.

"You're in Tornatoh," said a gravelly voice. "How are you feeling?"

Again, he was surprised this person seemed to care for his well-being. "Frankly, I hurt all over. Now I've answered your question. Let me be more specific. Where am I in Tornatoh?"

"Ah, you are a smart one, aren't you?" the rough voice almost seemed to be chuckling. "All right, you are in a safe-house—not very comfortable, I'm afraid, but at least off the System's radar."

"So, were you telling the truth before you grabbed me? Are you a friend?"

"An excellent memory for details, too. You've been in situations like this before, I take it?"

Laken was sitting upright now and trying to see his companion's face. "Who are you?" he demanded aloud.

"My name is Jakob," said the voice, and a small light appeared in his hand. "I was sent to protect you—by the Believers."

"So, are you one of the Believers, then?"

The man nodded, now that he could be seen in the light. "I needed to find you before you found your fellow travelers."

"Why?"

"Because your prison warden put a tracer on you."

"Oh—"

"Is the woman really your wife?"

Now it was Laken's turn to nod, but he suddenly found himself unable to speak.

"If you'd found them, you would've led the System trackers right to them."

"Are they safe now? Starla is my wife, and her uncle Stel is with her."

"Yes, I know these names—and their true ones, as well."

He felt a tight twisting in his gut. 'Have I betrayed them?' This thought seemed to boom and echo in his mind, which made his headache throb even more.

Then he felt a hand on his shoulder, a nonthreatening touch.

"They're safe with my partner. She'll take them to Johan when it's possible."

"Johan? Is he here? I never knew he came to Earth, let alone to Tornatoh."

"Sh-hh! He's in his own form of deep cover. You'll only see him if it becomes necessary. Please believe me."

"How long have you been working here in Tornatoh? What was your name—Jakob?"

In the small puddle of light, he could see the man nod. He appeared to be quite old, with gray whiskers on his cheeks, but there was a bright sparkle in his eyes.

"I've been many places in my work for the True King," the old man smiled. "One such place was Terres, where your wife's family comes from. My name has always been Jakob, however. I don't believe that's true of you, is it?"

"Uh, no. I have many names, but Laken is the one I've had the longest—and hope to keep."

"I know what you mean. I was blessed to find my ideal name on my first assignment. But few guardians are so fortunate."

"Finding my true self was a long journey for me," Laken sighed. "It took the love of my wife to help me."

"So that's why she's so dear to you."

His throat tightened at the thought of his wife, and he looked away from the man.

"No need to hide your true feelings," said Jakob. "I've had the same experience with my wife, Myra."

"Is she also your partner?"

"Yes, in the same way Celestia is your partner, as well as your wife."

Laken again felt a sense of panic as he heard the man say his wife's true name. He grabbed at him and managed to get hold of his shirt. "You'd better be telling the truth, old man."

"I am telling the truth." The man's voice was strained, so Laken knew he had a good grip on him. "Now, please—let go of me."

Laken relaxed his grip only slightly. "Prove it."

"You'll have to let me show you my arm," came the voice again.

He moved back a tiny bit more, and saw the old man reveal his forearm. There was the shape of a cross tattooed there. When he saw this, he let go of the man entirely, and pulled up his own sleeve to show his right forearm. "I have one of the marks, too," he murmured. "I must have received it during a former life that I don't remember."

"So, at least you can see we're on the same side," Jakob sighed.

Laken moved back out of the pool of light. "All right, you've convinced me—for now. Did you say you knew my wife's family on Terres?"

"Indirectly. I met her grandmother."

"Irina?"

"I believe that's her name. And I also met Raina, who I believe is now married to Jael?"

"Either you're a true Guardian—or you know too much."

"I didn't meet your wife there, however."

"Well, you're right about that. Celestia was never on Terres. She was born here on Earth—before—"

"Before the System came here."

"Right. So, what do we need to do next, Jakob?"

Again, the old man chuckled in his deep raspy voice. "Aren't you the anxious one? We have to wait until your tracer runs out of power."

"How long will that take?"

"Probably about six more days."

Laken felt his heart sink.

***

Jael was watching his niece Celestia's face carefully. She didn't seem to be showing any fear. 'But maybe she's just good at hiding it,' he thought.

Ever since Laken was taken captive, right after their ill-fated GAP-crossing, everything seemed to be going wrong. 'It's like a chain reaction,' he told himself. 'But that doesn't mean things will keep going wrong.' He wished he could convince himself of this statement, though.

Right now, the two of them were sitting on the ground in a grassy area. It appeared to be a popular place for the city's daytime inhabitants to take a break or eat a snack. They joined them, hoping to blend in. It helped that Celestia—'I mean Starla!', he mentally kicked himself—was already wearing a white coat, similar to many of the other workers sprawled on the lawn nearby.

Suddenly, however, his heart jumped into overdrive as a tall, willowy woman came towards them.

"Hello," she said in a pleasant voice. "May I join you?"

There was really nothing he could do except smile and nod up at her.

She sat carefully on the grass next to them. Jael saw his companion look up and try to smile at this newcomer.

"Are you two from around here?" their new companion asked.

"Yes, I'm Starla—and this is my Uncle Stel." He smiled at how calmly she was introducing them. "What's your name?"

"I'm called Myra." Jael actually found he was beginning to like the calmness and friendliness in her voice. 'Watch out,' he thought to himself. 'She could be a very skillful System agent.'

He decided to let the two women take charge of the small talk, since they seemed to be hitting it off already.

But he kept his ears attuned to the conversation, listening for any threats. Apparently, all was well, however. Once the woman who called herself Myra finished eating her snack, she rose to her feet and wished them both a pleasant day.

"What do you make of that?" he whispered when Myra was out of earshot.

"I don't think she had any ulterior motives. She was just being friendly."

"I sure hope so. She seemed to be overly interested in you."

"Well, I stuck to our script, didn't I?"

"Guess we'll see what happens tomorrow," he sighed. "But where are we going to sleep tonight?"

"Hmm. I hadn't thought of that. What do *you* think we should do?"

He mulled it over to himself for a few minutes, thankful she didn't interrupt. At last he shrugged, "I guess we do what Laken suggested—try to find a flat."

She stood quickly. "That doesn't sound easy. I sure hope we can find someplace that's safe."

These words were barely out of her mouth when the woman they'd eaten with walked by. "Did I hear you say you have no room for tonight?"

Her question was casual, but he didn't like the way she asked it so quickly. 'Has she been eavesdropping on us all along?' he wondered.

Starla answered before he had a chance to stop her. "We don't have a flat in the city yet. Do you have any suggestions?"

Jael cringed. Were they playing directly into the woman's hands?

"I have a two-room flat," Myra was saying. "You'd be welcome to stay with me until you can find something for yourselves."

"Oh, thank you."

'Starla is being much too naïve,' he groaned to himself.

"Come with me," the woman continued. "It's not far to my building."

'Much too convenient,' he sighed.

As it turned out, Myra did have a roomy and well-furnished flat. The second room had a large sleeping platform they could share.

"I don't mind sleeping with you, Uncle Stel, if you don't mind being with me."

"I'm sure it will be all right," he tried to smile. "It will be better when your husband arrives, and you two can be together again."

"When is your husband coming?" Myra asked.

"Uh—I'm not sure," she said quickly. "He was delayed and said he'd join us later. We were to find a two-bedroom flat in the meantime."

"If you two aren't comfortable sharing a bed, perhaps Starla could sleep with me."

"Oh, no," Stel said quickly. "We'll be fine." 'The last thing I need is Starla getting too familiar with this stranger.'

Myra spread an adequate supper for them in the part of the flat used for cooking. It was just one end of her bedroom, from what he could see. The food was good, but nothing fancy. In a way, this encouraged him. 'At least she's not trying to tempt us with wining and dining.'

Once they'd retired to their sleeping platform, he realized how exhausted he was.

"What do you make of all this, Uncle?"

"I'm not sure what to think, Starla." He made sure to say her undercover name clearly, just in case they were being listened to.

"She seems to just want to be helpful."

"I've lived a lot of my life knowing things aren't always what they seem," he sighed.

"Well, there wasn't much else we could have done tonight—unless we slept on the street or in a park, right?"

He nodded silently, not really wanting to think anymore. "Let's just try to get some sleep," he said at last.

***

Laken was trying to rest in the dark, tiny place Jakob claimed was his home. At least four days had passed, and he was worried about his wife. And he was tense about keeping out of sight during the day. How he wished he could take a walk in the sunshine.

Jakob came and went without letting any of his plans be known, which also made Laken uneasy. 'If he was truly a Guardian—like he says—he'd know he could trust me,' he often found himself thinking.

He began to lose track of how many days they'd been holed up in this place, when Jakob at last announced it was time to move.

"Has it been long enough for the power to wear down then?"

The old man nodded and half-smiled. "I can't stay here any longer," he added.

"Why not? Isn't this your place?"

"No—it's Johan's, and he has need of it."

Laken was startled. "Is Johan coming here? Why do we have to move?"

"I can't disclose all the details. But Johan has his reasons—as you should know all too well."

Now he could tell this was another test of his identity. "What? All this time and you still don't believe my story?"

"You haven't really told me much, you know."

"What more do you need to know, old man? I've said I'm a Believer and a Guardian—"

"And I've told you the same, haven't I?'

"Oh, I get it—if you believe me, then I can believe you."

"That's one way to put it."

Just as he was about to step closer to the man and try

to look into his eyes, there came a heavy pounding on the door.

"Quickly, follow me," Jakob whispered.

Knowing he had no choice now, Laken followed the man into a back closet, partially concealed in the darkness of the flat. To his surprise, the back wall of the small space moved when Jakob touched it. A stairway yawned into view, and they began descending it as quickly and quietly as possible.

"What?" he started to ask, but the old man shoved a hand over his mouth.

"Total silence."

Laken realized they'd reached the bottom of the stairs, and now there appeared to be nowhere else to go. 'Perhaps this is only a hiding room, and not a passageway,' he sighed to himself.

All he could do was stand in silence, listening to the banging sounds above them. He was panting and had to force himself to breathe normally. On its own, his body began taking steps to calm itself. 'This must be part of my old training ingrained into me,' he thought. 'I just wish there was a way to see if this man is telling the truth.'

Eventually, there were no sounds from the flat above them. The man tapped him on the forearm. This reminded him of the tattoo of the cross they both had.

"All right, I believe you," he whispered. "You have the mark of the True King, and so do I. What do we do next?"

"I think we need to stay down here for a little more time."

He sighed at this thought.

"You don't like the darkness, Laken?"

"I'm sorry. It's just I'm worried about my wife."

"She's better off away from you for a few more days."

"A few more days!"

The man made no reply, but patted his arm again.

After what seemed like forever, but was really only a few hours, Jakob finally appeared convinced it was safe to climb the stairs again. Laken's heart thumped loudly in his chest as they crept out of the closet and surveyed the tiny flat.

"What a mess," Jakob sighed as they saw what the searchers had done. Any dishes from the table were in pieces on the floor. The beds were overturned and stripped.

"What can we do now, sir?"

"I think it's time to go to Johan—if we can."

"So, you do know where he is, after all?" Laken couldn't keep anger out of his voice now.

"I've always known, but it wasn't safe to take you until after the power-pack of your tracer died."

"How do you know it's dead?"

"Because of this search. They came to the last place it located you."

"Oh."

"So now, you and I can try to make our way to Johan."

All Laken could do was hope this was the truth.

'At least the sun is shining,' he thought as they made their way down a narrow street.

Jakob was walking rather briskly ahead of him, and this made him wonder if he was really as old as he seemed. The man was looking around them frequently, which wasn't reassuring.

When they finally reached the end of the alley, he stopped right behind Jakob and looked cautiously over his shoulder.

"Is it safe?" he asked.

"I don't like the looks of those two men on the other side of the street," Jakob whispered. "But there's no other way to go."

"Where exactly are we going? Just in case we get separated, you know."

Jakob turned and smiled briefly at him. "Yes, you're correct. I need to trust you, also. We're going to a place called High Street, near the Temple. Have you ever been to the Temple of Unity?"

Laken shook his head. "No. I think Jael—or rather Stel—was there once many years ago."

"You can't miss the temple—it's the largest building in the city. And the Unity Tower is close by. So, if we do get separated, just head for the tower. All right now. Try to walk nonchalantly."

"Right," nodded Laken.

To start with, things seemed to go well. They walked onto the main sidewalk and began looking into various shop windows. The men across the way didn't pay any heed to them. But when they turned a corner onto another side street, Laken saw the men begin to move toward them.

"I think we're being followed," he murmured to his companion.

"Okay. At the next shop, duck inside, and I'll run. Hopefully they'll follow me instead of you."

"But won't they catch you?"

"Don't worry about me. You're more important."

This last comment surprised him, but there was no time to ask any of the questions popping into his head. When they reached the shop Jakob had indicated, he opened the door slowly and quietly stepped inside. No sooner had he done this, than Jakob gave a sharp cry, and began running up the next side street.

Laken was cowering behind a tall shelf in the shop, and no one seemed to have seen him.

There came a creaking sound. Apparently, the shop-keeper was coming out to see if he wanted to buy anything. It was too late to make a dash now, so he began gazing at the case he'd just been hiding behind. To his surprise it was full of brightly colored crystals.

"Have you found something that strikes your fancy?"

He tried his best to turn toward the merchant as

casually as he could. "I'm just browsing, sir. Perhaps I'll find something to show my wife."

"Is she coming to meet you here?"

This sounded like a leading question, and Laken decided talking about his wife was not a good idea. "Actually, no. She's in another city. I'm trying to find a gift to take back to her when I return home."

"Ah, a souvenir. The best thing would be one of these amethysts. Notice the deep purple color? These are only found in this region—around Tornatoh."

"Really?"

"Yes, sir. They were created when a volcano erupted east of here."

"A volcano?" He was doing his best to sound like a traveler on a casual trip.

"It was a few hundred years ago."

Laken nodded. That would explain why he hadn't heard of this eruption. It had happened after the Twenty-second Century—the time when he was last in this city. "Ah yes, I remember now. It's been a long time since I've visited your fine city. I think I'd like this pin." He pointed to a small clip with a deep purple stone.

"Very good choice, sir," the merchant smiled. "Will you be paying by credit or cash?"

Now Laken wasn't sure what to do—he had neither of these things. As he reached into his pocket, wondering how to get out of this predicament, he felt some hard circular coins with his fingers. Pulling them out, he looked up at the merchant. "Will this be enough?"

"Of course. Here let me wrap it for you."

Laken could tell by the man's eyes that the coins were more than adequate. 'Jakob must have slipped them into my pocket, just in case. I guess he is on my side, after all.'

As the man was wrapping the small parcel, he heard the shop door open behind him. The instant the package was ready, he grabbed it quickly. "Keep the change," he called over his shoulder as he quickly went out the door.

There appeared to be no one following him, but he walked briskly anyway. As he came to various corners, he tried to make random turns. But soon he realized he was totally disoriented.

'A fine problem. I've lost any potential shadowers, but I've gotten myself lost, too.'

He emerged from a short alleyway and looked downhill toward the inner city. Then he noticed the shining golden domes of the temple. And looming just beyond it was the towering spire he'd seen all those years ago—when Celestia first brought them here by crossing the GAP.

Resuming a brisk pace, he made his way toward the temple, as Jakob had instructed.

Just as he reached a more level stretch of road—he'd been descending rather steeply for several blocks—he noticed another man walking several meters behind him, and once again his heart began to pound.

'I shouldn't be reacting this much to danger,' he admonished himself. 'I've been trained for this kind of work.'

He began practicing the slow breathing/relaxation techniques he'd been taught somewhere in one of his past lives. The man appeared to be quite old and crippled, but it was difficult to tell if this was a disguise or not. He was drawing closer now, and Laken saw there was no way to escape crossing his path.

Taking a deep breath, he prepared some casual remark about the weather.

Just as the man reached him, Laken felt a fierce grip on his arm.

"Don't run," a raspy voice hissed.

"Oh, excuse me, sir." He tried to sound casual. "I believe you've mistaken me for someone else."

"No, Laken. I believe you're the one who's mistaken."

Hearing his own name, he felt his heart sink. 'I've been found out,' he sighed inwardly. He made no effort to escape as the man pulled him into yet another small side street. Then he heard the man begin to laugh.

"You really don't recognize me, do you Laken?"

He looked squarely at the old man, but there was nothing familiar about him.

"Perhaps this will help." As he said this, the man's scraggly beard became full and white, and his eyes began to sparkle.

"Johan?"

"Don't be so incredulous, my friend," he chuckled. Then he turned abruptly on his heel and led him up a sloping street to their left. Just as they reached the next corner, he saw the name, "High Street."

He didn't realize he'd said the words aloud until Johan looked back at him. "Yes, this is my back door in Tornatoh."

Following Johan into the dingy shop, Laken tried to get his mind back to proper functioning. Then he saw Jakob sitting across the room at a dusty table. "So you remembered my directions."

"Uh, most of them. But I have to admit Johan found me before I found him."

"Well, at least you're honest," both men chuckled.

"What about the others—uh, Starla and Stel?"

"They'll be along shortly—with Myra," came Johan's deep voice.

Just as soon as he'd said this, however, there came a shout and a scream from just outside the shop's door.

Jakob and Johan both were on their feet in an instant, looking each other in the eyes. Laken saw Johan nod and suddenly disappear in a shower of sparks. Jakob took Laken's arm and pushed him into a back room just past the table where he'd been sitting, but then the old man disappeared, too.

The next thing he heard was the sound of breaking glass. He wanted to jump out and help, but when he tried the door, it was locked. He couldn't do anything. Then the sounds seemed to calm down. A sound like running foot-steps went by the wall to his left. He thought he could hear a woman's voice calling, but couldn't make out the words.

Finally, he couldn't stand still any longer, kicked the door in, and pushed his way back into the shop, only to find it empty. Now he rushed into the street, and again saw no one. 'Have they all been captured?' His heart sank at this thought. 'After all this hiding and waiting,' he moaned to himself.

With nothing else to do, he ran uphill on High Street, panting for air. There was no sound now. Then suddenly, two hands grabbed him. For a split second he thought of punching at the face above him, but then he heard his wife's voice:

"At last, we've found you, Laken."

"Where are the others?" he gasped.

"Who?"

"Jakob and Johan."

"We didn't see them," she shrugged.

"Someone attacked the shop on High Street."

"I don't know anything about that. Johan must have run them off."

"Or just disappeared into a GAP, like he usually does," he sighed in frustration. "I just don't understand him."

"All I know is Myra just helped us cross a GAP to here."

"Jakob's partner?"

She nodded, "I think that's what she is."

"How did you find me? How long has it been?" His voice kept cracking as he tried to speak, and his head was throbbing again. "I don't know why I feel so weak all of a sudden."

"It's all right, Laken. Maybe you're reacting to being shut in for so long," she murmured in his ear.

"How did you know that, Celestia?"

"Myra told us they had to keep you in hiding until your tracker went dead."

"And how did you find me?"

"Myra helped us. She showed Jael—Stel, I mean— how to track you."

"The same way I can sense Jon," Jael's voice said in the shadows.

Laken took another deep breath before he could speak. "How long have I been gone?"

"From us? About two weeks," came Stel's voice again.

"We did find a flat, with help from Myra," his wife sighed. "And we've managed not to get into any trouble— aren't you proud of us?"

He found he could almost smile at her now.

"The flat's not far," she continued. "We can walk there, if you think you're strong enough."

"In a minute," he stalled for more time. "For some reason my head is really aching, and I feel dizzy. Now I know what kind of pain I must have put you through when I tried that Mind-merge with you—I'm so sorry." His voice cracked again and faded away.

"I forgave you for that long ago."

He could only sigh and lean against her. Then he felt the taller, leaner form of Stel on his other side.

"With both of us helping, do you think you can manage to walk?" he asked.

Taking another deep breath in an attempt to clear his head, he nodded.

"Okay," his wife said. "We'll take it slowly."

***

Laken woke gradually, still feeling slightly groggy. He was grateful his wife had found a flat with two bedrooms, so Stel didn't have to sleep in the same room with them. Reaching over to her, he took comfort in the ability to touch her without any qualms.

At his touch Celestia curled closer to him, snuggling like a kitten. "What should we do today, Laken?" she whispered.

"You're asking me? What I want to know is who the heck Jakob and Myra are."

"Stel says they helped his mother and Raina escape the destruction of Terres-City. They were friends of my Uncle Dominic."

"Oh, wow. That goes a long way back. Where are they now?"

"I have no idea. They said Johan had another assignment for them, and they left again while you were asleep."

"They seem to come and go a lot, don't they? And what are we supposed to do, Starla? You seem to know more than I do."

"Well, I'd say we get up, eat breakfast, and look for jobs," she murmured. "But you know that's not what I mean."

"I know. You mean how are we going to find your mother, right?"

In reply, she kissed his cheek.

"Now, dear," he teased. "Let's make this a proper kiss." He pulled himself on top of her and kissed her until she began to squirm.

"Hey, I can't breathe down here."

"Oh, sorry."

She used the instant he let go to sit up, and scoot toward the edge of the sleeping platform. He reached over and began making circles on her back with his fingers.

"You know I think better after—" he whispered.

She merely smiled as she turned back toward him, putting her arms around him.

***

Lying close beside Celestia on another morning, Laken was thankful their new identities didn't seem to be causing any red flags. A few more days had gone by, and no guards or soldiers came pounding on their door. Again, he felt relief wash over him.

'Hopefully the deep cover I've been able to bring over all three of us is working,' he thought. His mind began to relax again, and he reached over to pat his wife on the back. It felt so good to just lie here together in each other's arms. The soft warmth of her skin began filling him with indescribable peace, restoring his mind from his ordeal with the System Police.

"How did you fool the Questioner?" she said softly.

"I'm not sure exactly. It must have been some deep-cover programming within my mind."

She stroked his cheek and ran her fingers through his ever-lengthening black hair. "Well it's a good thing they took you instead of one of us."

"That's for sure."

They settled into silence again, but after a few moments he asked:

"Celestia, are you glad we waited until we were married to be intimate?"

"Of course I am," she murmured. "No other memories are in my mind when I'm with you. I think that's been a lot of my mom's problem through the years—being haunted by her past."

"I wish I was like you," he sighed.

"But you keep saying you don't remember your past lives. Is this just wishful thinking on your part?"

"Well, not exactly. I don't remember names or any details, just when I was sent to another place and time, when the True King required it."

"So, did you have any girlfriends in Tacoma, before I met you?"

He took in a quick breath, amazed at her candor. "Uh-huh—and now I regret that—a lot."

"But after we met, you didn't have anyone else?"

"No."

"So, in that sense you did wait and save yourself for me, when you knew that's what I wanted."

Now a warm feeling of reassurance crept into his chest. "Thanks for reminding me. You really do mean more to me than anyone else I've ever known."

She was drawing closer to him, and he pulled her into a long kiss.

"We just have to let the past be gone," she whispered. "And I think that's what we need to help my mother see. But with all her years of difficulty, I'm not sure how to do it."

"I think that's where we rely on the King's help."

"Of course. He can do beyond anything we can ask or think."

"I bet those words are in The Book, right?"

She just nodded and kissed him again.

CHAPTER 14
SECRETS IN TORNATOH

Perhaps it was the talk with Johan about The Book which rekindled a slight spark of curiosity in my heart. Whatever it was, I decided to do the only thing I could—without Shei getting angry—and headed back toward the Temple. There was no returning to the out-clave—it would only draw the System's attention to them. And apparently Shei's idea of finding me 'work' was to just keep me as his plaything. He said I lacked for nothing—I had food, clothing, and shelter.

'You can't really ask for more,' my annoying inner voice said. 'Life really has no meaning beyond this.'

I wanted to argue, but found I had no energy left to deal with such mental and spiritual conundrums. Maybe my doubting self was right—life was truly like a quote I'd read in an ancient book long ago:

"Life is a mere player, who struts upon a stage, full of sound and fury, but signifying nothing."

Now as I walked along the beach, I realized it was Shei who planted the Temple idea in my mind. 'You're just letting him be your pimp,' my accusing voice was saying.

Listening to the waves crashing on the shore—the wind was strong today—helped to drown out this unwelcome voice, though.

I went to the main entrance of the Temple, where "The Temple of Unity" was emblazoned in golden letters across an imposing arched gate. Gazing up at them for a few minutes, I wondered if they could be real gold.

Once inside, I wandered dozens of corridors between tall marble pillars before I found anyone to talk to. Then I came to a table in an alcove, just off a huge central room.

"How may I help you, seeker?" a young woman asked. Her voice was sweet as honey—almost too sweet.

"I—uh—was wondering if there's any work I can do here? I don't even need to be paid—I just need something to do."

"Perhaps we could train you to help guide tours. Your name?"

"M—I mean Tina." I tried to keep my voice from quavering. Why was I feeling this fear in the pit of my stomach? Surely there could be no danger here in a temple.

"Please step in front of the Terminal," the young voice said. "We'll register your image so the system can analyze your ideal calling in the Temple."

This sent another stab of fear through me. Could this Terminal reveal my true identity? But I couldn't turn back now without arousing more suspicion.

There came a series of whirrs, clicks and chimes from the machine. No sensations touched me, though. Then she told me to step aside and scanned through the information the Terminal gave her.

She raised her eyebrows once in what looked like surprise, and I was afraid all had been revealed. But then she said, "I see you are well acquainted with Shei."

I nodded without a sound.

"Well, I don't think he'll mind sharing you with us. It appears you'll be very well suited to a guide position. Follow me, please."

She moved toward a door to our left. After she'd used her handprint to pass the security lock, she moved me close behind her into another alcove. The little room had bright red walls that seemed to shimmer and flow as I watched them.

"Here," she said a bit more loudly. "Can't you hear me?"

"I'm sorry," I mumbled. "Those colors are so beautiful. I've never seen anything like it."

"So, this is your first time inside the Temple?" Her voice was kinder now.

"I've never been here before. Only one other time, long ago, some friends and I visited the fountains."

"Ah, that explains it," she smiled. "Please take these robes and put them on." As she spoke, she handed me a bundle wrapped with shining gold ribbon.

I looked at it blankly for a moment, not sure if she was expecting me to disrobe right there in front of her. But when she saw my hesitation, she pointed toward a door to my right.

Just nodding, because I was afraid my voice might crack if I tried to speak, I walked quickly through the door into a small dressing room. Taking off the slim tunic Shei had given me, I began to pull the beautiful scarlet robes over my head.

There was a mirror at one end of the room, and once I put on all the articles of shimmering red clothing, I turned to look into it. What I saw took my breath away. 'You look like a new person,' said my inner self.

"Definitely younger," I said back to the voice that was always with me now. "Not bad for someone who's been eeking out an existence in the wilderness."

Suddenly I stopped my voice, fearing perhaps listening devices could hear me. After a few moments of my heart racing, nothing happened, so I turned back toward the door and stepped out.

The woman was standing there patiently, but when she saw me, she smiled broadly and clapped her hands. "You look fabulous!" she cried. "I'll certainly be rewarded for bringing you into the Fold."

Not sure what this meant, I shrugged and tried to read some meaning from her eyes. "The Fold?" I finally asked.

"Yes, we're like a great family here. We are the sheep of his pasture and the apple of his eye—the people of promise."

"Oh? I don't understand what all that means."

"Don't worry. You'll learn what you need to know as you go along. Now come with me. I must take you to the commissioning service."

Again, I followed her through a seemingly endless maze of corridors and courtyards, until she stopped at last in a long, narrow room. It was not as large as the first central sanctuary I'd seen, but there were windows of brightly-colored glass in front of us. She led me to a low railing, separating the lower floor we stood on from a higher section just beyond. As she told me to kneel down, I noticed sparkling lights filtering toward us from the colored windows.

Deep resonant sounds began above me, and it felt like hands were touching my head, shoulders and neck. But when I tried to look upward, I couldn't see anything except the brightly colored sparks still flowing toward me. None of the sounds seemed to be words, but they could have been in another language.

When at last the sounds faded away, I felt a firm hand taking mine and raising me to my feet.

"Welcome to the Fold, Tina," said the voice of the young woman, now standing just behind me.

"Now what do I do?" I was feeling light-headed and confused.

"It will all come naturally when it's time," she replied. "For now, I'll take you into the reception area."

This proved to be a large open courtyard where colored waters danced in fountains. 'Now this is something familiar, at least,' I thought. 'We saw fountains like these when Jon, Jael and I came here with Soren and Dom. But that was thirty years ago at least. Much has transpired since then—the coming of the System, the persecution—'

"Ah, but that's all behind me now. I've begun a new life," I breathed to myself, as joy flowed throughout my body.

Near the largest fountain there stood a table laden with all sorts of luscious looking food. Walking toward it, I hesitated. Surely this was for some dignitaries and not for me. But just as I stepped up to it, a smiling young man handed me a plate.

"Help yourself," he said. "There's plenty for all new members of the Fold."

I must have looked like I was starving—I ate so much of the food, and washed it down with delicious sparkling colored water, wondering if this water came from the fountains. But by then the food and drink had me feeling a little woozy, so I sat down on a bench beside some flowering shrubs.

After I'd been there for several minutes, a young man also dressed in red came and sat down beside me. In my current state of mind, it didn't bother me at all that he hadn't asked my permission. Everything flowed along in a colored stream that I was floating in.

"Is this your first time?" he asked softly.

"My first day on the job," I replied.

He chuckled at this as though I'd made some kind of joke.

I was too embarrassed to ask why he found this funny, and soon it didn't matter anyway, for I swooned in a faint. The last thing I remember was his arms lifting and carrying me, but then everything went black.

***

When I awoke, I was still seated on the bench, but now I was wearing my plain beige tunic. No one else was in sight, so I stood up. Once the whirling dizzy sensation stopped, I walked gingerly toward a door like the one I'd first come through.

As I wandered the maze of corridors, I didn't see another soul. But I had a strange sensation many pairs of eyes were watching me. This made me walk a bit faster, and I felt sheer relief when I saw the arched gate I'd come in before.

'How long ago was that? Has time stood still, or has it all been just a dream?'

There was no way to discern the truth, for when I stepped out through the archway, the sun seemed to be shining in the same position as when I went in.

"Perhaps it was a Time-GAP or a Nexus?" I asked myself.

My inner voice was strangely quiet, and I felt like saying, "Why are you silent now when I could use some help?" But again, there was no reply.

I was barely aware of where I was going, so it didn't surprise me when I finally found myself on a strange street corner. After I stood there for what seemed hours, I heard a voice that sent chills down my spine:

"Mom? Is that you?"

Whirling around, I saw my daughter Celestia walking quickly toward me. No words would come out of my mouth, but she grabbed me into a tight embrace before I could speak.

"What are you doing, Mom?"

I shook my head, but still no words would come.

"Come sit down with me." She guided me toward a bench on the sidewalk, facing the street. "Are you all right?"

"Yes, I'm fine," I finally managed to whisper. "I have a new job, as a tour guide at the Temple."

"Really? How is that going?"

"Well, I just started today, and I'm not entirely sure what the job entails." 'At least now my tongue is working again,' I thought.

"Mother," she began, "We've come to take you back."

"Who's come?"

"Laken, Jael and me."

"Where are they?"

"They started a new job today. I hope to be working in the same building in a couple more days."

"Where's this?"

"It's at an infirmary close to the edge of the city."

"Well, I'm happy for you. It appears we've all found new lives here in Tornatoh."

"That's not the idea. We've only taken these jobs to hide our true identities. Our main purpose is to rescue you."

"Why on earth would I need to be rescued?" I actually chuckled at this thought.

"But Mom, your place is with your family."

"Then why didn't Jon come for me?"

"He and Ginna were whisked into a GAP before we had time to plan anything. We aren't sure, but we think Johan took them for something urgent."

"Yes, that sounds like your father, always in the thick of the battle and the intrigue."

"He's very upset that you ran away," she said softly. "So am I."

I turned then and looked into her dark brown, almost violet eyes—so much like her father's. "There's no need to worry about me. I've found a new life here. I'm part of what the Temple people call the 'Fold'. I don't need anything else—not people or things from my past—not that King who's supposed to take care of us, but never does."

"You don't really mean that."

Her eyes were blazing at me, so I looked down.

"What did I ever gain from all those years of deprivation? Nothing! I'm finished playing that game. From now on my life is going to be lived in the fullness of each moment. No worrying about truth, no regrets of the past, and no fears about the future."

Tears were filling my daughter's eyes, and for an instant I felt a motherly urge to brush them away. But then I stood up instead.

"Where are you going?"

"Back to my flat. I have a good life here, with no complications. All I really need is food and shelter—and that's what I have—the very things we had to struggle for so much in the wilderness. Why should I go back to that?"

She was still sitting on the bench looking stunned as I turned to walk away. I didn't feel any urge to hug her or even say a proper good-bye to my only child. Perhaps there was some kind of drug in that food from the Temple, something that drained me of all feelings of love.

I heard her say, "I'll be praying for you, Mom. And I'm going to keep waiting for you, so I can take you back."

"Don't waste your time," I called over my shoulder as I walked away.

CHAPTER 15
NEW MESSAGES

Laken gazed at his wife, thankful they'd found a place of employment where they could be together, an infirmary where many various ailments were treated. Celestia—'or rather Starla,' he mentally reminded himself—was drawing upon her experience treating accidents, injuries, and diseases in the out-claves of their Believer group.

Her first day, however, she'd been moody. He didn't know why until she finally told him about the encounter with her mother the afternoon before.

"We've got to help her," she said. "She's being sucked in by the System. You should have seen her. It was like she had no love for me, or anyone. Her emotions were all out of whack. I hope we can save her before she's gone too far."

He drew her away from her work station, just long enough to give her a quick embrace. "We'll do as much as we can. I think Johan has a plan."

"I sure wish he'd tell us what it is. I'm scared for her."

"I know. Just try to focus on our mission here. The True King will help us."

"I sure hope so."

His task at the infirmary was keeping of electronic records for all the patients and workers. He was glad his many experiences with all types of technology—in his various 'lifetimes' as a Guardian—made the task come naturally to him.

And he'd been able to convince his supervisor he needed Jael ('I mean Stel. I need to always use their new names!') So now Stel was his assistant, even though the man had little experience. Laken wondered if Stel had been adept with terminals in his early life on Terres, even though he had few opportunities to work with them.

Most of their days were spent in a closed office with lightly colored walls. All the electronics must be kept in a stable environment temperature-wise, away from dust and other possible contaminants.

This attitude toward technology amused him as he remembered all the stresses his own minitabs were put through in his many travels. 'But then these tiny computers were developed in a more advanced civilization than this one,' he reflected.

Laken was the only one of his companions who knew any of the origins of this civilization, and he also knew it wasn't time to reveal these facts.

"Laken, can you help me with this interface?" Stel's voice interrupted his inner dialog.

"Sure. Show me what's up."

Leaning over Stel's shoulder, he gazed at the floating holoscreen before them.

"I think we're getting some kind of interference. The picture keeps fading out and these nonsense symbols appear. Watch—"

Just as he said this, the picture of a patient's room several doors away flipped off and a series of angular forms scrolled across the screen in what seemed to be random order.

Stel reached over to press a key, but Laken's hand restrained him.

"Wait," he said. "Let it keep going."

"Do you recognize anything?"

"Shh! Let me concentrate"

"Sure. Sorry," Stel's voice merely whispered.

Then Laken quickly grabbed his minitab off the desk behind him. "There!" he cried after he'd pulled up a new screen on the tiny tablet in his hand. "Just as I thought. It's a code."

Stel didn't speak, having learned his lesson the first time.

For several minutes, Laken matched some of the figures with a chart on his minitab. His breathing grew faster as his excitement increased. Soon Stel also found himself holding his breath, and then having to catch it again.

"It's the ancient Greek alphabet," murmured Laken.

"Those angular shapes are an alphabet?"

"They were among the earliest forms of writing which used a small alphabet of symbols for sounds—so they could be rearranged into an infinity of possible words. It was much more efficient than pictorial writing, where each symbol stood for an entire word. Instead of needing thousands of possible symbols, the Greek language could be recorded and communicated by a mere twenty-six."

"I guess I'd never thought about it," whispered Stel.

"Of course, people rarely use any form of writing these days," sighed Laken. "Now the majority of communication is verbal, aural, and pictorial, with Terminals the chief means of connecting."

"That seems like a regression, doesn't it—going back to the older pictorial symbols, like China and Egypt used?"

He turned and looked into Stel's green eyes, seeing there a greater power of discernment than he'd noticed before. "That's right. I hadn't really thought of it that way."

By this time, he'd recorded each of the Greek letters on his minitab.

"You didn't record all of the shapes—"

"No, only the Greek letters. The rest are just gibberish to confuse any other possible receptors."

Working rapidly and drawing on his past knowledge of the language, Laken began to whisper words. "Record these on that other minitab I gave you earlier."

Stel had the tiny electronic device in his hand

immediately. Maybe he'd even reacted before Laken's order was given, anticipating what he was going to say. 'He has great powers of perception,' thought Laken, taking only a minuscule flash of his mind to note this for future reference. 'It's something that may be valuable to us later.'

"Danger is lurking," Laken began to whisper, staying close enough for the minitab to pick up the sound. "Dark force has moved to the center of the Galaxy. Must move quickly—need your help. Coordinates are-"

Abruptly he stopped speaking aloud.

"What? Did the message get interrupted?"

"No, but I don't want the coordinates to be recorded anywhere, even with us. I've filed them in my mind."

"Oh wow. You can do that?"

"It's not any more amazing than some of the things I've heard you can do. Right now, we need to get Starla. This is urgent."

"But what about helping my sister?"

"It'll have to wait until this emergency is handled. I'm sorry."

Before either of them could speak another word, a female figure moved into the sterile-looking room.

"I heard a call of some kind," said Celestia.

"You must have some of your uncle's perceptive skills," Laken smiled into her deep brown eyes.

"Well, *you* have hidden talents of your own—like being able to discern danger in advance. So, what is the danger now?"

"I'm not sure yet, but I have a strong feeling this message came from Johan. It says we need to help someone at the center of the Galaxy."

"Our Milky Way?"

Laken nodded and grabbed her hand tightly. He didn't even have to tell Stel to link them into a circle. Without another word, he closed his eyes and concentrated on the coordinates he'd been given.

***

When they emerged from the GAP, Laken found he was floating in empty space. But the next instant he saw a twisting flame of red, turning in the blackness.

"Where are we?" asked Celestia.

Before he could reply, Jael's voice rang out, "Is that the Serpent?"

"The same Red Dragon we saw when we were rescuing you." Laken's voice was tense.

"How are we breathing out here in open space?"

"I think we're in another Time Nexus."

As he said this, he saw the Red Dragon bank and begin to move directly toward them. "Ah—more victims!" he bellowed.

In the next instant a large black form appeared in the midst of the Dragon's path.

"Shadow! How did you get here?"

"No time to talk. Just grab onto his legs," came a small voice from above.

"Evin?"

"Yes, sir—quickly, climb up before he gets around us."

No sooner had they climbed on his back than the huge black dog landed with them all on what appeared to be an asteroid. The sky above was inky black and filled with brilliant swirls of stars clustered more thickly than any they'd ever seen.

"Can we talk yet?" Celestia's voice was shaking.

'Yes,' came a deep rumble in her head.

"Is that you I can hear, Shadow?" she asked. "I thought you only spoke to Evin."

'The necessity has arisen for more efficient communication,' the dog-voice rumbled.

"What's going on?" Laken cut in.

"The Dragon is trying to take control of our whole galaxy," came another voice, much more mature.

"Is that you, Dad?"

Turning, Laken saw his wife gripped in her father's tight embrace.

"The Dragon was coming right for us," she gasped. "How did we escape?"

"Shadow brought you into another Nexus, one the Dragon hasn't been able to penetrate so far," Jon replied.

As Laken's eyes finally moved from the amazing stars above them and began to focus on the scene around him, he made out another human shape. "Is that Ginna?" he asked.

"It's me," she replied, half-smiling. "Johan brought us four together."

"You, Jon, the dog and Evin?"

"Well four humans actually, so there are really six of us," came a new voice they hadn't heard before.

Blinking past Jon, Laken finally made out the shape of a shining white unicorn, with a blond boy on his back. "And who are you?"

"I'm Evin's brother, Dain—and this is Splash—"

Before Dain could say another word, a sharp cry came from Jael, "Splash? But he was a horse, not a unicorn."

"He's still Splash," said Dain. "Johan changed him."

The unicorn answered with a low whinny, and moved toward Jael, rubbing his muzzle on his shoulder.

"He's overjoyed to see you, too," Evin spoke up.

"Does he talk to you?" asked Jael.

"He talks to Shadow," Dain replied. "Then Evin passes the thoughts on."

"Okay! Enough of this talk; we need to devise a plan," Jon's voice came sharply.

"What exactly is going on?" Laken asked.

"The Dragon intends to accelerate the Black Hole at the center of the Milky Way, so the entire galaxy will be swallowed up in a matter of weeks, instead of the eons of time it should take."

"But what can we do to stop him?" asked Celestia.

"That's why we need to put our heads together and figure out a plan."

"That's right," Ginna spoke up. "Johan says he selected each of us for a specific gift we have. We need to find a way to harness each of these skills, so they work to our best potential."

"That's a mouthful," Laken realized he hadn't heard her speak with such authority. 'Apparently, she's much more than the quiet, pale woman I met when they were lost in the Twenty-second Century Time Well.'

"An easier way to say it is 'None of us is as smart as all of us.'," nodded Dain. "I learned that slogan in school."

"Shadow says we need to start brainstorming ideas," Evin chimed in. "We don't have much time."

"That sounds like the Shadow I remember," Laken half-chuckled.

It wasn't until they were all seated in a rough circle of stones that he realized he expected to see Danny with his sons, but then he remembered what Jon told him earlier—Danny had died back in his own time.

Laken knew why he himself was here—because Johan was familiar with his GAP-crossing abilities, from many past missions they'd shared. And Celestia was quickly becoming adept at the things he'd been teaching her. Jon had brought Ginna forward to this time in an attempt to reach Martina, but this failed when Martina fled their Out-clave.

'Johan apparently has a Plan B,' he mused, 'since he brought them here, and probably also fetched Danny's sons and their specially-talented animals.'

'You're correct,' came Shadow's voice in his head. 'Dain has been designated to take his father's place, except the roles are switched, since Dain is firstborn and Evin is the one who has Danny and Jael's ability to focus the GAP-crossings.'

"And what are you, Shadow?" he said aloud.

'I am a force—a helper sent by Johan.'

"Why isn't Johan here?"

"He had other urgent business," Jon replied. "Something about taking a backdoor into Tornatoh, to help Martina."

The catch in Jon's voice was all that revealed his intense emotion for his runaway wife.

"I'm sure it will help," Ginna patted him on the back as she spoke.

The familiarity between Jon and Ginna surprised Laken at first, but then he remembered how Jon had merged Ginna with Martina in a Time-GAP experiment over thirty Earth-years ago. 'There must be some residual of Martina still in Ginna's psyche which explains their link with each other,' he thought. 'I hope that's some comfort for Jon—until we manage to get Martina back.'

In the instant it took these thoughts to flash through Laken's mind, the rest of the group drew into a tighter circle. Shadow's idea of brainstorming appeared to be going around the circle, with each of them saying aloud any of their thoughts.

He was surprised, though, when Dain began, "I don't know how to defeat this powerful Dragon—he's the Devil himself, isn't he?"

"He certainly is," Jon replied. "But remember that song Johan taught us? 'One little word can fell him'."

"One word?" Evin sounded skeptical.

"The word of the Lord, who is Kristos—he's already won the war."

"Are you sure, Jon?" Ginna's voice sounded frightened.

"It says so in The Book, and I believe Johan wouldn't lie to us."

"Yes," Jael spoke up. "Johan gave us The Book—and it's been a good guide ever since."

"I sure wish we had a copy with us right now," Celestia sighed.

"We do," smiled Laken, pulling out his ever-present minitab. "It's all recorded in here."

"How do you manage to get that thing to work—no matter where we are?"

"It's from a civilization far more advanced than this one—powered by cosmic rays, and those are everywhere in the Universe."

"May I see it?"

"Sure, Jon."

As Jon took the card-sized tablet in his hands, it looked very small and insignificant, especially in light of all he knew it could do.

"It's easy to operate. Just push this tab and then speak, 'The Book'. Once it goes to that section of its library, say the name and section of The Book you want to see. It will display the words, or speak them for you, whichever alternative you select."

By this time Jon had directed the tablet to go to the book of *Joel,* then he said, "Here's what one part of The Book says about the last days of Earth:

> *'And afterward I will pour out my spirit on all people. Your sons and daughters will prophesy, your old men will dream dreams, your young men will see visions; and even on my servants both men and women I will pour out my Spirit in those days.*

> *'And I will show wonders in the heavens and on the earth, blood and fire, and billows of smoke. The sun will be turned to darkness, and the moon to blood, before the coming of the great and dreadful day of the Lord'."*

"That's really scary!" cried Dain.

"This is just one section of scripture," Jon said softly. "Beware of taking anything out of context. There are passages in several places echoing these same signs. But the part that Joel puts in the next chapter of his book is the part I hope applies to our situation:

'The sun and the moon will be darkened, and the stars no longer shine. The Lord will roar from Zion and thunder from Jerusalem; and the earth and the sky will tremble; but the Lord will be a refuge for his people'.'

"Well, that sounds more promising, at least," sighed Evin.

"We who place our trust in the True King have nothing to fear at the end of days," Jon said. "But we must look to him for our strength, not to ourselves."

"So, is that why we're so few against such a powerful enemy?"

"I think so. There are many places in The Book where it talks of a few overcoming what appeared to be an unstoppable army—with the Lord's help. You've read as much of this Book as I have, Jael. What do you say?"

"If we can't trust the True King, then there's no one in all the Universe that we *can* trust." Jael's voice was firmer than Laken had heard from him before.

"Aren't there places in The Book where the Word is compared to a Sword?" asked Evin.

"Sure are," Jael turned to him. "You remind me a lot of your father."

Evin turned red and looked down. "No, you remind me of him."

"Well, Danny is with us here in spirit, I'm sure," said Jon.

"I wish we had a sword now—like the one that spoke to the Dragon and made him fear us, when we were battling to rescue you, Jael." Laken said this quietly, but all could hear him, he knew.

"But don't you see?" Ginna spoke up. "The word 'sword' has the answer right in it—take off the 's' and you have 'word'!"

"That's so," Laken exclaimed. "At least in English."

"Shadow says we need to put our trust in the Lord's strong word—there's no other weapon more powerful," said Dain. The excitement in his voice showed how glad he was to hear the big black dog's thoughts.

"But why was the Dragon able to kill Stephan?" Evin asked. "You were there, Jon. What went wrong?"

"Well, there was a lot of confusion—and part of it was my fault for not keeping hold of what he'd given me to protect. I think that caused him to let his guard down just enough for the Dragon to attack."

"Don't blame yourself," whispered Ginna. "Stephan is now in a better place, I'm sure."

"But we need to carry on the fight against the Dragon, so his sacrifice won't be in vain," Laken said then.

"I wish we had a strong Guardian like Stephan here to help us," sighed Evin.

Suddenly, Shadow began to howl loudly.

"What's the matter?" Ginna cried.

"He says that he's a Guardian, too, and will do his best," replied Dain.

"And so is Laken," said Celestia, taking her husband's hand.

"I have a new assistant, too," he smiled at her. "My partner and wife."

Just as Laken said these words a brilliant pillar of light dropped among them from above. The figure in the center shone so brightly each of them hid their eyes.

"There's no need to fear!" came a voice like a trumpet.

"What is it?" Ginna cried to Jon.

But before he could reply the form softened to an image they all recognized.

"Johan!" cried Laken. "Boy, do you know how to make an entrance."

Now the figure shrank considerably, back to the white bearded man. "Sorry," he smiled. "The pillar of light is a faster way to travel, but it does frighten people sometimes. Now, I'm glad to see you're all here at last."

"All here?" Jon's voice asked.

"Each of you is an important part of the battle plan to stop the Dragon. Jon, I need you to join Evin on Shadow. You have the experience to best compliment Shadow's powers and help Evin."

Jon moved obediently to the young redhead's side. Shadow reached down and gave his face a quick lick. "Well, I guess Shadow agrees with your choice," he chuckled.

"Very well. Laken, you must assist Dain and Splash, our unicorn. Your extra powers from all your various lives will help them most. Dain has GAP-crossing powers he hasn't used as yet, but when the time is right, you'll know what to do."

Laken smiled grimly, for he—of all those present, besides Johan—knew how dangerous all this was going to be. He couldn't help looking back at his wife, wondering if he'd see her again in this life.

"Celestia, you and Ginna are both firstborn, and both have strong links to Laken and Jon—don't blush, Ginna," he half-chuckled, "You have very good reason to feel close to Jon, since you spent much time 'within' his wife."

"So, are you going to teach us to fly?" Laken heard a hint of hesitation in his wife's voice.

"I have a better idea," Johan smiled. He waved his arm upward and in a flash of light, golden wings appeared. These hovered above them for a few seconds, and then were joined by a flowing tail of many flashing colors. This vision finally settled in front of him in the shape of a huge bird.

"What is it?" Celestia breathed in wonder. "Wait! I saw a bird like this flying in the skies of Materna, the alternative universe. And even before that. I remember Annemarie trying to tell me about a bird like this she saw when we were in the Time Well."

Johan just smiled.

"I bet this bird's cry sounds like a hawk—"

She didn't get to finish her sentence before it let out a screech.

"Or an eagle," added Ginna. "Is this the bird we saw when you brought Jon and me to Maiar?"

"So, you have noticed her. Very good. My phoenix has been keeping watch over many of you in several times and places," the old man grinned. "Now she's up from the ashes to live again and help you battle the Dragon. Celestia and Ginna are to ride her, for the phoenix also symbolizes the female powers of the world. And her name is Ember."

As each of them stepped into the places Johan ordered, Jael soon found himself standing alone. Looking up at Johan, he sighed, "What about me? Is there nothing I can do? I know I'm not as strong as I once was, and that some of my powers have been lost-"

"Your mission is going to be the most difficult of all. The dangers aren't the same these others will face, but still there nonetheless. I'm taking you back to Tornatoh with me, to try and reach your sister."

"But isn't there anything I can do here?"

"Oh, there could be, I have no doubt. But Martina needs you more than these. Long ago on Terres, you were the only one who could reach her and bring her out of the dark bondage the Redlarks placed on her. And I'm praying you'll somehow be the one to rescue her from darkness again—where many others have failed, myself included."

With that, Johan turned in a complete circle, making eye-contact with each of the newly-designated warriors, and spoke these final words, "You each must have the Shield of Faith to extinguish the Dragon's fiery darts."

As he said this, a shimmering shape appeared strapped to each of their arms. Then the old man took Jael's hands and closed his eyes. In a flash of sparks, the pair disappeared.

CHAPTER 16
THE BATTLE

Laken looked into the eyes of each of his companions and saw the fear lurking behind the anticipation. His wife and Ginna were seated astride the feathery back of the strange phoenix Johan called Ember.

He and Jon decided to place their mounts, Shadow and Splash, in the forward position, so the phoenix was placed to the rear of them.

"I think a broader frontal attack is the best to start with," he said. "The women and Ember can be our rearguard." What he didn't add was he was putting greater trust in this creature Johan had given them, as his own natural tendency was to put more trust in Johan himself, his own Guardian through many eons of battles.

'I just hope Johan's trust in me is merited, since he's placed me with the least experienced pair—Dain and Splash,' he thought.

Just as they formed up, there came a rumbling and crashing sound above them. Then the sky seemed to shatter, and in the middle of their line of sight he appeared—the daunting Red Dragon.

"Ah-ha!" he roared. "So, Johan thinks you can stand against me? What a farce."

Laken was expecting fire to come raging from the Dragon's mouth, but instead the beast banked and began to flap his massive wings.

"What's he doing?" Jon's voice asked.

"Follow him!" shouted Laken. "He's trying to beat us to the event horizon of the Milky Way's Black Hole."

Shadow didn't have to be told twice, and the shining white unicorn followed right on his shoulder. Laken could hear the screeching cries of the phoenix behind him.

In an instant the rocky asteroid where they'd been standing disappeared. Now they found themselves in a whirling cloud of stardust and gases, all spiraling toward a yawning empty spot before them.

'I wish I knew exactly what he plans to do,' Laken thought. 'But apparently even Johan isn't sure what the evil Serpent has in mind. All we know is that it has something to do with accelerating the actions of the Black Hole—so that the Galaxy will be swallowed up in a shorter time.'

Even while these thoughts were whirring through his head, Laken saw the terrible beast turn and face them.

"You are powerless!" he hissed through his gleaming golden teeth. "There's no power in the Milky Way that can stand against me!"

"So you'd have us believe!" Laken shouted back. "But we have a power on our side that goes back to the very dawn of time—before you were even created, you Father of Lies."

"Oh, do you still buy the old myth that I was created? How quaint! I'm merely the opposite side of your so-called Creator. He's what you foolish humans call the good, the white, the true. But those things would have no meaning without me—the evil, the black, the false. We are one and the same, the Yin and Yang."

"That's another of your lies," came Dain's tense voice

'How am I hearing him?' Laken wondered.

"You've been propagating that lie since the day you were cast down from Heaven," Evin's voice called out.

'Are the sounds traveling in the void of space or sent somehow through Dain? They must be communicating telepathically, the way Jon says he and Jael could,' he finally realized.

"Next, you'll be using your favorite lie—that you can make us gods," Dain's voice somehow echoed back to him, deflected by the spiny red scales on the fearsome beast's huge chest.

The Dragon made no reply to any of them. Instead, he sent a column of smoke and fire from his nostrils. Their mounts barely had time to dart away from the white-hot flames.

While Shadow, Splash, and Ember scattered, Laken

saw what he'd most feared. The Dragon had managed to separate them.

"Come to me!" he shouted. "Celestia, Evin, we must stay close." He felt a slight sense of relief when he saw his companions moving back toward him. But when he turned his gaze back toward the Dragon, he shuddered at what he saw.

The Serpent was blowing thick black smoke from his mouth, and when the haze cleared, there stood a beast—the most fearsome thing Laken had ever seen. It had several heads, each with horns jutting from them. Its body was the combination of a swift leopard, a powerful bear, and a cruel lion. With a huge roar it launched itself toward Shadow.

Laken tried to follow, to protect Evin and Jon, but the Dragon exhaled another burst of smoke—this time fiery red. From the midst of this came a beast with two horns like a huge goat, and it charged directly for him. Dain reacted quickly though, and the unicorn flew away into the overhead spirals of stars, moving just ahead of this new attacker.

He had no time to look back to see what was pursuing Celestia and Ginna on the phoenix, but he could hear the bird's battle cries—and hoped this meant they were holding their own.

'This must be the Dragon's unholy trinity,' he thought. 'We have to find a way to call the True King's Trinity to aid us.'

But these thoughts were snatched right out of his mind, as though the Dragon could somehow sense them. He kept pressing Splash to gallop as fast as possible, and the unicorn responded with surprising speed. His hooves danced among the stars as he twisted and turned, evading each of the horned beast's charges with his own single horn.

Then words jumped into his mind, 'Slay them with the sword of your mouth.'

"I heard that—it's Evin!" Dain cried. "What does it mean?"

"Turn Splash so we can face the two-horned beast," Laken replied to his partner.

"If you say so, Laken. But he'll be able to charge us for sure if we stop."

"Trust me, Dain. I know where my directions come from."

And so, Dain pulled back on the unicorn's mane, causing him to turn and face their foe. Apparently, the beast hadn't expected this, for it stood in confusion for an instant.

"Charge, you fool!" came the terrible roar of the Dragon's voice.

But before the other beast could move, Laken cried out with all his might:

"Be gone, you false spirit! I rebuke you in the name of the true Holy Spirit of God, whom you mock."

"Noo-oo!" the beast wailed. A golden light seemed to shoot out from the unicorn's horn, and another joined it, pouring out of Laken's mouth. These two fiery beams caused the beast to disintegrate before their eyes. Nothing remained but a whiff of gray smoke.

Once their pursuer was gone, Laken turned to see where the others were. Shadow was flying with all his hidden skill, evading the many-headed beast. Once Jon saw what Laken did, he also turned Shadow to face their pursuer.

"You dare to mock the True King," Jon's voice rang out, "With a mere parody of the sacrifice he made for the sins of all of us."

"There is no other way to be saved." Evin's voice was surprisingly loud now.

"Be gone in the name of Kristos," Laken added to their shouts.

As all three of their voices joined together, the many-headed beast began to break apart. Each of its heads became a separate demon, and so did the remainder of its body. As soon as the demons saw they were alone and disconnected, they fled into the dark sky above.

"Stop!" roared the Dragon in vain.

The huge red Serpent veered away from Shadow and Splash, bereaved of his assistants, but still roaring and spouting fire.

"You have not defeated me yet!" he screamed.

Laken cringed with fear as he saw the Dragon closing in on Ember. Before anyone could make a move, the Serpent sent a stream of white-hot fire directly toward Celestia and Ginna. Their mount barely managed to outrun it. In fact, as it wheeled back around to face the Dragon, a trail of fire was rising from the phoenix's tail.

"Quickly," Jon's voice shouted. "Come to Shadow."

Before Laken could move a muscle, the phoenix dashed to the huge black dog's side. In a flash, Jon jumped onto Ember's back, and shoved Ginna and Celestia onto Shadow.

"Take them as far away as you can," he called to Evin, and Shadow obeyed as soon as the words left Jon's mouth.

Jon was trying to turn the bird into another attack position, but by now the flames were creeping onto its wings.

"Ah ha!" the Dragon's voice chuckled with pure evil. "Now you must come with me. You will help rather than hinder me, and you have no choice."

Then as Laken watched helplessly, the Dragon's lethal wings ripped through the flaming tail of the phoenix, and it began to fall toward the spiral paths of stars. The Dragon pulled in a huge breath, causing the bird to move dangerously close to its gaping jaws. Just as it seemed Jon and Ember would both be swallowed alive, the phoenix suddenly exploded in a flash of blazing feathers and sparks.

Now Jon was floating helplessly in empty space, as the Black Hole drew him nearer to the event horizon. An evil laugh filled their minds as the Dragon glided in closer to his prey, but just as the red beast reached Jon, he sent out a flaming arrow thrown from his bare hands, piercing the scaly hide.

"Where did that come from?" Laken heard himself asking.

"Evin's saying Johan gave it to him, just before he left," Dain told him.

"You shall never win, Father of Lies!" Jon's voice had more volume than seemed possible. "For your power is based only in hatred. My Lord's power is love—greater love has no man than this, that he lay down his life for his friends."

Now the Dragon was also spiraling out of control toward the threshold of the Black Hole. Jon was balancing precariously on the edge. He ducked to avoid the Serpent's flaming bulk, and Laken pushed Splash as near as he dared.

"Careful," came Dain's voice. "Evin says we need to keep out of the event horizon. Beyond that, there's no return."

In the next instant, Laken dove off the horse and tried to grab the Dragon from behind, to keep him from knocking Jon into the hole. But the Serpent twisted, his scales scraping across Laken's body, from head to toe. Searing pain shot through him and he could see blood spurting from his wounds out into space.

With a toss of his head, the Dragon shook Laken off

like an annoying fly. And then he pulled Jon down with him into the Black Hole.

"No!" Laken screamed.

But Jon and the Dragon crossed the threshold, and there was no force in the universe that could stop their long downward spiral to the singularity. No one even knew what awaited them there—if they would ever reach it—or just continue to fall into eternity?

Splash and Dain flew beneath him before Laken even realized it. Dain's arms had a firm grip on him, and he was pressed onto the unicorn's back in front of the boy.

His eyes seemed unable to focus, his mind clouded by the blow of the Dragon. All he could do was lean forward into the mane, clinging for all he was worth.

"Come with us," came Evin's voice dimly in his mind.

"Hurry, Dain," Celestia called. "You've got to escape the Black Hole's gravity."

Laken could feel the presence of Shadow beside them, more than he could see him. Something wet kept filling his eyes. He wasn't sure whether he wanted to know if it was blood or tears.

Now Dain was helping him get a grip on Splash's horn. A ripple of energy surged through the unicorn. Was he going forward or falling backward? He couldn't tell with his blinded eyes.

'Lord, help us all,' he thought.

Then everything went black. The last thing he re-membered was a small hand tightly gripping his.

CHAPTER 17
BACK TO THE CITY

Jael opened his eyes to brightness. It still was difficult for him to adjust quickly to light. 'Probably a carryover symptom from the long years in the Time Nexus,' he sighed to himself. Once his eyes were settled, however, he gazed in amazement up the steeply climbing street before him. Everything in his line of sight was made of bricks—the walls, the pavement—even the sidewalks.

"Do you recognize anything?" Johan's voice asked.

"Well, I think I may have been here once before, but it was a long time ago."

"You're correct. The first time you came you'd been told you needed 'tickets' to go into the Temple of the Way."

"And the second time was to find out why the fountains there did nothing for us."

"There was an old man in a shop just up this street," said Johan.

"Yes, High Street," Jael nodded.

Before another word was spoken Jael was astonished to see Johan transform before his eyes into the bent, grizzled old man they'd seen that day so long ago.

"Was that old man you, Johan?"

The balding man gave a low cackle, sounding more like a chicken than a man. "What do you think?"

"Am I allowed to say what I truly think?"

"Of course, you are."

"Well, if you're so old and wise, why don't you give us all the information we need."

"Such as?"

"Well, when our spaceship needed repair, and we stopped on your planet, you told us how we might find Maia. But your directions were very vague. Why didn't you tell us outright where Maia was? You knew more than you were telling us, didn't you?"

"Some things are learned better when we experience them for ourselves. I could have told you more, but then you wouldn't have learned from the adventures you had."

"I guess so. But did you know Earth wasn't going to be the wonderful place we hoped for?"

"Actually, there are still things I don't know about Earth and Maia."

"Are they the same place?"

"That's one of the things I don't know with certainty, Jael."

"Why not?"

"The King has his own ways of doing things, and he doesn't reveal everything to me either. He reserves the right of knowing the future for himself."

"The way you didn't tell us everything—Oh, I see! He wants you to learn on your own, too."

"I guess you could say so. There are some things about the plans for the End that even the King himself doesn't know. It's in his Father's hands."

"Who is the Father?"

"He's also called the Creator."

By this time, they reached the grimy door to the little shop. Johan turned the latch and the squeaky door swung open. Dust motes flew everywhere, sparkling in the sun. Again, Jael shielded his eyes from the bright light. Once the door was closed, however, the light didn't hurt as much because the windows were so covered with dust and dirt.

"What are we doing here?"

"We're going to wait for your sister—she'll come here eventually. She always does when her mind gets the most troubled. For she has reached the dark night of the soul."

"What does that mean?"

"It means she'd gone beyond what she thought she believed, and is lost in the dark—for now."

"How can we help her?"

"We can try various things, but most must come from Martina herself."

"Like what?"

"Well, in my experience, people who reach this place of unknowing do one of two things. They either run away from it, desperately seeking any solace they can find. Or they face it and move through it to the other side."

"What's on the other side?"

"A new faith," said Johan.

"But right now, my sister is running away, isn't she?"

"Yes, I'm afraid she is. And I'm still working on a plan."

Jael sighed, "Is there any hope?"

"We should never give up hope, young one."

"I don't feel so young anymore."

"Yet you are compared to me," the old man chuckled.

Jael took a long breath, trying to clear his mind of the fear pulsing inside. "While we're waiting, could I ask you some other questions?"

"Of course, but I don't guarantee I'll be able to answer them."

Jael sighed and seated himself on a low stool near a cluttered workbench. "I just want to know why we're here—back in the city and trying to hide from the System again. It's like my childhood on Terres. I feel like I've come full circle, and all that's happened to us—my family and me—has come to nothing."

"Are you sure?"

"Well, we fled Terres to escape the System, to find freedom and hope. When we finally found Earth, we thought our search was over—that we'd found what we sought. But now it seems we didn't."

"Did you learn nothing in your journeys?"

"I guess we did learn to trust and love each other. Jon and I discovered a deep connection between us. But Martina seems like she's lost everything we learned. She's back here in the city again—even though it's not Terres-City. I haven't seen her yet, but I have a feeling she's gone back to the life she lived before, using drugs and playing games with casual sex."

"And if she is?"

"Then it seems like all we went through has been pointless."

"But the story isn't completed yet, you know. There may still be hope around the next corner."

"How can we know what the future holds?"

"We don't."

"I remember Feier telling us that once. He said since we couldn't know the future, there was hope. If we knew exactly what was going to happen, then there'd only be hopelessness—nothing would be new or surprising, because we knew all along what was going to happen."

"Your feier-cat was very wise."

"I miss him."

"I'm sure you do," the old man half-smiled.

"So—how can I know which way to turn when everything is a dark unknown?"

"Well, it is true that sometimes one has to begin the next steps even before they can see the light ahead," said Johan.

"Before we can see the light at the end of the tunnel?"

"That's one thing people call it."

"But how do I know which way to go, if everything is in the dark?"

"You have to go with what your previous experiences tell you."

"Oh." Jael looked at the grimy floor, unable to meet Johan's eyes.

"Now do you see why I couldn't tell you everything all at once? You needed to have those experiences in order to be prepared."

"I guess I see what you mean. But some of the things we've gone through seem so hard—like Raina being raped as a child. Or my being captured, so my family thought I was dead for nearly eight years."

"Has nothing good come out of any of those things?"

"Well, maybe some—Raina and Daiah became fast friends because of the experiences they shared. And since I've been freed from captivity, our family is much closer than they might have been otherwise."

"You see?"

"Yeah, I guess. But Johan, why do some trials have to be so painful?"

"That's how humans learn the most—in the school of tribulation."

"But what about my sister?"

"What about her?"

"Well, she seems to have broken under the weight of her experiences. She's fallen into deep depression like our mother did. Wasn't there any way to prevent that?"

"There's no point in looking back at things we can't change, Jael. What you need to think about is how to help Martina now. Not the 'what-ifs'. Her life is what it is, you know."

"All right. But what can I do?"

"How did you and Jon get her to 'come back' when she was in bondage to the Redlarks?"

"We just kept loving her and trying to get through to her."

"There you are."

"So that's what it's going to take this time, too—just love?"

"Yes—love, not 'just love'."

"Could I ask you some different questions?"

"Of course, you can ask me anything, but—"

"I know, you may not answer them all."

"So, what else would you like to know?"

"I'm confused about all the alternative universes Jon and Raina have tried to explain to me. They said they met my father, Stephan—but he was from a different universe. And now there's the Black Hole at the center of our Galaxy. How does any of this fit with what I was taught by my family—from The Book?"

"Do you remember the conversation we had about the beginning of time?"

"Was that when we were on your little planet?"

"Yes, my Maiar."

"I do remember discussing how the Universe began and whether there was a Creator, but now I wonder more about how it will end.

Johan merely smiled.

"The world has changed so much since we first met," sighed Jael. "Now I feel old and tired. Does life have any meaning at all?"

"To me that's the saddest state of mind anyone can have: that life is meaningless. Let's move on to the other end—from creation, to the end of the world as we know it."

"Seeing the Milky Way Black Hole has certainly made me wonder what the Universe all about. Will the world just end in a flash—or in silence?"

"Actually, these two questions aren't so far apart, after all," Johan smiled more. "Physicists have been unable to explain what is happening in a Black Hole. Both the precepts of Quantum/Particle Physics and the General Theory of Relativity totally break down when it comes to trying to understand Black Holes."

"So how do scientists even know they're there?"

"With increasingly sensitive telescopes they've been able to see the effects of Black Holes—how they even keep light from escaping, how they affect other stars around them. Even though we can't see them or explain them, still there is evidence of their existence. And more than this, it's now believed the center of every galaxy is a Black Hole."

"So, does this mean every galaxy will eventually be consumed?"

"Some believe that eons in the future, when all the stars have burned out, the only thing left of our Universe will be Black Holes."

"That's depressing," sighed Jael.

"Well, there's another theory about Black Holes."

"Really?"

"This one says that on the other side of the Black Hole's singularity—or its center—where theoretically all the laws of physics cease to apply, a new universe is being born. Some scientists say the other side of every Black Hole is a White Hole, where another Big Bang is happening."

"Doesn't this give the System another chance to explain away the need for a Creator?"

"Some would take that opportunity. But it isn't always a valid assumption."

Jael sat for a few minutes shaking his head. "This is too much for my weakened brain," he smiled slightly. "For me, it makes more sense to believe there is a God who created us and cares about us. If I didn't have that, I think I'd be in despair."

"I believe each of us, at some point in our life, has to make a decision. We either believe and trust in the Lord, or we don't."

"It seems to me there's more evidence pointing to the existence of a loving creator."

"For those who are willing to examine all the evidence," Johan nodded.

"Why wouldn't they want to examine all the evidence, if they're truly scientists, as they claim?"

"I believe pride stands in their way. Others haven't been allowed to see all the evidence. Sadly, some scientists push aside evidence which doesn't agree with their prior assumptions. But we have a more important task ahead of us, Jael."

"What task is that?"

"The task of getting your sister to reawaken to what she believed in, before the enemy pulled her back into her well of despair."

Jael suddenly found tears forming in his eyes. "I hope we can reach her. It was difficult enough the first time—all those years ago on Terres."

***

After that long discussion, Jael's mind whirled with even more questions. 'Why is it the more I try to understand the cosmos, the harder it gets?'

For what seemed like several days, he and Johan sat

in the dusty shop and talked. But sometimes they just sat, because his mind was too tired to take in any more.

Once Martina happened by when they were sitting on the low bench. But she seemed to be in a daze, and Jael wasn't sure she even recognized him. She acted as though she'd never seen him before. For a long time after she left, his heart ached.

"I don't think I can handle this," he told Johan. "This hurts as much as the day we learned our oldest brother had died in a shuttle crash."

"Your brother Stephen?"

Jael could only nod.

"Please don't lose hope, Jael. While there's life there's hope."

"I've always wondered what that old saying meant," he sighed.

"It depends on who's saying it," the old man said quietly. "For someone who's hoping a dear friend or relative will see the truth—"

"Oh, I see. It means as long as the person is still living, there's hope they will change."

"It can also mean as long as we remember our redeemer lives, then we can have hope in him."

"I'm trying to hold on."

"I heard another saying once that may help," added Johan. "When you feel you've reached the end of your rope, let the Lord tie a knot in it."

Jael stared at the old man quizzically for a few minutes, and then he finally smiled. "I think I see. The Lord really is the only one who can help us hold on, isn't he?"

Johan patted his back. "Now you see, and what we must do next is help Martina see as well. But before we can do that, I think you need to see what's happened with your friends who've been battling the Dragon."

"Are they all right? Has anyone been hurt?"

Johan took one of Jael's hands and held it close to his chest. "Can you sense anything?" his crackly voice asked.

He closed his eyes and began to feel a dark terror. Flashes of fire from the Dragon were all around him, followed by swirls of stars being drawn ever closer to a yawning emptiness.

"Is that huge void a Black Hole?" he whispered.

"Yes, that is *the* Black Hole, the one at the center of the Milky Way."

"I can't see anything but black now," he cried, feeling sudden panic. "Jon's been pushed or dragged into the hole—by the Dragon!"

"Are you sure?"

"As sure as I can be, but wait. There's a faint speck of light ahead. That shouldn't be the case in a Black Hole—"

"Unless the theory is correct of the other side being the beginning of a new universe."

"Now I can hear some kind of chanting. It says, 'Behold I make all things new.' What does this mean?"

"Perhaps in every ending there is a new beginning."

Jael looked sharply into the old man's shining eyes. "Have you known this all along and never told us?"

"No, I'm not the Lord. I don't know any more about these deep mysteries than you do."

"Now I can feel Jon again. He's still alive, and he's in a good place. Not just good, but uh—different in every way from the place we're in. It's like everything is the opposite of here."

"I think your friends need to hear this. Let me take you to them."

CHAPTER 18
AFTERMATH

Ginna felt like she'd been weeping for years. When her eyes finally stopped enough for her to open them, she realized she was back on the asteroid from which they'd begun their mission.

Fearfully, she looked into the inky sky above them and saw the Black Hole in the same place as it had been before. This gave her a moment of relief, but then the terrible ache returned to her chest.

"I can't believe Jon is really gone." She didn't realize she'd spoken aloud until she felt a trembling hand touch her shoulder, and heard a voice:

"I can't either. We must still be in the part of grief called denial."

"Celestia? Is that you?" Ginna's eyes were blinded again with something hot and wet.

"Yes, it's me." The hand now pulled her into a firm embrace.

After a long time, they stepped back and looked at each other.

"Where are the others?"

"Evin and Dain have gone back to their home in Colorado."

"With Shadow and Splash?"

"Yes, Shadow was able to take them back—all four of them survived the battle."

"I wish I could have gone with them—or at least said 'good-bye'," Ginna sighed. "Is Splash still a unicorn?"

"I don't know for sure, but he'd probably draw too much attention in the Twenty-first Century, if he was." Celestia patted her back. "Anyway, Shadow said he'd been commanded to take them back as soon as possible."

"Probably because it's so dangerous here," she said. "At least I know they're safe. Though I hoped they might help us with rescuing Martina."

Celestia sighed, "I guess Johan has his own plans for that."

"What about Laken? Is he—"

"I'm fine—just exhausted," came the welcome, familiar voice.

"Luckily for you, Celestia," she sighed, not recognizing the angry pain creeping into her voice.

Laken stepped into her sphere of vision then, and this first view of him made her gasp:

"Laken, you look awful!"

He tried to smile at her, but all she could see was the streaks of dried blood all over his face, arms, and clothing. As she looked closer, she saw most of his clothes were ripped, and some hung in mere shreds from his shoulders. His hair had fallen out of its usual ponytail, and some of the ends were singed.

"I'll be all right," he said at last.

Celestia was clinging to her husband now. "But Jon really is dead?" she asked.

"I'm afraid so," he said. "The Dragon pulled him into the Black Hole."

Ginna hid her face in her hands, as the vision of Jon's last moments flashed through her mind.

"Something strange is happening, though," Laken continued. "It seems the Dragon's plot has been turned inside out."

"How do you mean?" Celestia's voice sounded very weary.

"Well, you know no one has ever come back out of a Black Hole, right?" Laken began.

"Of course—once something passes the event horizon the gravity is so strong nothing can escape—not even light," Celestia replied.

"At the bottom of the Black Hole is a point of the most intense gravity possible."

"The singularity, right?"

Laken nodded to his wife, but looked over at Ginna.

"Some have speculated that the singularity is actually a portal."

"A gateway to something else—like a Time Portal?" she asked

"Right, but not just time—space as well. Some have theorized the other side of the singularity is an 'anti-black hole' or a White Hole—the opposite of what's here on this side."

"So, what could it lead to? Another universe? I mean we know about them, don't we?" said Celestia. "We were in one with Stephan, when we fled the attack on Luna."

"That was an alternative-universe, but not everything was the opposite. An anti-universe would have opposite forces in everything—positive electrons, negative protons—"

"You mean like anti-matter? I heard about that in physics class," said Ginna.

"Perhaps. No one knows for sure."

"Laken, I can tell you one thing," came an unexpected voice from behind them.

"Jael! How did you get here?" Ginna cried.

"Johan just brought me back."

"Where is he?"

"He said he couldn't stay. But he *is* going to come back for me. He says he needs my help in reaching Martina."

"Figures," sighed Ginna. "Johan never seems to answer all our questions."

244

"He'll be here when we need him," said Laken. "So, what were you going to say, Jael?"

Jael's face was shining with a strange light as he began to speak. "I can feel in my heart that Jon isn't truly dead—he's just moved into a better place—on the other side."

"You mean Heaven?" Celestia's voice still quavered when she tried to talk about her father.

"No, not that," Jael insisted. "He's been transformed—into something else—on the other side of the Black Hole."

"In an anti-universe?"

"I guess so. It's the opposite of here—no evil—no Dragon."

"How can you be sure of this?" Laken asked.

Celestia was gripping her husband's hand so tightly that he had to pull it out of her grasp. After he'd flexed his fingers, though, he placed the hand gently on her shoulder.

"Jon and I have a unique bond, remember?" Jael was saying.

Celestia nodded. "I remember what Daiah told me—how when the System captured you, Jon thought you were dead because he wasn't getting any thoughts or feelings from you—the link was broken."

"But that was because I'd been taken to a Time Nexus—where all time was standing still."

"And the feeling you're getting now isn't the same?" Laken's voice was tense with suppressed excitement.

"I guess that's one way to put it—the opposite. I feel

Jon's presence flooding my mind with joy. Wherever he is, it's a truly wonderful place."

"Does this mean what I think it might?" Celestia stepped closer to Jael. "Instead of destroying our Galaxy, the Dragon has inadvertently opened a portal to a better place? Can this new portal be used by anyone? Does it mean we can all escape to this place—and that the Dragon's plan has backfired?"

"Maybe this was the King's plan all along," said Jael excitedly. "I remember hearing that he can work all things out for good. So maybe even the Dragon's plots can be turned around."

"I have no idea," Laken shrugged. "I need to discuss this with Johan. Right now, I think it's best if we all get some rest."

"But Laken," Jael said. "Perhaps this is what The Book talks about when it says, 'Death is swallowed up in victory,'."

"I always thought that was just about Heaven," murmured Laken. "How are things any different now than they were before? We're still waiting for the True King's return, and it sure doesn't seem like it's happened yet."

Jael stepped over to Laken and looked him directly in the eyes. "There's another verse in The Book that talks about something like this."

"What is it?" Laken gasped and slumped to the ground.

Jael drew himself to his full height and began to quote the verse he'd learned by heart so many years ago:

'Listen, I tell you a mystery. We will not all die, but we will all be changed—in a flash, in the twinkling of an eye—at the last trumpet.'

"That part about all being changed seems to fit with the idea of an anti-universe," Celestia said, moving closer to her husband, checking his breathing, and holding his hand. "All we can do right now is wait, though. We all need to recuperate from this battle, especially you Laken. You need to let me tend your wounds. Remember, I'm Starla, the healthcare worker."

"They're only scratches from the Dragon's scales."

"And I'm sure his scales are totally harmless—NOT! Don't argue with me. I've already lost my father, and I'm not going to lose you, too."

He sighed and tried not to roll his eyes as she led him to a shelf of rock nearby and sat him down again.

'So is Jon truly lost to us—or not?' thought Ginna. 'This is really confusing. I sure hope Johan can shed some light on this—before we have to break the news to Martina.'

With these painful thoughts echoing in her mind, she lay back on the cool rocky surface, looking up at the shining swirls of stars spiraling their way toward the still-mysterious Black Hole in the sky above her. Sleep was a long time coming.

***

When she next awoke, there was still no change in the sky. The Black Hole seemed the same size, as were the star-swirls overhead.

'Perhaps this is good,' she thought. 'At least the Dragon didn't make it speed up, like he said he would. Maybe Jon's being pulled in with him made a difference.'

She'd barely opened her eyes when she saw Jael coming toward her. Close behind him was Johan.

"So, you finally decided to help us?" These angry words were out of her mouth before she even realized she'd thought them.

"I know why you feel this way, Ginna." The old man's voice was calm and he didn't show any anger on his face. "But sometimes we have to learn things for ourselves and not merely follow the directions of others."

Ginna just stared at the ground.

"We need your help now," Jael said to her. "I need you to help me reach my sister. She's in a very dark place."

"Why me? I don't have the strength of Celestia, or the abilities of Laken."

"But you've had the experience of living inside Martina's mind for several years of her time. No one else can duplicate that," Johan said.

"Well, okay, if you really think I can help. Yes, I'll come with you to—"

"To Tornatoh, the place you once went with her to find Celestia and your daughter."

"And the place called Toronto back in the Twenty-second Century, when we got trapped in a Time Well, with Celestia."

"That's not the only thing significant about this ancient city, is it?" Johan was looking directly into her eyes.

"Well—it was the place Garek and I were married by a Justice Judge. Though we later had a formal ceremony, back in my time."

"I bet you miss him, don't you?" Jael said softly.

"Of course, I do. I think of him nearly every hour of the day. I'd rather be going home—like Dain and Evin did." There, she'd said it.

"I understand," said Jael, looking into her eyes. "I'd like to go back to my home with Raina, too. "But my sister needs us first."

Seeing the pain in his eyes, Ginna knew she owed it to him and Martina to help them.

Reaching over, she took his thin hand in hers, realizing how frail he still was. 'Well, if he can face this in his weakness, so must I. Lord, please help us.'

"Okay," she sighed. "I'm coming with you, and I'll do what I can."

CHAPTER 19
FROM THE DEPTHS

If I was really honest with myself, I could admit where I was and why. But I knew that kind of honesty would just leave me in deeper despair. And so I refused to look at it. I just got up each morning and dressed in the clothes Shei left in the flat for me.

Then I walked to the Temple, trying to think of it as only a job. How could I face the truth that I was now what I'd always feared? Each day as I guided pilgrims through the glittering red corridors, I began to actually believe what I said—that this Temple was the residence of the gods.

"There are many pathways," I'd hear my voice saying. "Each one in its own way leads to the truth."

Soon, I was leading others in rituals, and my beliefs from my past grew thinner and thinner. I shudder now when I think of some of those rituals.

Still, many times afterwards, I was haunted by strange and disturbing dreams. Some were just bizarre—like one in which I was trying to pull a scab off a sore on my arm. When it came off, I began to ooze some white puss. But before my eyes, the blob of white morphed into green writhing snakes. And these kept growing until they consumed everything around me. I expected to be the next thing they devoured, but then I woke, sweating and shaking in fear.

Each time I finally reached the end of myself, I went back to the little shop on High Street. Johan was always there, listening to my rambling fears and excuses, patiently trying to help me find myself again.

Then one day, when I pushed open the dusty door with the squeaking hinge, I couldn't believe my eyes. My younger brother was sitting on the bench beside Johan.

When he looked up and smiled at me, I saw the old familiar light in his green eyes. A sharp pain shot through my chest as I remembered how much he looked like our long-dead brother Stephen.

"Oh, Jael," I moaned. "Why have you come to torment me with memories of my past?"

"You don't remember, do you?" he sighed.

"Remember what?"

"That you saw me here just a few days ago."

I shook my head in confusion. "I haven't been here for ages," I finally managed to say.

Johan looked over at Jael and shrugged at him. "I told you she wouldn't remember that first time you saw her."

"What? Have I been sleep-walking?"

"Or perhaps drugged-walking says it better," sighed Johan.

My face started to burn with anger. "Don't try to tell me what to do, old man."

By this time, Jael stood and moved to my side. "Will you come take a walk with me?" he whispered.

I nodded and turned away from Johan. "Just don't let that nosey old man come."

"No, he's staying here," said Jael, as we turned our backs to him. "We're going to walk down to the lake."

I nodded. "It's beautiful down on Lake Street."

Once we were outside the shop, Jael quickly took my hand. "Let's go all the way to the shore." His voice sounded excited, much more like the little boy I remembered.

So, we went past the temple and its gushing fountains, and I was thankful I didn't have to explain my job to Jael. When we got to the lakeshore it was crowded with people, some walking along the water's edge and others actually swimming in the waves.

"They're hardy souls," Jael chuckled. "I think that water would be too cold for me."

"Oh, but it's a warm day," I laughed. "You'll be surprised how good the lake water feels." And before he could reply, I ran out far enough to throw myself into one of the incoming waves.

"Hey, wait for me, Tina."

As I turned and saw him running toward me in the water, I realized my so-called 'new name' was the one he'd used for me when he was a child—'Tina'.

Soon we were laughing and splashing each other like children.

At last, Jael pulled himself up to his full height. Standing beside him I was surprised to see his face just above mine.

"You've really grown, Little Brother," I laughed.

"Well, it's been a long time since I've seen you," he smiled.

"So why did you come to this city?"

"Just to pay you a visit."

"You know I have a flat here," I said. "You could come and stay with me, instead of staying with that silly old man."

"I'd like to. But I'll need to stop by the shop and get some extra clothes I brought."

"Well, if you insist. But I have everything you'll need—food, bedding, and I'm sure Shei could get you some new clothes. He's gotten me lots of new clothing—"

My voice tapered off as I saw the confused look in his eyes. "Who's Shei?"

"Oh, he's just a new friend I've made here," I said quickly. Maybe having Jael stay at my flat wasn't such a good idea, after all. I couldn't think of a good way to explain Shei to him. Deep inside I knew it wasn't right, though I refused to admit it.

Somehow, Jael must have read my thoughts, for he said, "You know, I've got a good bed at Johan's. You wouldn't believe it by the mess in front of the shop, but he has a pretty nice flat in back. Maybe it's better if I just stay where I am for now."

I knew he was giving me a graceful way out, and I hugged him quickly. "I still want you to come see my place sometime. I'll get it tidied up, and maybe I can take you there next time. Uh, are you staying long?"

"Yeah, I'll be here for several days. Just come back by the shop as soon as you can."

By this time, we'd waded out of the water, and were picking up colorful stones on the beach. Hoping to change the subject, I grabbed an especially bright green stone and called to my brother:

"Wow, look at this one."

He came to my side, smiling. "Oh, that is a beautiful one, Tina. I've always liked greenstone the best."

"Green is the color of life," I nodded. "This greenstone is very revered in many cultures."

"I remember the natives in Indonia especially prized it. Didn't they call it 'Jade' ?"

"That's right. I do remember."

I turned and stared into his green eyes, as I said this. 'Am I remembering more than I want to? Memories can be dangerous.' I told myself. 'Just live in the now.'

"I think my favorite shade of green is the color of your eyes," I murmured.

He just smiled.

"I guess I'd better go now," I said with a sigh. "I uh— have an appointment."

He nodded and continued smiling.

'He wouldn't be smiling if he knew what this appointment is,' my inner voice said.

"Oh, be quiet, mind," I muttered to myself. "All I do is show people the Temple."

'And deny your faith in the True King.' This voice always insisted on having the last word.

"Please come see me again soon," he said, giving me a quick hug. Before I could reply, he began walking up the road by the temple and turned onto High Street.

***

Later, as I lay on the bed in my flat, I heard Shei come in and close the door quietly. He didn't say a word or bother to ask if my day had gone well. He just climbed into the bed beside me and began to pull me to him. I had no desire for him now, but I knew what I must do.

That's the reason I didn't go back to the old man's shop for several days. I just couldn't face the people who loved me, for I knew I was totally undeserving of that love.

I was very surprised the next time I went into Johan's old shop. There were three people to greet me.

"Ginna?" My mind had trouble believing my eyes. "How did you get here?"

"The same way I got to your Wilderness Out-clave." She was trying to smile casually, I could tell.

"Jon?"

She shook her head.

"I brought her here," said Jael.

"But you're not a GAP-crosser."

"No, Ginna is."

"Oh, that's right. But I bet you had some help from this nosy old man, didn't you?"

"Yes, I helped," said the crackly old voice.

"Why didn't you bring Jon with you?" I found those words out of my mouth before I could stop myself.

"So you do remember Jon?" asked Jael.

I nodded my head, but suddenly didn't want to speak. Something about the look in Ginna's eyes sent fear into my bones.

"What's wrong?" I asked, looking from one to the other.

None of them would meet my gaze, even Johan.

"You're all hiding something from me, aren't you?"

In reply, Ginna took my hand in hers. "Let's go for a walk," she murmured.

"Oh, I get it." I was staring at Jael. "First you take me off alone on a walk—and now Ginna does. You all must be trying to get me to come around by being buddy-buddy with me."

"Please," sighed Jael. "I just wanted to have some fun with you—like old times. And we did have a nice time down by the lakeshore, didn't we?"

"All right, I'll go with Ginna. It must be her turn to 'work on' me." As I turned to go, I caught a glimpse of tears in Jael's eyes and felt sorry I'd caused him pain, but not enough to apologize.

Ginna and I went down to Lake Street and wandered among the vendors' shops and stalls. She seemed to enjoy looking at the pretty baubles and trinkets there. Either that, or she was really good at faking it.

Eventually though, we reached the end of the street. Beyond us was a grassy area with dunes behind it.

"Does any of this look familiar?" she asked.

"Well, I remember seeing it when we first came looking for the fountains—"

"Was that when I was 'within' you?"

"I think so."

"I have another memory of this place, too," she smiled. "When I was back in the Time Well with Celestia, this is where Garek asked me to marry him."

"Why did you have to bring him up?" I snapped suddenly.

She turned and stared at me in surprise. "What? Are you jealous? I thought you'd decided you loved Jon more."

I stalked away from her, onto the dunes and toward the shoreline.

"Wait, I'm sorry. I didn't mean to make you angry."

Hearing the pain in her voice, I turned and looked back at her. She was running through the sand, trying to catch up with me, and I waited until she reached my side.

***

I could hear my voice babbling, but the words made no sense. There was an aching in my chest I'd never felt before, and tears blinded my eyes. I'm not sure how long I lay, curled into a miserable heap. Finally, I began to sense Ginna's hand on my back, and heard her voice:

"It's okay. I understand what grief can do—I've been there. And I know how it feels to want something so badly that's far beyond your reach."

'What is she talking about?' I wondered to myself.

"You can cry on my shoulder all you want," she said, and I felt her pulling me toward her.

"But you have no idea what I've done," I managed to say at last. My words were finally coming ungarbled. "I've betrayed Jon, Jael, Celestia—everyone. I've been so selfish. I thought I was the only one in despair. And the more I tried to hide from it, the worse it got."

"You can still come back. It's not too late. Jael and I still care enough to be here for you. Celestia and Laken will come, too—if you want them to."

"But what about Jon? Doesn't he care enough to come?"

She was staring at me quizzically. "Didn't you hear what just I told you?"

"What did you tell me? When?"

"When I caught up to you here on the sand, just before you collapsed."

I kept shaking my head. "Sometimes I blank out, I guess. I don't remember. What is it?"

By now her face was beginning to look very pale. I even noticed her hands beginning to shake.

"Are you okay? What's wrong? What have I forgotten now?"

"I told you just a little while ago—Jon is gone. The Red Dragon took him down with him."

"The Dragon?"

"Yes, the Evil One, the Serpent."

"Didn't they battle him when they found Jael?"

"Yes, you are starting to remember."

"And Celestia and I—we went into a safe place—with a crimson dome."

"But then the Dragon came back with a new scheme. He wasn't defeated entirely. Johan gathered those of us he felt could defeat him. There was a battle— Jon was there with Laken and Celestia and my nephews-"

"Danny's sons?"

She nodded, but her lips were pulled into a tight grimace.

"Did they defeat him?"

"Well, we're not exactly sure what the outcome will be," she sighed. Then she took my hands firmly in hers. "Please be strong, Martina."

I tried to nod my head, but it felt like a piece of lead.

"Jon rescued Celestia and me—when our mount was set aflame by the Dragon. But the Dragon dragged Jon down with him into the Black Hole."

"What Black Hole?"

"The one at the center of our Galaxy."

"So he's—"

"We don't know if he's dead or not. Jael can still get some sensations from him."

"And maybe he can bring him back?"

"Nothing ever comes back from a Black Hole, Martina. It's the ultimate gravity source of the universe. The matter inside it has become so compressed that nothing can resist its gravitational pull."

"You told me this already?"

She nodded silently.

"What's the point of giving me false hope?" Now my voice was rising in anger. "You should just come out and say it. As far as we're concerned in this world, my husband is dead."

She nodded again. "I'm sorry. I cared for Jon, too." Tears were coming down her cheeks, just like mine.

But now rage filled me. "I thought you were supposed to help me," I screamed into her face. "All you've done is brought me more hopelessness and despair."

I wanted to jump up and run from her—perhaps out into the lake where it was too deep for anyone to come and save me. But my legs refused to hold me up. As soon as I tried to stand, I collapsed.

I could feel her hugging me and stroking my hair.

"Mother," I whispered. "Where are you? I need you. Why can't I come be with you—and Father, and Stephen, and Darien? Why have you all left me here alone? And now even Jon is gone."

***

What I hadn't said to Ginna—but wanted to—was she'd also taken Garek from me. I was such a mess by this time that even when I tried to mourn for Jon, I kept seeing Garek's face instead. And this made me feel even worse.

'What's wrong with you?' my accusing voice would ask. 'You don't even love your husband like you should. Instead you turn your thoughts to a man you had an affair with.'

I kept trying to tell this annoying voice to go away and leave me alone, but it never did. "I must be totally insane," my own voice told me, during the few times I was coherent.

Most of the time I just curled into a tight bundle of pain, spending all my time lying on the bed in my flat. Even Shei couldn't reach me. I kept turning my back on him, too.

"Tina, what can I do to help?" he'd say.

At first, I thought he cared only because he was missing his paramour. But gradually I began to notice little things he did, like bringing me a cup of tea, or gently massaging my aching shoulders and neck. 'Maybe he really cares in his own way,' my thoughts began to say.

It must have been one of those better days when I heard myself saying to him, "You've been a good friend, Shei."

His face registered surprise, then he replied, "How can you have any good feelings for me?"

"What do you mean?" I moved toward him but was dismayed when he stepped away.

"You know as well as I do—I'm just using you. Can you be that naïve?"

"But Shei—you are a good lover."

"Love isn't part of the picture," he shrugged. "We're just having sex, not making love. Besides don't you realize I get paid?"

"Paid for what?"

"For providing your services to the Temple."

"Oh, I know that. But it doesn't really matter. I can sense you care about me more than you realize."

This time he looked even more puzzled and took a small step toward me. "I've been told this could happen—it's called Stockholm Syndrome. Sometimes, a captive begins to fall in love with her captor—as a kind of defense mechanism. But I'm not worthy of your love. You should love the people who really care about you—like your brother or your friend Ginna."

"You've met them?"

"They've been here almost every day since you collapsed."

"They have? Why don't I remember?"

"I'm no physician. But I'd say you've been away in some dark place of despair."

"And depression," I added.

"Perhaps you don't feel you can reveal your true self to those closest to you."

"Oh, Shei." I let him pull me into his arms. "You are my only safety in all the world."

As I spoke these words, I reached up and tried to kiss him, but he turned his face away so all I caught was his cheek.

"Please," I murmured. "I need you."

"I can't take advantage of you when you're like this," he sighed. He managed to pull me onto his lap and began rocking me like a child. "When you come back to reality, then I'll know."

But I didn't hear the last of his words because my mind shuttered its windows on the world. I went back into the darkness again.

During some of the darkest times, I must have been having nightmares, for I often awoke screaming or in a cold sweat. Most of the time I didn't remember my dreams. But occasionally fragments were still in my mind—images of flames, blood, and violence.

Sometimes, all I remembered was confusion. In many of these dreams I was wandering through a maze of small rooms, connected by trapdoors and secret staircases. In some, I was wandering lost in a market, where vendors had their stalls in secret corners of a warren of tiny rooms and passageways.

Often when I awoke, I felt relief that it had been only a dream. But more often, the fear and hopelessness seemed to swallow my mind, and I couldn't distinguish reality from dreams at all.

Perhaps some of the nightmares were a result of the pills I kept taking. I have no idea if Shei was giving them to me—or if I was sneaking them. But it didn't matter. My mind was a dark blank, and most of the time nothing got in. I refused to eat, hoping I might starve to death. Sometimes I wondered if I had enough pills to kill me, if I took them all at once. But somehow, I never did. Perhaps Shei was monitoring my meds, after all. Or more likely I didn't even have the desire to do anything—either to help or harm myself. I was just numb.

CHAPTER 20
GINNA'S CHOICE

Ginna was walking along the shore with Jael, as they did nearly every day, rain or shine. She still found the fresh, moist air here to be reinvigorating, especially after the dingy shop on High Street.

"How can Johan stand to always be in that grimy place?" she asked Jael one day.

"I don't think he stays there all the time."

"But we never see him out here."

"Oh, he uses his own 'back door'," Jael had smiled.

"You mean he crosses the GAP to some other place?"

"I'm sure he does."

She sighed deeply now, remembering this earlier conversation. "I wish we could just cross the GAP to anywhere we want to go."

"What's that?" Jael seemed to have been deep in his own thoughts.

"I was thinking about Johan and how he can come and go as he pleases."

"Well, it may not be entirely as *he* pleases, you know. He's a Guardian, so many times he's summoned to a task."

"Yeah, I guess I forgot. Still, I'm getting tired of hanging around here—waiting for something that may never happen."

"You mean my sister coming back to sanity?"

She nodded, regretting she'd dragged him down into her negative thoughts. "I shouldn't have brought her up. I'm sorry."

"She's always on my mind anyway," he sighed.

"Do you think anything can reach her?"

"My love reached her, back on Terres. But we were both much younger then—not yet world-weary. We could still stir up some hope within ourselves."

"Don't you have any hope now?"

"What little hope I have seems to be dwindling daily."

She stopped suddenly and reached for his hand. A tiny shiver passed through his hand into hers.

"Danny?" She couldn't believe she was sensing her dead brother, who was from an entirely different time and place.

"Can you feel him?" Jael whispered.

"Has this been happening all along?"

"No, it just started when I woke up this morning. I know he's dead and buried in the Twenty-first Century, but somehow a bit of his presence must have been lying dormant inside me."

"And today it awoke?"

He nodded and then pointed to a rocky outcrop between the dunes and the beach. "Let's sit down here."

"Can you read any thoughts? Perhaps Danny can help us figure out what to do about Martina. He was always the most perceptive one in our family."

"That's what my siblings often said about me," Jael sighed.

"Well, Jon did say Danny was a forerunner of you."

"Right now, I'm not getting anything but a tiny sense of his presence—nothing else."

Ginna leaned her back against the stony cliff behind her and closed her eyes. In her mind's eye she could see her younger brother—just as he'd been when they first moved to Colorado, a shy brown-eyed blond that the bullies in the school found an easy prey. 'I defended him, though,' she smiled to herself. 'And the bullies got the message.'

"Ginna?" Jael's voice interrupted her memories. "I think I'm losing my faith."

"What do you mean?"

"Well, I can't seem to pray anymore. It feels like God has left me."

"But in The Book he tells us, 'I will never leave you or forsake you.' You know, I think you're the one who so often quoted that—especially when we were wandering lost in the Galaxy, trying to find Maia—Mother Earth."

"When we found it, though, the problems were still

the same. I thought at first the King must be testing us. But now it seems it will never end."

"What will never end? The world—or our troubles?"

"Both, I guess."

"Well, you know The Book warns that as this world draws to a close, there will be many who scoff and try to make us believe the King isn't returning. But he's warned us, so we can be prepared to fight against these challenges."

"I know. I remember telling Martina—and later Raina—about that. But what if I can't believe it anymore myself?"

"That's the little voice in your mind lurking in the dark and whispering, 'There's no way out.' But it's a lie. Don't believe it. I know how it feels, though—I've been there many times."

"You have?"

"Lots, especially when I was struggling to be a good single parent to my daughter, only to have her turn her back on our faith. It was almost enough to make me want to die."

"But things are better now, aren't they?"

"Yes, they are—when I'm actually in my own time, with my loved ones."

"Including Garek?"

She only nodded, her voice lost in a wave of emotion.

"I'm sorry we messed up your life to try and help my sister."

"Please don't feel badly. I came because she needs me."

The he suddenly jumped to his feet and gave a high-pitched cry, gripping her hand in a fierce hold.

"Ouch! What's the matter?"

"I'm sorry. I just had to grab something, so he wouldn't take me away."

"So who wouldn't take you?"

"I think it was the Serpent, or one of his demons." Jael was sweating and panting by this time. She began to massage his arms, and pulled his head down into her lap.

"Breathe long slow breaths. Think of the most beautiful, calm place you can. The Serpent is gone, remember?"

Gradually his breathing returned to normal, and Ginna did her best to calm herself also.

At last he murmured, "How can we know for sure the Dragon is really gone—is what The Book tells us about God is really true? What if it's just a story or myth someone made up?"

"Jael, you saw the Evil One with your own eyes."

"I got a glimpse—yes. But I didn't see the battle, remember?"

She took his hand gently. "I know. I think Johan was right in keeping you with him. You're still weak from your captivity."

"Yeah, I know," he sighed. "It makes me feel so useless sometimes."

Now she pulled him into her embrace. "That's why

the evil ones can get to you. But keep on being brave. I know the King still has plans for you."

"Please help me. I think I'm sinking into the depression that runs in my family."

"You're just emotionally exhausted. I would be too, if I was facing what you are. Especially after all the other things you've been through."

As she collected her thoughts, she continued to slowly massage his temples, and run her fingers through his blond hair. Again, she felt the quick electrifying sense of her younger brother's presence—just for an instant. But then it was gone.

"I know you and Johan have talked a lot about the creation and the beginning of all things," she said at last.

"And about the end times, too."

"In one place in The Book, the King calls himself the Alpha and Omega."

"What's that?"

"They're the first and last letters of the Greek alphabet."

"Oh, yeah. I remember Laken using that alphabet when we got an encrypted message from Johan."

"Well, the King used them to mean 'the Beginning and the End'—and he's everything in between, too. Even if we try to hide from him, he still sees us. He never sleeps, The Book says."

"That means he's everywhere, doesn't it?"

She nodded. "So, you can't lose God, if he never loses sight of you."

Now Jael smiled slightly. "I guess you've convinced me. I'm afraid to let any of my doubts and questions out when I'm with the others, especially my sister. So, I'm really grateful that I can truly be honest with you."

She smiled and sighed. "I'm glad, too. Having questions and doubts isn't a sin, you know. It can be a way to help us grow—by seeking the truth more deeply. Then we can know why we believe what we do."

"Now, if we can just help Martina see this," he sighed.

***

Ginna was looking out of Johan's shop window, watching the sun rise over the sleeping city of Tornatoh. It was an exceptionally colorful sunrise, and she wondered about a saying her father had told her so long ago:

'Red sky at morning, sailors take warning. Red sky at night, sailors delight.'

"The second part seems to show true more than the first," she said to the window. "For red skies in the morning can result in good days, too."

"What's that?" came Jael's voice.

"Oh, just thinking of some old proverb my dad used to say."

"Do you miss your father?"

"Actually, I haven't seen him for over thirty years. He's just a small memory now—I think my mind has covered over that pain."

"Especially since you've found Garek?"

"That's a big part of it. And my relationship with my daughter has been healed."

"Do you miss them?"

"Of course I do. I wish I could go home to them right now."

"I'm sorry my problems are keeping you here," he sighed, then continued, "Do you think the Dragon was truly swallowed up by the Black Hole?"

"Johan says he was. And he also says the anti-universe on the other side is the opposite of here, with no evil."

"But why do bad things still exist here, if the Dragon is gone?"

She turned and looked into his eyes, amazed that he'd said her very thoughts aloud. "I asked Johan that," she sighed. "He says there are still remnants of the Dragon and his demons which need to be dealt with. Then Kristos will be able to make this world new also."

"Do you think my sister has a demon in her?"

"I hope not. It seems more like some demon is whispering lies into her ears."

"And maybe there's a demon holding onto her feet and trying to pull her down?"

"That could be. There have been times in my life I've felt like I was trying to pull a heavy load behind me every time I moved."

"I've tried everything I can think of," he said, casting

his gaze to the floor. "Now that she knows Jon is gone, she seems to have lost her will to live altogether."

"I know," she sighed. "But I think there is one thing which might break through to her. I'm just not sure I'm prepared to do it."

"What's that?"

"Well, I think Martina still loves Garek."

"But he's married to you. You shouldn't have to give up what God has given you."

"What I'm thinking of wouldn't quite do that," she whispered. "I keep getting this thought that perhaps Garek was brought into our lives for other reasons than just me."

"He did help Annemarie come back to herself."

"More than that."

Her voice cracked, and he turned and looked into her eyes. "I think I know what you want to do. You're going to merge yourself with my sister again, aren't you?"

She nodded silently, speechless for a moment.

"You're willing to let Martina live inside you, so she can be with Garek."

At last she found her voice. "It's the only thing I can think of."

"But what a sacrifice you'd be making, to share the love of your life with another."

"Still, ever since that first time Jon merged us, I've felt like Martina has always been a part of me—even when we were each in our own bodies. And this time, she would be 'within' me—instead of the other way around."

"You've never done this before. Jon never reversed the roles. Are you sure it will work and won't kill you? This is all topsy-turvy. Besides, we don't have Jon anymore, with his abilities."

"But we do have you, Jael. And we also have Laken and Celestia."

"I notice you didn't mention Johan," he murmured.

"I'm not sure he'll approve."

"How are you going to do this thing without Johan interfering?"

"I think that's where you can help me."

"Oh, you mean create a distraction."

"That's right."

"I don't think we can keep Johan from knowing, no matter what we do."

"But isn't it worth a try—to save your sister?"

"Well—yeah. Of course."

"Then let's get our plan laid out, okay?"

He merely nodded this time, for his voice was lost in emotion.

CHAPTER 21
LAKEN'S TASK

Laken and his wife had just crossed the GAP to Tornatoh with Johan, and the weather was wicked. Cold wind whipped his hair and stung his face with icy spray. He saw they were now beside the lake, the one called Omato in this time. The last time he'd been here was 900 years ago, when he was trying to figure out how Celestia had learned to cross the GAP. In fact, she'd crossed to this very city, to get them away from uncontrolled looters in earthquake-stricken Tacoma.

As the cold drops of ice and rain blinded him, he reached out and called his wife's name, "Celestia, are you there?"

Then a cold hand gripped his arm. "I'm right here. But this is no beach day. We've got to get to some shelter." Her voice was coming in gasps.

"This way," a deeper voice called. "Follow me."

"Is that Johan?" His words were ripped out of him by the lashing wind.

"I think so," came Celestia's voice, seeming far away. "Come with me."

"Can you see anything?"

"Not really. But Johan's voice came from this way."

He tried to move toward her voice. But then a much stronger gust of wind knocked both of them off their feet.

"I'm sorry. I can't even walk in this gale. We'd better just crawl," he gasped. "Hold onto my foot, so we don't get separated."

Her ice-cold hand grabbed his right ankle, as he began to inch his way forward in what he hoped was an uphill direction. 'Up has to be toward the shore instead of the water's edge,' he told himself.

As he eased forward, he made sure he wasn't losing the grip of his wife's hand. By now his teeth were chattering hard. The wind was tearing away any body heat they could muster.

Then he heard Celestia trying to talk. "I can't go much farther. My knees are getting all skinned up from this rough sand."

"Just stay with me," he managed to mutter. "I won't go as fast."

"But I can't keep holding on. My hands are so cold they can't grip anymore."

He stopped his forward motion then, and turning, he pulled her into a tight embrace. "Does this help any?" he asked.

Her teeth were chattering so much she couldn't even reply. Instead she just clung to him, trying to catch her breath.

"Do you think you can crawl again?"

He felt her head nod.

"Then, you go first, and I'll hold onto you. I don't think it will be any colder, and this way you can set the pace."

"Why has Johan abandoned us?" she asked sharply.

"I think we just got too far behind," he sighed. "And he can't see or hear us in this storm."

Just as he said this, though, a shape appeared ahead of them and a voice called, "There you are!"

"We're sorry," came Celestia's voice. "We aren't as strong as you are."

"But I'm just an old man," his voice chuckled.

"I'm not so sure about that now," she retorted.

Before they could say anything else, strong arms wrapped around both of them, and in an instant their feet left the sand. The next thing Laken knew they were standing inside a dusty room.

Blinking his eyes, he tried to get them to return to normal sight, and finally, he was able to focus on their surroundings.

"Have I been here before?" his wife was asking, before he'd even formulated the words.

"I don't think so," said Johan. "Your mother has been here several times, however."

"My mother—Martina?"

"Yes. And I'm hopeful she'll return again in the near future, so we can find a way to extricate her from the mess she's gotten herself into."

"What mess?"

"She's given herself back to the System." As he said this, Johan took her hand gently.

"You mean she's been captured?"

"No, my dear," Johan continued. "She's gone over voluntarily. There's great danger in trying to rescue her. The System doesn't like to give up their converts readily."

"I guess I do remember that from some of my other lives," Laken sighed.

"What can we do then?"

Laken was glad his wife hadn't asked her usual question about what he remembered from any of his past lives. 'It's hard to explain it to her,' he sighed to himself. 'Sometimes the memories jump into my mind, seemingly from nowhere. Then they disappear again, back into the oblivion of forgetfulness.'

While these thoughts echoed in Laken's head, Johan's voice continued, "Patience, my girl. We will find some way to reach her. A good possibility has just presented itself, in fact."

"What's that?" he asked.

"Laken, you must be patient, too," Johan chuckled softly. "By the way, I'm sorry about the storm. I must have miscalculated my arrival day."

"Why couldn't you just bring us to this room in the first place?" Laken couldn't keep the edge out of his voice.

"I'm sorry, but this place is shielded," said Johan. "I normally don't let anyone cross the GAP in or out."

"Shielded?" asked Celestia.

"Yes, you're safe here. Besides, the battle with the Dragon is over, and hope has re-entered your world."

"That's really hard to believe," said Celestia. "It seems like the Dragon has won—you yourself said he *did* speed up the Black Hole—and dragged my father in with him."

Johan looked her full in the face. "What you don't realize, is the True King is Lord of all. He can use even bad things to fulfill his plans. What looks like evil to us can be turned completely around, bringing about good."

"But that makes it sound like the King is evil as well as good," Laken protested. "Like the Yin and Yang the Dragon talked about."

"No, the King doesn't cause the evil—the Serpent and his kind do that. But then the King can turn their wicked plans back on them, and bring good about instead."

"This is really hard to understand," Celestia sighed.

"Especially now when we're so exhausted from battles and storms," added Laken.

"Right now, the two of you need to get some rest before our next task."

With those words, he led them through a doorway to their left. Once inside the next room—which wasn't nearly as dusty as the first one—he showed them a sleeping platform with several blankets.

"You may sleep here. There's no need to think about anything else right now, my children."

Laken and his wife sat down on the soft cushions. Before any other thoughts came to him, he hugged her, laid down and fell into a deep sleep.

***

Laken stood in the warm sun and surveyed the reflection of the Temple of Unity in the still waters of Lake Omato. It was hard to believe that only a day ago, this shore was being ripped and torn by howling winds and icy rain. The only signs of the storm's passing were the scattered piles of debris, some high above the present water's edge.

"Look at how much stuff the storm brought in," said Celestia. She bent down to pick up a piece of driftwood. "See how its edges are all worn to curves."

"Wind and water can be very powerful," he nodded.

"The weather today is totally opposite of yesterday."

"You know, all this flotsam and jetsam—"

"What?"

"Oh, those are old words for debris tossed up by the sea," he laughed. "What I meant to say is that life is like this shore."

"How do you mean?"

"Some days we're at peace and the world is all wonderful and bright, but other days are stormy."

"Like when we're having troubles or feeling fearful?"

He nodded. "It's these stormy times in life which cause all the junk inside us—that we didn't know was there—to get tossed up on our life's beach."

"Oh, I see. When times get rough, a lot of bad stuff comes to the surface."

"Not all of it's bad, though." As he said this, he reached down and picked up a shining pink stone. "Look how pretty this pebble is."

She took it from his palm and gazed at it wordlessly.

"You know I'm no angel, don't you?" he murmured. "I've done a lot of wrong things in my past lives. Even though I'm a Guardian, I'm still just a human, like you."

"I know," she sighed. "No human is perfect. Maybe I haven't done any outwardly terrible things, but I've thought them. Isn't that just as bad?"

"The Book says so." He patted her gently on the shoulder and left his hand there.

"Why did God make humans flawed?"

"That's the age-old question," he muttered. "I've been

taught he gave us free-will so we could truly love him by choice—and not be like programmed machines."

"But our first ancestors blew it, didn't they?"

"That's how the story goes. The Book isn't an account of great deeds humans have done. Instead, it's a saga of human failure—and the Lord's enduring love and patience with us in spite of everything."

She laid her head on his shoulder, and he saw the shining dampness in her eyes. "Do you think that's what happened to my mother?" she whispered. "Has old junk from her life been tossed back up by her emotional storm?"

"I'd say that explains it very well." He took her hand as he said this, and was surprised at how cold her fingers were. He pulled her to him and gave her a long kiss. "We'll find some way to help Martina, I know it."

"I sure hope so. Johan sounded like he had an idea."

"I think he does, but I don't know what it is yet." He saw her face cloud with confusion, and decided it was time for a little diversion. "You know, this scene hasn't changed much since the last time we were here."

"That's pretty amazing, considering that time was 900 years ago. But I think the lake looks smaller."

He turned and smiled into his wife's brown eyes. "I suppose that's true. I get immune to some of the details."

"Because you've been time-traveling so much, I suppose," she sighed. "So, did Johan tell you why he wanted us to come here?"

"Not exactly. But everyone else has left the Nexus where we battled the Dragon. There wasn't any need for us there."

"Because my dad disappeared," her voice broke and she buried her head in his tunic.

"Jael and Ginna are here in Tornatoh, too" he said softly, stroking her long hair. "This morning, Johan said he had a task for me, but he wasn't at liberty to discuss it."

"Perhaps he didn't want to talk to you with me around."

"I don't think that's the problem. There was something he's hiding, though. He acted like I'd know what to do when the time came, but he had to keep himself out of it."

"I wonder why."

"It's like he wants to help someone, but doesn't want that person to know he's doing it."

"That sounds confusing."

"Johan can be quite mysterious, I've found—from working with him down through the ages."

She lifted her head and looked into his eyes. "You can be pretty mysterious yourself."

"I even confuse myself sometimes," he grinned. "Living in different times and then not remembering much about them can be difficult."

"I get confused with just the little GAP-crossing I've done." She stood, took his hand in hers, and began leading him down toward the water's edge. "The first time I was here was in my own time, but the second time was far in the past."

"With me."

"I was still afraid of you then."

"I know."

She stopped suddenly, pulled his face down toward her and kissed him. "I'm not afraid of you anymore, though."

"Maybe now it's my turn to be afraid of you," he laughed. "You are so full of surprises."

"Like what?" She didn't wait for him to answer but ran down into the shallow water on the shore.

There was no need for conversation while they played and splashed each other in the cool water. Once they'd grown tired and settled down on the dry sand just above the water line, he put his arm around her and pulled her to him.

"I wonder why I love you so much," she whispered as she rested her head on his chest.

"I wonder the same thing, too—about why I love you—out of all the other people I've met in other lives," he nodded.

"Do you believe in fate?"

"How?"

"Well that somehow we were destined to be together—of all the people in the world?"

"That's a lot of people, if you count all the times I've lived."

"Well I'm not going to worry about that. Let's just make the most of the time we do have."

He drew her face up toward his and kissed her deeply. Then she snuggled into his embrace, and they lay in the warmth of the sun on the sand.

***

Laken woke with a start. 'I must have fallen asleep.' He looked around, but no one else was in sight. The sun was sinking low on the western horizon.

Shaking Celestia, he woke her quickly. "We need to get back to High Street," he said. "I don't know where this day went. I hope Johan won't be angry with us for being gone so long."

"Well, he didn't give you a certain time frame for this task, did he?"

"Not really. He said we had the day to use as we pleased."

"Then you shouldn't worry." She grinned slightly, but then a cloud seemed to cross her face. "I feel like I'm missing something," she said at last.

"What do you mean?" He lay back on the sand again, enjoying its warmth as the air around them cooled.

His wife sighed before she spoke again. "Well, before I was hearing the King speak to me sometimes, telling me what he wanted me to do. Like when he sent me to help Ginna and Annemarie."

"You did some amazing things, all right."

"It was the King's power, not mine. But now I don't seem to hear anything. Is he angry with me? Have I failed in some way?"

He reached up and grasped her hand, then pulled himself up to embrace her. "Don't ever think that. God loves us all the time, but he doesn't always talk to us. Sometimes he tells us things through other people, or in his word, The Book."

"Maybe he's angry because I've been doubting his care. All the troubles with my mother seem to have weakened my faith. I thought trials were supposed to make us stronger."

He looked into her deep brown eyes a long time before he replied. "I don't believe God is angry when his children question him. He understands we're just limited beings."

"I really hope you're right."

He put his arms around her and held her tightly. "Just let me take care of what Johan has entrusted to me. I don't know what it is yet, but I hope it'll help us reach your mother."

"I know, but I feel so helpless now, like I've been left out in the cold—the way it felt in the storm yesterday. Lately it seems like others are doing the main work—you, Dain, Evin—"

"Look at it like you're having a break," he whispered.

"I guess so. I'm just being selfish and silly, aren't I?"

"Well, we all have times of doubt. But I know your heart is in the right place." He gave her a quick kiss on top of her head. "And so does the King. We never know what may be around the next bend, as an old saying goes."

She turned and looked into his eyes. "Thanks, Laken. You know you're the best thing that's ever happened to me—in whatever world we're in."

He chuckled and stood, pulling her up with him. Just as they both reached their feet and rubbed the sand off their backs, he saw Ginna walking toward them.

She waved but didn't call out, so they waited for her to catch up.

"Where's Jael and Johan?" asked Celestia.

"Oh, they had something to work on in the shop." She was trying to make her voice sound casual, but Laken could sense the tension hiding underneath.

"What's up?" he asked cautiously. "Do you need something from us?"

"You could say that," she said and shuffled her feet in the sand, making small ridges. "Come with me."

Without another word, she started back along the shore toward the temple. He and Celestia followed, wondering what all this meant. Once they reached the base of the temple wall, she led them to a small circular door.

"This is where Martina works," Ginna said softly.

"Is she here?" Laken asked.

In reply, Ginna placed her ear on the center of the

door and listened. "Yes, and I'm glad. Usually, she's guiding tours for pilgrims."

Celestia looked at them in confusion.

"You mean you still don't see, Celestia?"

"What? Is my mother working as a Temple Guide? But why would she do that? She's a Believer."

Gently Laken took her hands in his and murmured, "I'm afraid she is. She's trying to turn her back on all her past—and her faith."

"No," Celestia moaned.

Laken grabbed her arms firmly when she tried to break away and run.

"You might as well face it," he said.

"How could she do this—to Dad and me?"

"She's been in the pit of depression so long she has no idea what's right or wrong anymore," Ginna sighed. "All she knows is the prevention of more pain. But no matter what she tries, nothing works for long—not even the drugs she takes."

Laken saw the tears streaming down his wife's cheeks and reached up to brush them away. "I'm guessing you have an idea of something that may help, right Ginna?"

"I hope so, but I need you to help me, because I've heard Celestia say you're a forerunner of Jon."

"That's one way Jon and I described our connections. But my relationship to Jon wasn't at all like his and Jael's."

"We don't need that kind of link for this," Ginna went on, her voice still barely above a whisper. "Jon was the one who did it before, long ago when he drew us—my brother and me—into the minds and bodies of Martina and Jael."

"So that's what you're up to."

"What are you two talking about?" Celestia's voice was still confused.

"I'm going to take Martina into myself this time," Ginna said. "That way she can live in my world, with Garek."

Laken felt a rush of energy course through him. 'This is what Johan was talking about,' he thought.

Then he saw the total shock on Celestia's face as she finally realized what Ginna meant.

"You're willing to give up your own life and love, to try and help my mother? Ginna, I could never ask so much of you."

"But you're not asking me," Ginna replied calmly. "I'm volunteering. No one is forcing anything on me. This is the thing I can do to help, and I choose to do it—for love of the one I've lived 'within' through many trials and tribulations."

"Mom would never ask such a thing of you either."

"Sh," murmured Laken. "You know this is all Ginna's idea—isn't it?" He turned and looked into the older woman's brown eyes, noticing the hints of gray beginning in her hair. "You're sure you want to do this?"

"As sure as I can be. Will you help? Will you merge Martina and me together again?"

"I guess I can. Especially since you two were merged before."

"But this time it will be the opposite. Before, I was in her body. Now she needs to be in mine."

"Does it make any difference—really?"

"I think so. She needs to be in me, so Garek won't know anything about it. He loves me, and I pray he still will. Except that by being 'within' me, Martina will also experience his love."

"And you think this will heal her? Bring her back?"

"What do you think?" Ginna turned a level gaze toward him.

"It may bring her back to reality, because she'll see the world as you do. The only problem is she'll be back in the Twenty-first Century."

"Oh, so I won't be able to pop over for a visit, will I?" Celestia said.

"No. I'm sorry," Ginna sighed. "But this is the only thing left to try."

Just as she said these words the round door opened, and Martina stepped out onto the beach sand.

"Hello? Celestia, is that really you?"

She pulled her mother into a tight embrace. "So you do know who I am?"

"Yes, I have a daughter, but her father has died." There was total desolation in Martina's voice—and Laken could hear it all too well.

"M-mom?"

"What?"

"Ginna would like to take you with her on a journey."

"But I'd rather stay here in the city." Martina's voice had the stiff, unfeeling sound of someone who was drugged. "I have a flat and a job, you know."

Ginna spoke up quickly, "The place I have in Colorado will be much more comfortable and healthy. I'd love for you to come visit me."

"Well, if you insist. But I can't stay long. Shei needs me."

"Shei?" Celestia mouthed to Laken.

"He's my friend here in Tornatoh," Martina mumbled.

"A rather intimate friend, I think," Ginna added.

"Do I need to go pack my belongings for this trip?"

"No," said Ginna. "I have everything you'll need at my house. Just take my hand, all right?"

As she was about to grab Martina's hand, they heard a voice calling to them from the shore.

"Oh, no," Ginna sighed, "It's Johan and Jael."

There was no help for it now. All they could do was stand as the two came up to them. Laken saw Johan was his livelier self, with the long white beard and dancing eyes.

"I know what you're doing, Ginna," he smiled.

"Please, don't make me stop," she sighed.

"What do you want, Nosey Old Man?" snapped Martina.

"Ah, I'm glad to see you're alert," he smiled.

Silence fell, until at last Jael spoke, "Johan thinks you have a good idea, Ginna," he said.

"Really?" She felt relief wash over her like a cooling rain.

"There is one thing that must happen first, however," Johan continued. "Martina needs to be aware of what she's really done—and what she must do next, facing the darkness. She must turn and stop running. Let's walk down to the edge of the water."

Soon all five of them were walking just above the water line. Occasionally a large wave would wash up the sand, and they either had to get their feet wet, or dance quickly up to higher ground.

Then they stopped together just above the reach of the waves and sat down on the warm sand.

"What do I need to do, Old Man?" asked Martina, weariness in her voice.

"Let's just think about it, and while we do, I believe Jael has some verses from The Book he'd like to share with us."

Silence settled around them for a few minutes. The only sounds were the incoming waves breaking on the shore and the cries of a few gulls.

"We all like sheep have gone astray," Jael's voice came softly. "Each of us has turned to his own way."

Laken took his wife's hand. Martina had closed her eyes, and he saw Ginna resting her head on her own knees.

"Your sins have caused a separation between you and the True King," whispered Jael. "Do you remember, Sis? How it was with the Redlarks?"

Martina shook her head and brushed away tears.

"Look, Mom—you can cry again," Celestia murmured, her voice hoarse.

"I'm not sure which pain is worse." Her voice quivered and then faded away.

Jael was sitting close beside his sister now. "Martina, I still love you—we all do—but especially the Lord. He's waiting for you to reopen that door you slammed in his face. Just like you did back on Terres, after Jon and I rescued you from the Redlarks."

"But Jon is dead!" she wailed.

Celestia joined them, pulling her mother into a close embrace. "He's in a beautiful place now."

"Yes, I've felt him, sis."

"Are you sure?"

"Positive," he nodded.

"I wish so much I could go to be with him," she sighed.

"That time isn't here yet," said Johan in his deepest voice.

"I know." By now Martina was shuddering with her sobs. It was all Jael and Celestia could do to hold her.

"What do you know?" Ginna asked softly.

"I know there's no good in me. I'm like King David in The Book."

"The one who took another man's wife and had the man killed to cover up his sin, right?" Laken spoke up.

"That's true," sighed Johan. "But even this wasn't an unforgivable sin. The Lord did forgive David when he confessed. I bet Jael knows the words."

Jael nodded and began to speak slowly, "It's in a song David himself wrote, Psalm fifty-one:

'Have mercy on me, O God, according to your
unfailing love blot out my transgressions. Wash
away all my iniquity, and cleanse me from my sin.'

Then Martina's voice joined with Jael's:

"'Against you, and you only have I sinned, and
done this evil in your sight…Let me hear joy and
gladness, let the bones you have crushed rejoice'."

Laken saw his wife begin to weep as she heard her mother's voice. Soon she was moving her lips, too. And before long all five of them were speaking the psalm:

"'Create in me a pure heart, O God; and renew
a steadfast spirit within me. Do not cast me away

from your presence; or take your Holy Spirit from me. Restore to me the joy of your salvation, and grant me a willing spirit'."

By this time, Martina was lying flat on the sand, her eyes staring up at the sky. Jael and Celestia were still sitting on each side of her. "I repent in dust and ashes," she sighed, almost to herself. Then her voice grew stronger: "Lord, I'm not worthy to receive you, but only say the word and I shall be healed."

"Receive the forgiveness of the Lord, my child," said Johan, placing a slightly trembling hand on her forehead. "Now you're ready to receive the gift Ginna has chosen to give you."

"But I feel like there's a weight in my heart," sighed Martina. "Shouldn't I feel forgiven?"

"Don't put too much trust in feelings. I've told you this before," said Johan. "Feelings can change too easily and deceive us."

"What *should* I trust, Old Man?"

"Trust in the True King—for he is always true to his word. Jael, tell her that other Psalm you know, number thirty-two."

"Right, sir. David wrote this one shortly after Psalm fifty-one, scholars say." He turned and looked into his sister's eyes. "It begins like this:

"So don't fear, sis—the Lord has forgiven you."

Martina was trying to wipe the flood of tears from her face as she hugged her brother tightly. "Come visit me, Jael," she whispered.

"I will," he nodded, but he glanced up at Johan with questioning eyes. Laken saw the old man made no motion to indicate an answer to this silent question.

Quietly, Laken stepped toward the two women and helped both to stand. Then Ginna moved into the spot where Celestia had been, taking hold of Martina's right hand. Seeing this, Laken took her left hand, then linked his own left with Ginna. Celestia stepped back away from their circle. Jael and Johan also moved away, and suddenly disappeared into a GAP.

The three who were joined began to shimmer with a silvery light. The last rays of sun were fading from the horizon, and Laken began to chant:

"Behold, I make all things new…Heaven and Earth will pass away, but my words will never pass away…"

The last thing Laken saw of his wife was when Martina and Ginna seemed to flow into each other.

"Laken!" he heard her scream, "Don't leave me here alone!"

For an instant, he knew she was experiencing the utter desolation her mother had been feeling. Then he felt the beach sand under his feet again. As soon as his shape became distinct, she leaped into his arms.

"Don't ever leave me like that again." She was sobbing loudly onto his shoulder.

"Hey, it's okay. I'm back. And so is Ginna—back in her own time and place."

"And my mother?"

"She isn't fully aware yet—it will take time for the drugs she's been taking to wear off."

"But she'll be all right?"

"I think so. It's a very brave and generous thing Ginna has done."

"I know," she sighed, still clinging to him. "I'm just glad I still have you, especially now that I've lost both my parents."

"You haven't really lost them."

"I know," she sighed into his chest. "But I can't go to where they are."

"Not yet, anyway," he smiled.

CHAPTER 22
BE THOU MY VISION

Be thou my vision, O Lord of my heart
Naught be all else to me save that thou art.
Thou my best thought, by day or by night.
Waking or sleeping, thy presence my light.

Laken woke to the sound of this song going through his head. Where had he heard it? Was it at a Gathering when he first came to the Indonia Out-clave? Or perhaps it was in some other life? It bothered him—how these unknown memories popped into his mind. What if they came at the wrong time?

'I know this is just one of the hazards of being a Guardian,' he sighed to himself.

Sometimes, he wondered why the King had chosen him for this task. He knew others who were stronger and more virtuous than he was—including his wife. Too often the temptations of whatever world he was in drew him away from his true mission.

As she began to stir on the sleeping mat beside him, he breathed a quick prayer, 'My Lord, thank you for sending Celestia into my life, even though I never deserved her love—or her forgiveness. And yet because she gave it, I more fully understand your grace to me, as well.'

The song continued to play in his mind, and he remembered the words of another verse:

High King of heaven when victory's won,
May I reach heaven's joys, bright heaven's sun.
Heart of my own heart, whatever befall,
Still be my vision, O ruler of all.

"I think I've heard that song before," a sleepy voice murmured beside him.

"Oh, I didn't realize I was singing aloud. Sorry if I woke you." He turned and kissed her on the cheek.

"I was already waking," she smiled at him. "Where did you learn it?"

"I'm afraid I don't remember."

"Another one of those memories you didn't know you had?"

He nodded and sighed. "It's kind of scary to think I don't know who or where I've been in other lives."

"I learned that song when I was in school, as a child in Celeton. We were told it was of Celtic origin."

"What's that?"

"It means it was originally from the British Isles—perhaps Ireland or Scotland. Maybe you were in one of those places in some other life."

"Anything's possible, I guess."

He reached over and ran a finger along her cheek. "You still look as beautiful as the day I first met you."

"Well, we're both older," she laughed. "Although it's hard to put a number on people who have crossed so many GAPs."

"Age is only a number," he smiled. "It doesn't really matter. We're just here—where we are. That's one thing I learned long ago, in some of my early missions—to live in the now, whenever that time may be."

She sat up and pulled him to her for a long kiss. "There! That's what I felt like doing in this moment." Then she looked around the small room where their sleeping mat was spread on the floor. "Where are we, by the way? I seem to have forgotten."

"That's not surprising," he chuckled. "We keep shifting around. Let me think-"

"We helped drive the Dragon into the Milky Way Black Hole," she said. "And my dad-"

Suddenly her voice disappeared.

"I'm sorry. Maybe I shouldn't have brought any of this up."

"No. It's part of where we are," she sighed. "Let's see—after that we came here to Tornatoh to try and help my mother—"

Again, her voice dissolved, and she hung her head.

"Oh, Laken, everyone I love has left my life except you."

He made no reply, but gently stroked her mussed hair.

They sat there together for a long time with her head resting on his shoulder. Then at last, he turned to look into her deep brown eyes.

"You definitely have your father's eyes," he whispered.

"And my mother's hair," she sighed, trying to comb out some of the tangles with her fingers.

"I love your hair," he chuckled softly.

"Even when it's like this?"

"Especially when it's like this."

Just as they were sinking into silence again, there was a light tap on the door. "May I come in?" The voice was low and gruff, so they knew it was Johan.

"Come in," they said together.

As the old man with the white flowing beard entered, Laken finally realized where they were—in the flat at the back of the little shop on High Street.

"Did you sleep well?" he asked.

Celestia nodded but didn't try to speak.

"I had some strange dreams," admitted Laken.

"Do you need to share them?" Johan asked.

"Uh—not yet, sir," muttered Laken. He hoped to tell them to his wife first—alone.

"He woke me with a song," murmured Celestia. "It began, 'Be thou my vision'—"

"Ah yes—an ancient Celtic hymn." The old man's eyes danced.

"What does it mean?" she asked.

"It's asking the True King to always be our guide and our light. It prays that he'll take us to our true home at last."

"You mean Heaven?"

"Oh, yes. But there's even more to be said about visions."

"My parents told me about the vision they saw of Heaven, when Eli took them to the Fountain in the Desert. I wish I could have seen it."

"Those things and many others even more wonderful will you see when the Son of Man returns."

"But when will that be?" Laken cut in quickly. "Why does he keep delaying?"

"Ah, his time is not ours, you know. He's above and beyond time, in fact. He sees time as though he's looking down on one continuous river—seeing it all, from the tiniest trickle at its source all the way to its mouth where it joins the ocean."

"That's so hard to imagine," she sighed.

"We're limited to the space and time we're currently in, aren't we?" said Laken.

"That's so—even those of us who can take shortcuts and jump across space and time," the old man nodded.

"Then why did my parents get to see a vision of Heaven?"

"The Lord must have known they'd need that glimpse to help them through the trials ahead."

Celestia's head was still down, trying to hide the tears, but Laken saw them, and brushed at them with a thumb.

"It's good to cry," whispered Johan. "Tears bring healing."

She nodded. "I know. Mom sometimes said she was too numb to cry, even when she wanted to."

"Each of your parents is in a better place now."

"But what happens next?" Laken couldn't help asking.

"You always were the anxious one," Johan rumbled. "To be honest, I'm not sure what *is* around the next bend."

"As the old saying goes," Celestia chuckled.

"I do think I should tell you the Milky Black Hole has been accelerated," Johan added.

"Oh, no! Does that mean the Dragon succeeded after all?"

"Not exactly. And your father may be a part of bringing the True King's plans to fruition."

"How do you mean?" asked Laken.

"Well, our Galaxy—this world as we know it—will soon come to an end."

"Then we did fail?"

"No, please let me finish. Now that we know there's a new anti-universe on the other side of the Black Hole, everything is different. Because of your Jon, we know that what we saw as the end is really a new beginning."

"Wow!" Laken nearly bounced with delight. "So, when this world is consumed in fire, as The Book says, it will be changed into a new heaven and earth."

"Just like it says in The Book," nodded Johan. "There is no need to fear."

"But will we still exist as ourselves?" Celestia asked, sounding confused.

"Our spirits will go on," Johan smiled. "You will still be you, and Laken will still be himself, but you'll need new heavenly bodies for this new heavenly world."

"And this is going to happen soon?" Laken asked.

"It seems so. But of course, no one knows the exact time—only God the Father."

Silence settled around them, and Celestia sat up, looking around their sleeping room. "Where's Jael?" she suddenly asked.

"I've taken him back to his wife," the old man smiled. "Someday you'll see them in the new world, too."

"Oh, I'm so glad. Raina really needs him. She's had a very rough pathway in her life."

"They need each other, Laken murmured softly into her hair.

"And I need you, Laken Meta."

After they sat in silence for awhile, Johan suddenly clapped his hands.

As Laken and his wife looked up in surprise, he grinned. "Now I need to take you two to your own places."

"Our places?" Laken had a sinking feeling. 'He can't mean he's taking us to separate places, can he?' The thought of being away from his wife sent a stab of pain through his chest. Looking over at Celestia, he saw the same fear in her eyes.

"Don't fret. The True King has need of both of you, and he knows you work better together than you do apart."

"Boy, you had me worried for a moment." Laken let his held breath out in a *whoosh*.

"But where do we belong?" Celestia asked. "It seems like we've been all over the Milky Way—and beyond—but no place has ever become our home. We're just wanderers in a world where others have roots."

Johan looked into her eyes. "This is very true, my dear. You have been privileged in this way."

"Privileged? I don't see how. Everyone else has a home and a family, but us."

"But we do have each other," Laken said quickly. "Is that what you meant, Johan?"

"That and more." The old man took each of their hands, Laken on his right and Celestia on his left. "You have no true home here because no one really does. Our ultimate home and destiny is to be with the True King in his Heaven."

"Like the last verse of the song Laken was singing when I woke," she sighed: *"High King of heaven, when victory's won, may I reach heaven's joys…"*

"Focus your hopes and dreams on that, Mr. and Mrs. Meta." His voice echoed around them, as though they were standing in some great hall, instead of the tiny flat.

Then Laken felt a breeze wafting his long, unbound hair, and he opened his eyes. What he saw took his breath away. All around them were bright colored fountains and flowering plants of every size and shape imaginable. There was no chill—or heat—in the atmosphere around them. Everything looked and felt perfect.

"Where are we?" he whispered to Johan.

"The True King has brought you to a resting place," the old man murmured. "You've been through several battles and are in need of recuperation."

"Is this Heaven?" Celestia's voice sounded incredulous.

"Not quite. Think of this as one of the anterooms of Heaven," Johan chuckled. "Your time to pass on through will come, but not quite yet, I'm told."

"Told? By the King?"

The old man's eyes flashed as he nodded to Laken.

"So that means the King still has work for us to do, right?"

"Yes. But for now, you need to regroup and prepare— by sitting here and taking all of this in. None of us knows exactly what will come next, but we do know God has it in his hands."

"Sometimes it's hard for me to keep hold of that," sighed Laken.

"He knows our every weakness," the old man smiled. "But he still has a plan and purpose for you. Here, sit and rest."

Just to their right, a low bench appeared. It was made of some kind of translucent white stone, and when they sat down, it held no chill. In fact, the material seemed to yield and mold to his body, so he felt more comfortable than any time in his life.

Turning to his left, he saw Celestia nestled close to him, smiling. "This feels perfect somehow," she whispered.

He nodded silently.

Johan stood above them and placed a hand on each of their heads. Then his deep voice seemed to float down to them, as from a cloud:

"The Lord watch between you and me, while we are absent one from another."

Laken hardly noticed when his voice faded away.

"I wonder what happens next?" Celestia murmured.

"I haven't a clue. Every time we cross another GAP, I think we'll be entering the battle for the end of the world."

"But the world just seems to keep on going, doesn't it?"

He nodded and gripped her hand. "I hope I never have to face the end without you."

"Me, too. I wish we could stay here in this wonderful place forever."

"So do I."

"What should we do?"

Just as she asked this question, they felt the presence of other people nearby. Looking up, Laken's heart warmed with pleasant surprise.

"Isn't that Jakob?" he asked his wife.

"Well, I recognize Myra." She jumped up and ran to hug the tall slender woman.

"I'm glad to meet you both at last," Myra said.

"And I finally get to see you two together. This is my husband, Laken."

"Yes, we've met," the man smiled. "We're also here in the waiting place."

"Do you know what we're supposed to do next?" Celestia asked.

"I don't think we're supposed to do anything—until the King tells us to," Jakob smiled. "We're supposed to just be—to be ready."

"That's right. He told us that way back in Jerusalem—when we were prisoners in the Citadel. And then he sent us to your time, Celestia—and that's the best thing to ever happen in any life."

Jakob and Myra smiled at them and began to move on. "No, please stay," Laken said.

Once all four were seated on the white bench, it felt just as comfortable as before, almost as though it grew to accommodate them all.

"I still wish we could just stay here," Celestia

murmured, leaning against Laken. "Do you think there really will be an end of the world?"

"Nothing lasts forever," he whispered to her.

"Are you sure? I mean isn't there supposed to be eternity?"

"I guess so," Jakob put in. "But I don't think our limited minds can understand that concept. Some things we must leave in the King's hands."

"I know," she sighed.

"Like the end of the song in my head when I woke up today," said Laken.

"If it really was today."

"Doesn't matter. The song said, *'Heart of my own heart, whatever befall'.*"

"In other words, no matter what happens."

"That's right," he smiled. "The ending says, *'Still be my vision, O Ruler of All.'*"

"That's reminding us to keep our eyes on him," Myra said.

"Yes, and then we'll learn what we need to know, *when* we need to know it," Laken added.

Celestia reached a hand up to touch his cheek. "Then, I'm going to stay right here, until I'm told it's time to move," she smiled.

Just then, a brilliant light flashed above them, followed by a huge thunderclap. At first the sound was so loud they wanted to cover their heads.

Music began to reach their ears, and words became decipherable:

Lo, he comes with clouds descending,
Once for every sinner slain;
Thousand, thousand saints attending,
Swell the triumph of his train:
Alleluia, alleluia, now our Lord returns to reign.

And then they heard a voice saying, "Don't let your hearts be troubled. Trust in God, trust also in me. In my Father's house are many rooms; if it were not so, I would have told you. I am going to prepare a place for you… I will come back and take you to be with me."

"But Lord, how long?" Laken heard his wife murmur.

"Yes, Lord," he added. "It seems we've been waiting forever."

"Oh, my children, not forever!" There was almost a chuckle in the booming voice that answered them. "Behold, I *am* coming soon!"

CHAPTER 23
HOME AWAY FROM HOME

Ginna and Garek were sitting on the front porch of the little brown house on the edge of Deer Path, Colorado. The breeze was wafting coolly through their hair.

"These nights don't come very often, do they? Most times it's too hot or too cold to sit out here."

"Sorry I can't control the weather like they did in your century," she giggled.

Taking a sip of wine, he smiled into her eyes. "Oh, I don't need all that extra technology to complicate my life. I prefer it here—and now. Seems like there's more freedom in this time."

"I'm glad you feel that way," Ginna sighed with contentment. "I couldn't do much to change it."

"Do you think Jon or Jael may come back here again? And if they did, would you want to go?"

She looked down at her hands for several minutes, wondering how much she should disclose in her answer.

Besides, she wasn't really sure what she *would* do if one of the GAP-crossers came back to this Twenty-first Century.

"Hey, what's wrong? Did my question upset you?"

"Not really. It's just I'm not quite sure what I'd do. For one thing, Jon won't be coming back. He was pulled into the Black Hole in the battle with the Dragon."

"I guess you haven't told me about that yet." Garek's voice was full of disbelief. "You mean Jon is dead? I didn't even know."

"It's more complicated than that," she sighed. "From this point in time, he hasn't actually been born yet."

"Hey, this is really confusing."

"That's one reason I didn't bring it up. It really doesn't affect us here and now." Though while she said these words she was thinking to herself, 'I can never let him know the whole story—of how Martina is living 'within' me. That's a secret I *must* keep—for all three of our sakes.'

She reached over and took his hand before she spoke again:

"Besides, Jael has worries of his own, so I never want him to feel the need to come back here. I think things are better left as they are—them in the future, and us here in the past."

"But that leaves me as the only one who isn't in the correct century, you know."

'You aren't the only one out of their own time,' she thought.

By now her hands were getting clammy, and she could feel the twitch in her left eyelid which always acted up when she was nervous. Trying to step away from this uncomfortable subject, she stood and walked over to the porch rail.

"With Danny gone, there's really no reason for Jael to come back—and he can't cross the GAP alone, anyway, since he's not firstborn," she added.

"What about Danny's sons? I seem to have picked up hints that they've done some GAP-crossing of their own."

"Well, yeah, but that's with Shadow—their big black dog. Since the Dragon's been defeated, I don't think they'll be needed."

"Okay, I'm confused again. The Dragon is the Devil, right?"

She nodded, encouraging him to go on.

"If he's not defeated until the future, he's still around now—isn't he."

"He's been around since Eve took the forbidden fruit in the Garden."

"So that's more than just a mythological story?"

"I believe it's true. It explains why humans can never be basically good."

He sighed and moved to stand beside her. "I spent a lot of my life hoping human beings were intrinsically good, and if we could just educate them, all would get better."

"But it hasn't turned out that way, has it?"

"Unfortunately, no—not in my time or yours. Though since I've lived in both, I think your time is actually better than mine."

"That's how I feel. Things will go from bad now to worse in the future," she sighed.

"So, will the world of the Thirty-first Century get better since the Dragon is gone?"

"I hope so. Shortly before I left, Johan told us—"

"Us—who?"

She took a quick breath, afraid she might give herself away. "He was talking to Laken and Celestia, and me."

"Okay, so what did he tell you? I've never met this old hermit, you know."

"He's very wise," she said quickly, glad to shift the subject. "He doesn't know everything, or so he says. I think he withholds information sometimes, saying we need to learn some things for ourselves. Anyway, he was telling us there are three forces working to pull humans down into the darkness and away from God."

"And those are?"

"The Devil, the World (or what some in your time call the System), and humankind's own selfish nature."

"So one down—the Dragon—and two still to go."

"Johan says people can't change overnight. It will take time for those other two forces to be overcome."

"It seems to me the big battle was won, but now come

all the little skirmishes with soldiers who haven't heard the war is over."

She chuckled as he said this. "You know, I've heard stories of lone soldiers still fighting on—such as isolated Japanese in the South Pacific, after the world war ended."

"I've heard of that, too. I wonder if it will be the case with this war."

"But we aren't in that future yet. We're back here nearly a thousand years before."

"It seems like the Devil isn't as strong here as he will be then."

"I wonder if there's anything we can do to help our friends in the future," Ginna said quietly.

"I don't think we can do much from here."

"But each person should do what they can," she added. Her heart began to race, as she realized these words weren't her own. 'Martina? Is that you?' she said to her mind.

'Yes, I think I'm finally back. And now I know what a generous thing you've done for me. I'll never do anything to jeopardize it—or you and Garek.'

Just then, Garek took her hand and rubbed his thumb across her knuckles softly. "I guess that's where prayer comes in," he whispered. "If we keep in touch with the Lord, we'll be ready and able to do what he calls us to do."

She nodded in reply, and standing up on her tiptoes, she kissed him gently.

***

The evening sky was beginning to fill with stars on another night a few weeks later. Ginna was happy when Garek suggested they go to the little community church where David was ministering now.

As they got out of the car in the parking lot, she saw Annemarie waving to her from the church door.

"I've saved you a seat, Mom and Dad."

Garek smiled as his daughter spoke. "This is the only place in all the universe where I want to be," he whispered to Ginna.

Once they were settled on a bench, close to the front of the little sanctuary, Ginna saw Annemarie's guitar sitting on its stand just to the left of the lectern.

"Look," she whispered. "I think Annie is going to sing tonight."

He grinned at her and patted her hand.

First David stepped to the lectern, opened the Bible, and spoke, "Today is a day to give thanks for the many blessings the Lord brings us in our lives. Sometimes those things don't seem to be blessings at first—but rather trials and tribulations."

'He has no idea what kinds of tribulations we've seen, does he, Ginna?'

'Martina?'

'Yes. Don't worry, I won't give you away. But it's been

hard sometimes, hasn't it? Waiting for those trials to finally turn around into blessings?'

"And so," David's voice was saying, "My wife has a hymn to share. It was written during one such time. The people who wrote it had been through much persecution, but now at last were freed to worship God unhindered once again."

Annemarie stepped up to the front and put the guitar's strap around her shoulder. Then she strummed her opening chords, and her voice rang out clear and strong:

We gather together to ask the Lord's blessing;
He chastens and hastens his will to make known.
The wicked oppressing now cease from distressing:
Sing praises to his name—He forgets not his own.

As her daughter was returning to her seat, Ginna's eyes filled with happy tears. 'I never thought I'd live to see this day,' she said to herself.

Garek turned to smile at her, and whispered, "Pretty talented daughter we have, huh?"

She nodded and took his hand. "I've received so much more than I ever expected. There were so many dark years."

"But since we've been through those dark times, the light we have now is all the more precious."

She just leaned into his shoulder. And deep inside her mind she heard a quiet sigh:

'I understand now what it means to be truly saved by the Lord's grace. He gave me his love freely—especially when I'd done nothing to deserve it. In fact, I've done almost everything wrong.'

'Don't say that,' Ginna said in her thoughts. 'I'm really no better than you. We're both learning to face the great unknown, as well as the darkness within.'

'None of us can ever do enough to earn the Lord's love. He just gives it, and the most we can do is live in gratitude. It says in The Book that we can love because he, the True King, loved us first'.'

'I know, Martina. He's helped me learn through many years of hard lessons, too.'

"That's why I can love you as a true friend, Ginna. And why I thank you with all my heart for letting me be a part of your joy.'

CHAPTER 24
POSTLUDE

Ginna was surprised to hear the knock on the front door. Garek was napping in the back bedroom, and she wasn't expecting anyone. When she opened the door, she was even more surprised to see a lanky, red-haired young man.

"Evin?"

"Yes, Aunt Ginna, it's me."

"Is something wrong?" There must be something going on, for her nephews didn't visit much, especially since they'd graduated from high school and gone on to college.

Dain, the older of her deceased brother's sons, had been attending the university in Boulder for three years now. Evin, who graduated with honors from high school, was now attending Colorado State, in nearby Fort Collins.

"I'm okay," Evin murmured, but Ginna could see trouble in his eyes.

"Well, come in." She made her voice sound casual, as

though this visit was exactly what she'd expected when she awoke this morning.

Evin tried to smile as he stepped into the living room and planted his lanky frame on the floral couch.

"Would you like something to drink? I have cookies I baked this morning, too."

"A cup of coffee and cookies sounds great." He was still trying to smile.

She had the few minutes in the kitchen to compose herself, as she got two cups of hot coffee. Soon there were two steaming mugs on the coffee table, along with a plate of cookies.

"Chocolate chip, my favorite. You must have known I was coming," said her nephew.

"Well, if I did, it was only subconsciously. You boys haven't been by this old house in quite awhile."

"I'm sorry," he dropped his gaze. "I've been busy, I guess."

"Hey, it's okay. You have a lot going on now, and only so much time to do it. So, to what do I owe this visit?"

He looked directly into her eyes as he spoke this time. "I'm worried about Dain. Ever since we got back from the GAP-crossings he's been really quiet. He used to talk to me about everything, but now he's shutting me out of his life."

"How do you mean?"

"Well, when we were in high school, we'd double date. Taking a couple of girls out for dinner or a movie—and to school dances, of course. But now, he never wants to talk about who he's dating. It's like he doesn't want me to know."

"He is in Boulder, and you're in Fort Collins. Maybe he just has a different circle of friends now."

"I guess so. But still, he used to tell me about what he was doing, and now there's no communication at all."

As he said this, a sharp pain stabbed across her mind. She remembered this pain from the mind-blending she's experienced when she was traveling with Celestia long ago. Perhaps some deeply-buried memory was forcing its way out—like it had then. Putting her hand to her forehead, she closed her eyes.

"What's wrong?" Evin's voice was panicky. "Are you sick?"

"No, I just felt a sudden headache. It's okay."

"I didn't know you got headaches like that. Dad did—uh, before they found the cancer."

She saw the fear growing in his eyes. "Don't worry, it's not that kind of pain. It's more like I just remembered something that I wanted to forget."

"What do you mean?"

"Well, if it's the one that came to me before, it's a painful one. From back when my parents got divorced."

"Oh, yeah. Dad won't ever talk about that. Or about his father, who left you guys and never came back."

She was shaking her head now, as words began to flood her mind:

"How can you do this to us, Tim? You said you loved me. We have two children now."

"What did you say?" Evin asked, interrupting her thoughts.

"I think I'm reliving a conversation my mother had with our father. His name was Tim Parker."

"And he was my grandfather?"

She nodded. "He divorced my mom when I was about eleven. Your father was only seven. Our dad never used any of his visitation rights, and both of us wondered why he totally disappeared from our lives."

"And you never found out why?"

"Actually, I did. Later. When I was about seventeen. It was a crazy time. I was pregnant, and I had no idea how it happened."

"Wasn't that something to do with the GAP?"

"Yes, it happened when I was 'within' Martina. She met Garek, and—"

"Dad did tell me about that."

"Good. Then I won't have to explain it all."

"So, if this isn't the painful memory, what is?"

"It has to do with your Grandfather Parker, my dad. He told our mother that he was leaving her for a lover, but it wasn't another woman. It was a man."

"My dad never mentioned that."

"That's because he never knew, Evin. Mom made me promise not to tell him."

"I guess being gay or bisexual was harder to understand back then, wasn't it?"

She nodded, trying to keep her eyes on him. "Things have changed a lot in the past forty years, that's for sure. If my parents had lived now, maybe it wouldn't have been so hard."

"Your mom must have been really upset, if she left that kind of memory in your head.

"I guess so. I was more hurt by the divorce than the reasons behind it. I loved Dad, and it was hard to lose him, especially the way he just cut us off."

"I hope Dain doesn't cut me off. I need to find some way to let him know I understand. Do you think he's gay, too? Is that why you told me this memory?"

"I have no idea, Evin. It just came out. It's been buried in my subconscious for a long time. It only resurfaced one other time, when Laken—"

"Oh yeah, the one who helped us defeat the Dragon."

"Yes, he did this mind-reading thing with me," she sighed. "You know, Dain has always been a sensitive and caring young man."

"Yeah. He really values relationships, and he empathizes better than I do."

"Those are often seen as feminine characteristics, I've read."

"I know," he nodded.

"I'm not sure what to tell you," she sighed. "My generation has a different world-view than yours."

"Well, Dain is still my brother, and I love him. I wish there was some way I could let him know that."

She reached across and took his hand. "I'm sure you'll find a way. I hope I haven't made things worse by telling you this."

"It's okay. I'm an adult now.

This brought a smile to her lips, hearing this nineteen-year-old sounding so grown up. "That's true. You've been through things no one else in this century has—like battling the Red Dragon in the center of the Milky Way."

"That's not something I tell my friends," he grinned.

"I don't tell friends how my daughter was conceived, either."

He drained the last of his coffee, and seemed ready to leave. But then he took a deep breath. "There's one more thing I wanted to tell you. It's something no one else will understand, except maybe Dain.

"What is it?"

"Shadow is missing. I think he's gone off to die alone."

"Oh, I'm so sorry." She reached over and took his hand.

Before she said another word, he grabbed her into a tight hug. 'Doesn't matter if he's almost twenty,' she thought. 'He still needs some comfort—like any child.'

"What makes you think he's dead?" she asked, once he relaxed his grip on her.

"Well, I've read animals do this sometimes when they know the end is near. And it seems like Shadow has been limping and showing his age lately. He doesn't play, or chase sticks I throw anymore. He sleeps most of the time, and his muzzle is turning white. I thought Guardians never got old," he muttered.

"Maybe they have to find another form when the body they're in gets old. I don't know much about any of this. Didn't Shadow tell you anything?"

"No." She could hear heartbreak in his voice now. "He's only talked to me a little since we came back from the big battle with the Red Dragon—you were there."

"Yes, I was trying to stay on the back of a phoenix and hanging on for dear life. I don't think I was much help. Jon took our places—Celestia and I—so he was the one pulled into the Black Hole."

"I think those events were what the King meant to happen all along. Shadow did tell me that. And he said Jon was *not* dead, but instead had made it possible for others to pass through the portal to the other side of our Milky Way's Black Hole. But after a few months, Shadow stopped sending me messages. He began to act like an ordinary dog."

"Did he tell you anything else?" She wasn't sure she wanted Shadow, a Guardian in the form of a dog, to know her deepest secret.

Again, Evin looked into her eyes, and she saw the same color and shine she'd always seen in her brother Danny's eyes. Before she knew it, tears seeped into her eyes.

"I'm sorry if this is upsetting."

"No, please tell me. It's just you remind me so much of your father."

"Usually people say that about Dain, not me," he dropped his eyes.

"Well, they're only looking at the surface features. I see my younger brother every time I look into your eyes."

"Well anyway, Shadow did tell me about you and Martina—what you did for her."

"Oh." Suddenly this was all she had the breath to say.

"You're an amazingly loving person. That's why Shadow said I should come to—if he was ever—uh, you know—"

"And now you're sure he's gone?"

The redhead nodded mutely, tears glistening in his eyes.

"So, you know my secret, but Uncle Garek must never know," she whispered hoarsely.

He nodded again. "Have you heard anything from the—future?" he asked at last.

"Not for a few years now. Sometimes, I used to hear Celestia in my dreams, but that was long ago, when you were just starting high school. I don't ever hear Martina's voice in my mind now—at least not when I'm awake. I'm beginning to wonder if she's gone, too."

"Wouldn't you notice if she suddenly left you?"

"I used to think so, but it's happened so gradually. I wonder if somehow her love for Jon has drawn her to where he is. She kept saying in my mind that she still loved Garek. And in a way, she did. But it wasn't like the love she and Jon shared. That transcended space and time. I know because I experienced it what I was 'within' her psyche."

"That kind of goes with one of the last things Shadow told me."

"What was that?"

"He said the time for crossing the GAP to the future was drawing to a close."

"Really?"

"He thought all of those times the GAP-crossers came to you guys were—uh—during the time they were first on Earth, before the System came back."

"And that time is gone?"

"Yeah, it seems to be. I think maybe they've all followed Jon into that Black Hole—through the Portal."

"You mean they've all been lost?" Her breath and pulse were racing now.

"I don't think they're really lost. Shadow hinted they were now in a brand new, totally opposite place. He called it the Anti-universe."

"Does this mean they've gone to Heaven?"

"I'm not sure, but he said it's a wonderful place. He kept telling me not to be sad—that we'd all be together again somehow, someday."

As he said this, he reached out, took her hands, and placed them on his head. Her fingertips began to tingle, and she opened her eyes wider, looking directly into his.

Before she could even speak a bright flash filled her mind, and then she could smell and taste something too delicious to be real. Musical sounds began to ring in her ears. Her arms trembled, and her eyes filled with tears of joy. Then she dropped her gaze—and everything disappeared into thin air.

"Did you see it?" he whispered.

"Yes, I think so. What is it?"

"I don't know what to call it. Shadow showed it to me and told me I'd know when it was time to share with you. What do you think it means?"

"It seems to be a wondrous place—more beautiful than any mere human can imagine," she said softly.

"It was like that for me, too. I guess Shadow wanted us to know they were all okay."

"Who's there? Did you see any faces?" Now her heart was pounding as though it would burst out of her chest.

"No, but I have this feeling everyone we've lost is there—whether they came from the future or this time."

"Your dad, too?"

"It seems like I could hear him. I felt his presence—or something. I think I met Grandma Lauren, too." His voice dropped to a mere whisper.

"You never knew her. She died before you were even born."

He nodded, and lifted her hands from his head. "Still, I'm sure it was her. She reminded me of you."

"Oh."

"Shadow said someday we'd meet even those we never knew, for they're part of our beings and inheritance—past, present and future."

"So perhaps you'll see Shadow again someday."

He brushed at his cheeks and tried to smile.

"And Shadow told you the GAP-crossings were over?"

"For now," he said. "They've all moved into another existence, and it's impossible to cross the GAP from there to here. At least that's the best I could make of what he told me."

"It does feel a bit lonely now, doesn't it?"

"You mean—because we know they can never come back for us?"

"I feel like an orphan," she sighed. "But I know I shouldn't. I have you and Garek. Still, it feels strange. I hope Martina has finally found herself and come out of depression."

"If she's left you, then maybe that's a good sign."

She nodded and sighed, "I miss her sometimes, but if she's happier now, then it's for the best."

They sat in silence for a long time then, each trying to sort through their own thoughts.

Ginna recognized a deep emptiness in her heart as the silence continued. And then she remembered when she'd felt this before.

"Evin, I think I know some of how you feel. It's like

when Martina and I were separated the first time—after I'd been 'within' her for so long."

"It feels like half of you is gone, doesn't it?"

She nodded and reached for his hand. "When I had to come back here without her, I felt desolate, but then I was also confused about being pregnant."

Now it was his turn to squeeze her hand reassuringly. "It's like I can't remember a time when Shadow wasn't in my mind. But now he's gone. Do you think perhaps he's gone to that Anti-universe, too?"

"I hope so," she sighed. "I've been having this empty feeling a lot lately. That's why I feel Martina has left me."

"Maybe someone else took her with them—like Laken and Celestia."

"Or Shadow—"

She looked into his eyes and sighed. A stillness settled on them from above like a gray fog, and she suddenly noticed she was looking up into his face. 'When did you grow so tall, Evin?' she said to herself.

Still the silence enveloped them until he finally spoke again, "It makes me want to know when the Lord's Second Coming will be. Then we *know* we'll be with the True King, and all the Believers, forever."

"That's true," she smiled slightly. "But it hasn't come yet—and no one knows when it will be. And from what we've seen, the world lasts for at least another thousand years."

"There have been a lot of strange and foolish cases in the past of people who thought they knew when the Lord was coming," he added.

"That's for sure. Many people have been deceived, or at least confused, by so-called prophets who claim to know."

"Why do you think the Lord is taking so long?"

"Well, the Bible says he's not willing for anyone to perish—or die without him. He *is* waiting for a time only he knows. But he also tells us to always be ready—not to be caught napping."

"A few months before he died, Dad told my brother something we should never forget," he murmured. "What is it?"

"He said to always be prepared—*'Semper Paratus.'* He made a drawing in our barn that says it, too. Dain showed it to me right after the funeral. I'd like to take you to see it sometime, if you'll come."

"Certainly I will," she said quickly. Her heart began to race again as she thought of seeing something written by her deceased brother.

Evin wasn't finished yet, however. "Another time Dad told me, 'The day you die—whether it's soon or late—before the Lord comes again or not—that's your Second Coming Day, *your* Day of the Lord.'"

Again, they sat in silence, this time holding onto each other's hands.

"I'm so glad you shared all this with me."

"It's what Shadow wanted," he half-smiled.

"You know, I'm certain your big black dog has gone off to that Portal himself," she murmured.

"I hope so."

"Either way, you'll see him again, I think."

He smiled a bit more. "And I still have Splash to ride. He's not a unicorn anymore, but he's a good horse. Want to come horseback riding with me, Aunt Ginna?"

"I'd love to."

EPILOGUE

I, Jael, have been appointed to speak for my family and friends—given a last opportunity to communicate with your world. Jon and Martina said that it should be me because I was the one who began the telling of this Saga, *The Peaks at the Edge of the World*.

Yet, don't think this is the ending of the stories, for in every end there's a new beginning—on the other side of the singularity, or portal. The only difference is someone in your world will have to tell them, for all of us from this story have moved to the true "Beyond" – far past any of the things we before considered "the edge of the world."

We thought we knew more answers than we really did. At first, our hopes were set on climbing the towering Peaks on our planet Terres. Then we tried to get beyond our planetary bonds. As we wandered through charted— and uncharted—spaces in our galaxy, we found another goal to strive for—the location of Maia, the planet most thought mythical. And so, at last we found our way to Mother-Earth.

But this was not the true Maia (or mother) after all. In a few short decades the System 'rediscovered' this lost place and began to subjugate it all over again. I became a prisoner of this dark force rising, and languished in a prison so deep that time had no meaning—it was a Time Nexus. When I was rescued, through valiant efforts of friends I knew, the dark force had taken the form of a dreadful Red Dragon. Even my son, Jace, did battle with this beast.

Now all these things are behind me. In fact, I can turn in the Circle of Time and see them back there—some bright and shining moments, and others dark and fearful. The Dragon has been sent to the Lake of Fire where he belongs. And each of the dear ones in my life has been transmuted into this new place of opposite-life and anti-matter—the Anti-universe.

At last, I understand that our original search for Maia was not accurately focused. Maia, as we now know, was the eldest of the Pleiades, the seven sisters, and the seven-fold Spirit of the Creator God, who gave birth to all the universes. So, when we thought we'd found her, we finally realized we needed to search beyond her to the true source of all life—the Creator.

And because our Creator is above and beyond the material universes, we need to move our awareness into a higher plane, as well.

When I look around, not with physical eyes but

mental ones, I sense each of the bright bodies around me. Some call them stars, but they're higher beings—and so much more than mere gaseous globes of atomic particles. Each one I look on has a unique blend of brightness and colors of the visible and invisible spectrum. And because I'm one of them now, I can recognize each as a person I knew in the old world we inhabited before.

Yes, each one has come here in their own appointed time—my parents, my siblings, my wife and son, and dear friends, old and new. A fresh flash of energy courses through me, and all around me, each time a new one comes to this promised place.

Some call this place "Heaven" but it's much more. No one can find words that fitly describe it. Each person, hearing or reading these words of mine, will have to wait until his or her time comes to fully understand all this—all the wonders of energies, lights, sounds. Ancient poets were the closest when they talked of 'the music of the spheres'.

It's good to be reunited with Daniel, my forerunner from the Twenty-first Century. We were as close as any two friends could be, for he lived 'within' me, experiencing all I felt and did, for several years. He and his son were among the ones who came to rescue me from the Time Nexus and the Dragon.

I think it no coincidence that both our names end with 'El'— the Hebrew word that means 'god and lord'. For throughout our lives, both together and apart, we've sought to point others to the True Lord, who loves his people beyond all measure.

Our watchword is from The Book, in a section written by another Daniel:

"And they that be wise shall shine as the brightness
of the firmament; and they that turn many
to righteousness, as the stars forever and ever."
— Daniel 12:3

As I watch another 'star' join us, I remember a vision I had long ago, as a child in the Redlarks Camp of Terres. I'd gone there to find my runaway sister, but she had no memory of me. And so, I sought to find meaning in the Pavilion of the Priests. I remember vividly the part of the vision when I was thrown against a huge stone looming out of an ocean, and I broke apart into numberless stars. But in this vision, I myself—Jael—ceased to exist.

However, that last part of the vision was false, for even though I shine with the stars now, I am still of the same essence I was before. I haven't merged with some vague entity or oneness. Each of us is as unique and individual as we always were. And an even greater wonder is this: though there are stars beyond trillions, the Creator knows each of us by name.

I am still Jael.

The biggest difference now is I can look upon the things of God with more understanding. At some wondrous times, I can even hear the Voice, as it moves across the underlying music of the spheres, and among the sons and daughters of the morning:

> *"Beloved, now we are the sons of God, and it does*
> *not yet appear what we shall be: but we know*
> *that, when he shall appear, we shall be like him;*
> *for we shall see him as he is."* — I John 3:2

And so we know, as we are known.

"VOICES IN THE PAST"

CHAPTER ONE
MAGIC IN THE NIGHT

I like to watch my shadow on the ground as I walk, the wind tossing my curly hair upward and outward. I can see the ends of it waving against the dry buff of the grass on the school playground. I guess short hair isn't so bad, after all. At first, it felt strange to have it cut, after having long hair most of my childhood. But Mom says I look more mature this way. It's a non-descript brown, though. Dad says it's like his Aunt Ginna's hair. I wish I could dye it a rich burgundy, but my parents say I'm too young. A lot of kids my age dye their hair, but I don't want to argue with Mom and Dad, so I make the best of it.

Flinging these thoughts away, I toss my head back

like a wild horse and break into a run on the street leading home.

Today my younger brother Ian is meeting me halfway down the block and waving at me wildly. When I reach him, he pulls me into the exuberant embrace of a five-year-old, and begins a steady babble of questions:

"What did you do at school today, Cinda? Did you see any Hobbits down by the creek? Do you think we could take a walk in the woods after supper? Will we ever get to go camping?"

"Hey, slow down." I ruffle his curly red hair and watch the wind finish what I started. For an instant, I see our dad, who has the same color hair and greenish hazel eyes. "I can't answer twenty-million questions at once. And Hobbits are imaginary, remember?" I take a deep breath. "Where do you want me to start?"

He swings in beside me, holding my hand tightly. "It doesn't matter. I'm just glad you're home. I miss you on school days."

As I smile down at him, I feel the strong connection we've always had. The seven years between us always seem to melt away when we're together. I don't even care that my school friends think it's strange to be such close friends with a little boy, even if he is my brother. But of all my friends, Ian is the one I feel most comfortable with. I can talk to him about anything and know that despite his young age, he somehow understands.

Mom says he has some kind of sixth sense like our dad. Sometimes I ask her more about this, but she won't tell anything else. "Dad is the one who'll decide when you're old enough," is all she ever says.

One day this past summer, I met Dad in the driveway right after he got home from work and pulled him around the back side of the groundcar's charging station. "What is Mom talking about?" I demanded. "Are you psychic, or something? She thinks Ian has a sixth sense like you. What does she mean?"

Dad looked into my eyes for an instant, but then he turned his gaze down to the grass at our feet. "I wish your mom wouldn't talk to you about it," he sighed, almost to himself. "Look, I promise I'll tell you when you're old enough. It's complicated."

"But I'm almost thirteen already."

"All right," he smiled. "You can ask me again when you're a teenager, okay?"

I let out a deep sigh. Same old brush off. And he knows as well as I do that my birthday is eight months off.

Now as I remember this, I look down at Ian and see how his hair glows in the setting sun. There's something almost other-worldly about it. Why does he seem more than just a child?

Sometimes when we sit talking, especially in the back yard under a sky full of stars, the years fall away from us, and we become two beings existing in all time—traveling from star to star—instead of a twelve-year-old girl and a five-year-old boy.

I shake my head slightly as we walk up the driveway. Am I crazy, or is it just my imagination? Then I realize Ian hasn't re-voiced any of his many questions, and I look down into his face.

He smiles up at me and says, "You were thinking."

Just as simple as that. It's like he can somehow read my mind. Now I can see the shine of stars in his eyes. Tonight could be one of those magical nights, so I say, "Let's ask Mom if we can sleep out in the yard tonight. After all, it's Friday."

"A-a-ll right!" He draws the words out as he dashes through the back door ahead of me. "Mom!" I hear him calling. "Can Cinda and me get out the tent?"

"Ian, say it correctly: '*May* Cinda and *I* get out the tent?'," Mom is saying as I walk in.

"Oh, okay—may Cinda and I—can we please?"

Mom turns and shrugs at me. "Where did I go wrong?" She rolls her eyes, but I see the smile hiding there. "We'll see after supper, Ian," she adds. "Now wash up."

He grins as he runs for the sink. I can tell he's seen her smile, too.

After supper, Dad helps us get out the old canvas tent that looks like a square umbrella, and we set it up in the backyard. He doesn't say much, and I can tell he must be tired from a long week at work. I'm not exactly sure what he does, except that he works at an office in Denver and drives over an hour to get there. Most days Mom has to save his supper for later because he can't get home in time to eat with us. At least he got home early today.

"Dad?"

"Yes?"

"Can we go camping in the mountains someday?"

I hear him sigh and see how he tries to smile. "I hope so. We need a better tent than this one, though."

"Like what?" asks Ian.

"One with a real floor to keep the damp out and the warmth in," Dad mutters. "The nights get cold in the mountains. And we'd need a real zipper for closing the door—to keep out the insects."

"Have you ever been camping, Dad?"

He turns to me, and I see his eyes flash. "My brother Dain and I used to go when we were young. But now we're too busy with our jobs and families. Besides, Dain and his family live far away now, since they moved to Montana."

"Was your camping before Grandpa Parker died?" asks Ian.

I see Dad flinch as he turns toward Ian. He opens his mouth, but then closes it and just nods.

Silence floats between the three of us, and Dad rises to his feet. "I need to go talk to Mom. You two can handle things from here."

"Sure." I try to make my voice sound cheerful as he walks toward the house. "You need to remember not to ask about Grandpa Parker," I whisper to my brother as we crawl into the tent and begin to spread our blankets out to cover the grass.

"Yeah, I forgot."

I decide to change the subject. "I wish we could visit Uncle Dain in Montana. I've heard it's a really neat place."

"Me too."

"Yeah, I wonder why Dad isn't close to his brother," I sigh. "Seems to me they hardly ever talk."

I look up at Ian as I finish and see how the rising full moon is shining through his hair, looking like a halo.

"Do you think he'll ever let us go camping in the mountains, like he used to?"

"I don't know. It seems to remind him too much of Grandpa and how he died too young, before Dad was even in high school."

"It would be hard, wouldn't it, if one of our parents were to die soon?"

A chill runs down my spine. "Let's not talk like that. It might bring bad luck."

He doesn't reply but turns and looks wistfully at the blue-black of the evening sky. I move over next to him in the tent doorway, following his gaze. We sit in silence a long time, watching as the stars begin to appear one by one.

I hear a humming sound and realize it's my own voice.

"I wonder if the stars really sing," he whispers.

"You mean like the Bible says they did at Creation?"

"Yeah."

Quiet settles around us again.

"Cinda?"

"Huh?"

"Sometimes I can almost hear them, but not quite."

"Me, too. It's like you only hear them when you quit trying too hard. Then it happens, kind of by itself, just for a moment."

"I think this is one of those nights," he whispers.

I don't say anything, enjoying the silence. Instead I take his hand.

His voice comes again, "It's the kind of night that feels like Narnia is right across the yard. If you walked over there at just the right time, you'd walk into it, like Lucy went in through the wardrobe."

I draw a sharp breath. 'Lucy? That's Mom's name. Could there be some kind of connection?' But I push this thought out of my mind. 'Don't get carried away. He's just a child and has a big imagination,' I tell myself.

His voice begins to speak again, and it suddenly seems far away, even though he's still right beside me, "Maybe it's Middle Earth," his voice begins to quaver. "I feel like I can almost see it. Look—over there. I see something moving."

I follow his pointing finger and draw in a sharp breath. "Tell me what you see."

"It's an open plain of tall grass. With moonlight. And some huge animals moving—eating the grass, I think."

As I squeeze his hand more tightly I can see strange shapes looming where our house should be. But then I blink, and in that split-second it's gone. All I can see is our back porch.

"Wait," he cries. "Oh no, it's all gone."

I feel him trembling and pull him gently into my arms. "It's okay. I saw it too—the dark shapes and the tall grass."

"Did you really?"

I nod but wonder if I'm just echoing what he told me. Did I really see something?

While I'm rocking him on my lap, I begin humming a tune that just popped into my head.

"Cinda, what's that song?" he murmurs.

"I don't know. Do you?"

"No, but I have a feeling we will someday. This is kind of scary, isn't it? I wonder if things like this happen to other people."

"Except in books?"

"Yeah."

"Mom says you have something like Dad," I find myself saying, before I realize I shouldn't.

"We need to ask Dad about it." He almost jumps up.

"Not now." I pull him down into my lap again. "I've already asked Dad, and he won't tell me anything. He said to wait until I'm older. Besides, I think I've just filled your head with too many magical stories and books. They're only pretend, you know."

"I don't know," he sighs. "Sometimes they seem so real in my mind. And you said you saw what I did."

I try to think of an answer to give him, but my mind has gone blank.

"Tell me a story—please."

"Oh, all right. Which one would you like?"

"Tell me about how the morning stars sang together."

"Okay. Well, in the beginning of all time, God…"

His eyes are closed as he lies there with his head in my lap. But I know he can hear me as I speak softly into the night.

THANK YOU

Thank you for joining me. If you liked the story and have a minute to spare, I would appreciate an honest review or comment on the page or site where you purchased the book.

Reviews from readers like you make a huge difference to helping new readers find stories similar to The Peaks series: *Where All Worlds End.*

Thank you!

M. F. Erler

ABOUT THE AUTHOR

M.F. (Mary Frances) Erler is a music teacher, outdoor educator, and author of fantasy fiction and non-fiction. Her teaching career has spanned over 25 years, and she has been writing most of her life. Her first Christian-based science-fiction book, "The Peaks at the Edge of the World" has been re-written and revised in 2017.

Erler has been writing most of her life. In fact, some of the characters in *The Peaks Saga* were initially conceived in her youth. Her lifelong goal has been to bring spiritual ideas into fantasy-fiction, in the spirit of writers like J.R.R. Tolkien and C.S. Lewis. She enjoys public speaking and sharing her faith journey. She is an approved speaker for Women's Connections, a Stonecroft Ministry.

Now that she has published the ***The Peaks Saga,*** she is embarking on a new venture in historical fiction, where her modern-day characters time-travel back into the lives of their ancestors. So, in the future, watch for more tales in *Journeys Beyond the Peaks.*

Her books are designed to appeal to young adults and all who are young at heart. Among her many hobbies, Erler especially enjoys travel. She has been to several countries, including China, New Zealand, the British Isles, and Western Europe, as well as Canada, Mexico, Jamaica, and 43 of the 50 States. Her favorite mode of travel is cruising, but her current favorite place is her home in Montana.

Along with fantasy, true science, and science fiction, she is also a student of history, comparative religion, ecology, and music. Previous publications include non-fiction articles in *Today's Christian Parent,* and *Social Studies and the Young Learner,* as well as poems and short sketches in Standard Publishing Program Books. In addition, she has produced *Music in God's World,* a music curriculum for preschools, and *Wonders of Creation, an Environmental Education Curricula* for use in schools and camp settings. She has worked as a newspaper reporter and columnist, and was writer for various U.S. Forest Service publications, including being in charge of producing the book, *Targhee Lodgepole-Tragedy or Opportunity?*

She has a Bachelor of Science in Environmental Education and Biology from Colorado State University, and a Masters of Music Education from Concordia University-Chicago. In her senior year of high school, she was awarded a prize for her writing by the National Council of Teachers of English, the Quill and Scroll Award for Journalism, and a National Merit Scholarship.

Her love of singing has led to participation in many choirs and Acapella groups, which enabled her to perform at two International Sweet Adelines conventions in Nashville and Houston. She sang with these women's barbershop groups for 18 years. Hobbies include reading, singing, playing several musical instruments, and teaching piano and guitar lessons. She and her husband have two adult children. All make their home in the northwest.

You are invited to connect with the author at:
mferler@peaksandbeyond.com
Or follow her blog at PeaksAndBeyond.com
(MFErler.blogspot.com)

This book is dedicated to
ROCK-
Who has been an anchor in my life.
She has become a true sister,
in spirit if not in blood.